MAGIC

Voyager

ISAAC ASIMOV

MAGIC

The Final Fantasy Collection

HarperCollinsPublishers

Voyager
An imprint of HarperCollins*Publishers*
77–85 Fulham Palace Road,
Hammersmith, London W6 8JB

Published by HarperCollins*Publishers* 1996
1 3 5 7 9 8 6 4 2

First published in the USA by
HarperPrism 1996

Individual story copyrights appear after pages 273-275

A catalogue record for this book is
available from the British Library

ISBN 0 00 224622 8

Set in Sabon

Printed in Great Britain by
HarperCollinsManufacturing Glasgow

TABLE OF
CONTENTS

---

part one
The Final Fantasy Stories

part two
On Fantasy

part three
Beyond Fantasy

INTRODUCTION

ASIMOV . . . FANTASY?

As almost everyone on our planet knows, Isaac Asimov was the most prodigiously talented, productive, and renowned science fiction writer who ever lived. As everyone perhaps *doesn't* know, he also delighted himself and his readers by writing fantasy stories throughout his fifty-year career.

Like the great Victorians, whom he so admired and so resembled in both seriousness and industry, Isaac Asimov wrote to entertain as well as to instruct: to puzzle, to divert, and sometimes simply to charm or to dazzle. Asimov's fantasies were as often written to justify a pun as to illustrate a point. But they invariably honored his deepest tendencies toward rationalism and logic. Even his wizards were logicians; even his dragons obeyed the Laws of Thermodynamics.

And like the great Victorians, Asimov worked at his writing desk until the day he died. We have thought it a fitting memorial, therefore, to complete the monumental task at which he labored all his life, and to assemble in one volume for the last time, all the uncollected fantasy stories he wrote during his enormously productive career. May are whimsical, others are elevating, but all are entertaining and all reveal another fascinating side to the protean figure that was Asimov.

INTRODUCTION

Also included, on a more serious (but hardly somber) note, are the critical essays he wrote on the subject of fantasy. Toward the end of his days, Isaac Asimov was concerned with the prospects and condition of his beloved field of science fiction, well aware that it had become inseparably linked with fantasy both in the marketplace and in the public's imagination. Indeed, it was only shortly after his death that the Science Fiction Writers of America, the organization he helped found and nurture, officially became the Science Fiction *and Fantasy* Writers of America. In the essays collected here for the first time, Asimov expresses his hopes and fears for this marriage, which was one of convenience as well as love; and explores as only he can, the shifting, permeable but very real border between the two realms.

Finally, and most appropriately, we have included Isaac Asimov's previously uncollected articles that range beyond the formal field of fantasy to touch on such "un-scientific" subjects as luck and immortality, Biblical astronomy, the Universe's ultimate fate . . . and America's prospects for survival. A fantasy? The good doctor hoped not.

It is our hope that this farewell collection of Asimov's best-loved fantasies and writings on fantasy will take its place on the shelf as a companion to *Gold*, Asimov's final science fiction collection. Together, they form an integral and essential part of his legacy.

In one of his essays, Asimov quotes his friend Arthur C. Clarke's famous dictum that "science, sufficiently advanced, is indistinguishable from magic." The same might be said of the good doctor's own delightful tales—that occasional fantasy, gracefully presented by a masterful writer who happens to be a scientist, is . . . well, *Magic*.

THE PUBLISHERS

PART ONE
THE FINAL FANTASY STORIES

TO YOUR HEALTH

I SNEEZED.

George drew himself away and said, austerely, "Another cold?"

I blew my nose without doing myself much good and said (my voice rather muffled by the tissue), "Not a cold. Sinusitis."

I stared at the remains of my coffee as though it were its fault that it had had no taste. I said, "This is the fourth flare-up of my sinusitis in the course of a year and each time I lose my sense of smell and taste for a shorter or longer length of time. Right now I can't taste a thing and the dinner we've just eaten might as well have been composed of cardboard."

"Will it help," said George, "if I assure you that everything was superb?"

"Not in the least," I said, grumpily.

"I myself don't have these afflictions," he said. "I attribute it entirely to clean living and a clear conscience."

"Thank you," I said, "for your sympathy, and I prefer to think that you avoid these disasters simply because no self-respecting microorganism would consent to live on your foul tissues."

3

"I don't take offense at that unkind remark, old fellow," said George, bridling more than a bit, "because I understand that these afflictions sour the disposition and cause you to say things that, in your right mind (assuming you have ever been in it), you would not say. It reminds me very much of my good friend Manfred Dunkel, when he was competing with *his* good friend, Absalom Gelb, for the charms of the fair Euterpe Weiss."

I said, morosely, "Curse and blast your good friend, Manfred Dunkel, his good friend Absalom Gelb, and their mutual prey, Euterpe Weiss."

"That is your sinusitis speaking, old man," said George, "not you."

Manfred Dunkel and Absalom Gelb [said George] had both attended the New York Institute of Opticianry and a fast friendship had formed between the two young men. It is, of course, impossible for two young men to immerse themselves in the mystery of lenses and refraction, to tackle the serious conditions of myopia, presbyopia, and hypermetropia, to sit at the grinding table together, without coming to feel like brothers.

They studied eye charts together, designed new ones for those who were most familiar with the Cyrillic or Greek alphabets, chose ideograms for Orientals, and discussed as only two specialists could the intricacies of balancing the advantages versus the disadvantages of using the various accents, grave, acute, circumflex, and cedillas, for French patients; umlauts for German ones; tildes for Hispanics, and so on. As Absalom told me once, very emotionally, the absence of these accents was pure racism and resulted in imperfect corrections of the eyes of those who were not of pure Anglo-Saxon ancestry.

In fact, a Homeric struggle on the subject filled the letter columns of the *American Journal of Optical Casuistry* some years back. Perhaps you remember an article written jointly by our two friends denouncing the old charts. It was entitled "Eye! Tear that tattered ensign down." Manfred and Absalom stood back to back against the united conservatism of the profession and although they did not succeed in imprinting their point of view upon the field, it drew them closer together than ever.

Upon graduating they opened the firm of Dunkel and Gelb, having tossed a coin to see which name was to go first. They prospered exceedingly. Dunkel, perhaps, was a trifle better at grinding surfaces to perfection, while Gelb was an acknowledged master at designing spectacles in art-deco modes. In everything, they saw, as they were fond of saying, eye to eye.

It was not surprising, then, that when they fell in love, it was with the same woman. Euterpe Weiss came in for new contact lenses and as the two men eyed her (one cannot say ogled in connection with the truly professional manner in which they studied her lovely optics), they realized they had encountered perfection.

I cannot say, as a nonoptician, that I quite appreciated what that perfection consisted of, but each of the two waxed lyrical to me— separately, of course—and talked fluently of optical axes and diopters.

Because I had known the two lads since they were young teenagers wearing their first spectacles (Manfred was slightly near-sighted while Absalom was slightly farsighted, and both were moderately astigmatic), I feared the result.

Alas, I thought to myself, surely a sacred boyhood friendship would founder, as the two, grown into strong men, would compete for Euterpe who, as Manfred said, with his hands clasped over his heart, was "a sight for sore eyes," or, as Absalom said, with his hands raised to heaven, "where Euterpe is concerned, the eyes have it."

But I was wrong. Even in connection with the divine Euterpe, the two opticians, closer to each other than even the closest-set eyes, behaved in perfect amity.

It was understood between them that on Tuesdays and Fridays, Manfred would be free to date Euterpe, if such dates could be arranged, while on Mondays and Thursdays, Absalom would have his chance. Weekends, the two worked together, taking the damsel to museums, operas, poetry readings, and chaste meals at some convenient diner. Life was a giddy round of pleasure.

What about Wednesday, you ask? That showed the young men's enlightened attitude at their highest and most refined. On Wednesdays, Euterpe was free to date others if she cared to.

The passion of Manfred was pure, as was that of Absalom. They wanted Euterpe to make her own choice even if it meant that some lout who was not an optician might be gazing into her eyes— breathing sighs—telling lies—

What do you mean, you wonder who's kissing her now? Why do you introduce non sequiturs when I am trying to give you a coherent account of events?

All went well for quite a while. No week passed in which Manfred didn't play a snappy game of casino with the young lady on one evening, while on another Absalom would blow a stirring tune on a comb covered with tissue paper. It was a halcyon time.

Or, at least, I thought it was.

And then Manfred came to see me. One look at his haggard face, and it seemed to me I knew all. "My poor young man," I said, "don't tell me that Euterpe has decided that, on the whole, she prefers Absalom?" (I was neutral in this matter, old fellow, and was prepared to mourn if either young man got it in the eye, so to speak.)

"No," said Manfred, "I won't tell you that. Not yet. But it can't last long, Uncle George. I am under a handicap. My eyes are red and swollen and Euterpe can scarcely respect an optician with eyes that fall short of normality."

"You have been weeping, have you?"

"Not at all," said Manfred, proudly. "Opticians are strong men who do not weep. I merely have a case of the sniffles. A cold, you understand."

"Do you have them often?" I asked, with sympathy.

"Lately, yes."

"And Absalom, does he have colds?"

"Yes," said Manfred, "but not as often as I do. He throws his back out occasionally, and I never do, but what of that? A man with a bad back has eyes that are clear and pellucid. The occasional groan, the periodic inability to stand up, are unimportant. But as Euterpe stares at my streaming eyes, at the redness of the sclerotic blood vessels, at the flush of the conjunctiva, surely a feeling of repulsion must sweep over her."

"Ah, but does it, Manfred? By all accounts she is a sweet damsel with a melting, sympathetic eye."

Manfred said grimly, "I dare not chance it. I absent myself when I have a cold and lately, this has meant that Absalom has seen her far more often than I have. He is a tall and lissome young man and no maiden can listen to the stirring music of his comb and tissue paper without being moved. I'm afraid I don't have a chance." And he buried his head in his hands, being careful to avoid harmful pressure on his eyes.

I was moved myself, as though ten combs with ten tissue papers had struck up "The Stars and Stripes Forever."

I said, "I might be able to arrange to make you immune to colds forever, my boy."

He looked up in wild hope. "You have a cure? A method of prevention? But no—" The momentary flame in his reddened eyes died away, leaving them just as reddened, however. "Medical science is helpless before the common cold."

"Not necessarily. I might not only cure you, my boy, but I might see to it that Absalom was afflicted with constant colds."

I said that only to test him, for you know my rigid sense of ethics, old fellow, and I am proud to say that Manfred passed as only an optician could.

"Never," he said, ringingly. "I ask that I be freed of this incubus, yes, but only that I might fight fair and meet my adversary on equal grounds. I would scorn to place him under a disadvantage of his own. I would sooner lose the celestial Euterpe than do that."

"It shall be as you say," I said, wringing his hand and clapping him on his back.

Azazel—I may have told you of my two-centimeter extraterrestrial, the one whom I can call from the vasty deep of space and who will come when I do call for him. Oh, I have, have I? —And what do you mean I should tell truth and shame the devil. I *am* telling the truth, blast you.

In any case, Azazel tramped up and down the edge of the table, his wiry tail twitching and his little nubbins of horns flushing a faint blue with the effort of thought.

"You are asking for health," said Azazel. "You are asking for normality. You are asking for a situation of balance."

"I know what I'm asking for, O Divine and Universal Omnipotence," I said, trying to mask my impatience. "I am asking to have my friend avoid having colds. I've had you meet him. You studied him."

"And that's all you want? To avoid his having these nasty, rheumy, messy, phlegmy colds that you sub-bestial inhabitants of a worm-eaten planet are subject to? You think that it is possible to light one corner of a room without lighting the whole room? I'll have you know that the balance of the four humors in the specimen you showed me is badly, viciously askew."

7

"The balance of the four *humors*? Sanctified One, humors went out with Herodotus."

Azazel gave me a sharp look. "What do you think humors are?"

"The four fluids thought to control the body: blood, phlegm, bile, and black bile."

Azazel said, "What a disgusting idea. I hope that this Herodotus is very properly held in universal execration by your people. The four humors are, of course, four mind-sets, which, when balanced very carefully, cannot help but bring permanent normality and good health to the useless bodies of even such insignificant vermin as yourselves."

"Well, then, can you balance the humors very carefully in my verminous friend?"

"I think I can, but it's not easy. I don't want to touch him."

"You won't. He's not even here."

"I mean make contact astrally. It would require a ritual of purification that would take the better part of a week and be quite painful in spots."

"I am sure, O Essence of Perfection, that avoiding the astral touch would be to you a trifling matter."

As usual, Azazel brightened under flattery and his horns stiffened, "I dare say I can," he said, and he could.

The next day I saw Manfred. He was visibly glowing with health and he said to me, "Uncle George, those deep-breathing exercises you told me about did the trick. The cold was cured between one breath and the next. My eyes cleared up, whitened, cooled, and I can now look the whole world in the face. In fact," he continued, "I don't know what it is, but I feel healthy all over. I feel like a well-oiled machine. My eyes are the headlights of a marvelous locomotive that is racing across the countryside.

"I even," he went on, "have this marvelous impulse to dance to some seductive Spanish rhythm. I will do this and dazzle the heavenly and ethereal Euterpe."

He left the room, dancing, his feet spurning the floor with delicate steps while he cried out: "Eye, eye, eye-eye."

I could not help but smile. Manfred was not quite as tall as Absalom, not quite as lissome, and although all opticians are classically handsome, Manfred was not quite as classical in his handsomeness. He looked better than the Apollo Belvedere but not quite as much better as Absalom did.

This glow of good health, I thought, would redress the odds.

As it happened, I was forced at this point to leave town for some time, owing to an argument I had with a bookie who happened to be a rather low devil, impervious to logic.

When I returned, I found that Manfred had been waiting for me.

"Where have you been?" he asked peevishly.

I stared at him with concern. He looked healthy and fit, his eyes liquid and limpid, and yet—and yet—

"I have been away avoiding business," I said, carefully not going into details, "but what is wrong with you, my boy?"

"Wrong?" He laughed, hackingly. "What should be wrong? The beautiful Euterpe has made her choice and it is not me. She is going to marry Absalom."

"But what happened? Surely, you didn't get—"

"I didn't get sick? Of course not. I've been trying to get sick, you understand. I have walked out in chilly rains. I have put on wet socks. I have fraternized with people who had colds and who were suffering from rhinitis. For heaven's sake, I even courted conjunctivitis. —Anything to be sick."

"But I don't understand, Manfred. Why should you want to be sick?"

"Because Euterpe has a strong motherly streak. Apparently, this is common among human beings of the feminine variety. I hadn't known this."

I looked grave. I *had* heard this. After all, women had children and I knew for a fact that children were always ailing, drooling, dripping, sneezing, coughing, growing feverish, turning blue, and in other ways becoming repulsively ill. And it never seemed to affect a mother's love; rather the reverse, it would seem.

"I should have thought of that," I said, thoughtfully.

Manfred said, "It's not your fault, Uncle George. I stopped the deep-breathing exercises at once and that didn't help. It was Absalom, the poor fellow. His back went out altogether. He was simply pinned to the bed."

"He couldn't be faking, I suppose."

Manfred looked horrified. "Faking? An optician? Uncle *George*! Professional standards would not permit such a thing. Nor would our close friendship. Besides, one time, when I jumped on him unexpectedly and forced him to sit up, his howl of agony could not have been simulated."

"And this has affected Euterpe?"

"Unbelievably. She sits at his side incessantly, feeds him bowl after bowl of chicken soup, and sees to it that the warm compress over his eyes is changed frequently."

"A warm compress over his eyes? What good does that do? I understood you to say it was his back that was out."

"It is, Uncle George, but Euterpe understands, for we have taught her, that all treatment begins with the eyes. In any case, she says that it is her mission in life to care for Absalom, to see that he recovers, to make him happy and comfortable, and with that end in view, she will marry him."

"But, Manfred, you were a martyr to colds. Why didn't she—"

"Because I avoided her, then, unwilling to subject her to contagion, unwilling to become aware of the cold look of repulsion I fancied would be in her eyes. How wrong I was! How wrong!" And he beat his fist against his head.

"You could pretend—" I began.

But again there was that haughty look on his face. "An optician does not live a lie, Uncle George. Besides, for some reason, no matter how I pretend to be ill, I find that I don't carry conviction. I simply look too healthy. —No, I must face my fate, Uncle George, Absalom, bless him for a true friend, has asked me to be best man."

And so it was. Manfred was best man, and through all the long years since, he has remained single. There are times when I think that perhaps he might be reconciled to his sad fate. After all, Absalom now has three rather unpleasant children; Euterpe has gained weight and her voice has grown shrill and she is rather extravagant.

I pointed this out to Manfred recently, and he simply sighed and said, "You may be perfectly correct, Uncle George, but when an optician loves, he loves not lightly—but forever."

George, having sighed sentimentally, stopped talking, and I said, "Strange, but the only optician I know in some detail has never been seen without a woman; nor has he ever been seen with the same woman twice."

"A detail," said George, waving his hand. "I told you this story to convince you that I can cure your sinusitis. For a paltry twenty dollars—"

"No," I said, sharply. "My wife, whom I love very dearly, is a physician, and gets a perverted pleasure out of doctoring me. Make me symptom-free and she would probably go mad. Here, I'll give you fifty dollars. Just promise to leave me alone."

It was money well spent.

THE CRITIC ON THE HEARTH

I HAD BEEN BROODING A BIT DURING the course of the dinner with George, but I finally said, "Would you like to hear what Samuel Taylor Coleridge thought of critics?"

"No," said George.

"Good! Then I'll tell you. He said, 'Reviewers are usually people who would have been poets, historians, biographers, etc., if they could; they have tried their talents at one or at the other, and have failed; therefore they turn critics.' Percy Bysshe Shelley said almost the same thing. Mark Twain said, 'The trade of critic, in literature, music, and the drama, is the most degraded of all trades.'

"Lawrence Sterne said, 'Of all the cants which are canted in this canting world . . . the cant of criticism is the most tormenting.' Twenty-three centuries ago, the Greek artist, Zeuxis, said, 'Criticism comes easier than craftsmanship.' Lord Byron said, 'Critics all are ready-made . . . with just enough of learning to misquote.' He also said, 'As soon seek roses in December, ice in June, Hope constancy in wind, or corn in chaff; Believe a woman or an epitaph, Or any other thing that's false, before you trust in critics.' —I could go on and on."

"You are going on and on," said George. "What do you do? Memorize these things?"

"Yes, I have lots more."

"Don't quote them."

"I have two of my own comments. The first is that every critic ought to become a garbage collector. He will be doing more useful work and he will have a higher social position. The second is that every critic ought to be thrown into the fireplace."

"And become the critic in the hearth, eh? And all this, I gather, because one of your miserable productions received a truthful review from some hardworking artisan who had been forced to read through your swill."

At this point, a brilliant idea crossed my mind. "George," I said, "have you ever known a critic and tried to help him?"

"What do you mean?"

"Well, you have bent my ear most grievously with your tales of your little demon, what's his name, and the miseries he has inflicted through you on innocent victims. Surely, there has been an occasion when you have inflicted the miseries on someone well worth it—a critic, in other words."

George said, thoughtfully, "There is indeed the case of Lucius Lamar Hazeltine."

"A critic?"

"Yes, but I doubt that you have ever heard of him. He doesn't work with your kind of trash, as a general rule."

"And you tried to help him?"

"I did."

For the first time in our long acquaintanceship, I made no effort to abort one of his stories. "Give me all the details," I said, gloatingly.

Lucius Lamar Hazeltine [said George], although a critic, is a most remarkably handsome young man. In fact, I have never known anyone more handsome than he except for myself in my somewhat younger days.

It is to his good looks entirely that I attribute his ability to remain a critic for ten long years and yet retain an unscarred face and an unbroken nose. As you, of all people, know very well, critics are constantly faced with the possibility of being struck with generous force by writers who object to being described as "meretricious purveyors of organic dreck."

Hazeltine, however, had so nearly the look of an angel from heaven with his clear, blue eyes, his golden curls, his pink complexion, his beautiful nose, and manly chin that one could see writer after writer striding toward him with malevolent intent, only to waver and turn away. They did not want to be responsible for spoiling perfection. Undoubtedly, they cursed their own weakness, and it must have occurred to them that if one among them, but one, were to consent to bang up Hazeltine a bit, his perfection would be gone and the rest could then pounce on him with unrestrained fury.

However, none wished to be the villain of the piece.

For a while, the hopes of the writing fraternity rested on Agatha Dorothy Lissauer. Perhaps you have heard of her. She writes murder mysteries that delve ferociously into the inner workings of psychotics. Her stories are so replete with details of the most repellent sort that even critics find themselves irresistably drawn to her. One critic said, "For slime, Agatha Dorothy Lissauer cannot be touched." Another said, "Horrifying disgust fills every sentence."

Naturally, a delicately nurtured young woman would feel glee and delight at having her work described in this fashion and, at a meeting of the Crime Writers Association, she was the only writer to stand up and defend the art of criticism, to the slack-jawed astonishment of every decent writer in the place.

It was, however, Lucius Lamar Hazeltine who taught her better. He had ignored her first dozen books totally, but her new book, *Wash Your Hands in My Blood,* seemed to attract his attention. He said, among other things, "*Wash Your Hands in My Blood* attempts to upset the stomach and at times I became aware of a very mild feeling of nausea, but nothing more than that. I find myself astonished that any young woman cannot do better. The book might as well have been written by a man."

On reading this, Agatha Dorothy Lissauer burst into tears and then, afterward, her lips set firmly, and, a cold, hard look in her glorious eyes, she went from livery stable to livery stable pricing horsewhips.

Hazeltine, she knew, was a member of the Critics Congregation, a gathering of the profession who met in an obscure tenement in the wilds of the South Bronx, where they felt, quite justifiably, no one would dare follow them. Ms. Lissauer, however, caught up in the grip of stormy emotion, threw caution to the winds. It was her intention to find the Congregation, wait till Hazeltine emerged and then, showing no mercy whatever, whip and lash him into a bloody pulp.

This she would certainly have done, cheered on by a happily drooling membership of the Crime Writers Association, until she actually came face to face with him. She had seen photographs of him, but had never seen him in three-dimensional proximity.

The sight of his lovely face changed everything for her. Throwing away her horsewhip, she collapsed in tears. I might have mentioned that Ms. Lissauer had the same heavenly beauty that Hazeltine had, except that her hair was russet, and her eyes a heavenly brown. Her nose was tip-tilted, her lips bee stung, her complexion a delicate peach and, to be as brief as possible, the two fell instantly in love.

I met Hazeltine not long afterward. We were good friends, partly because, as a critic, hardly anyone would speak to him, and he was always grateful to me that I consented to do so. —But then, you know me, old man. Hazeltine was generous with his luncheon hospitalities and I am the kind of person who is a true democrat. I will accept refreshments from any hands, however lowly.

"Lucius," I said, "congratulations. I hear that you have won the heart of the loveliest writer in all the world."

"Yes, I have," he said, with an oddly strained expression, "and she has won the heart of the loveliest critic in all the world—myself. It is, however, an ill-fated love. It can never be, George."

"Why not?" I said, puzzled.

"She is a writer. I am a critic. How, then, may we love?"

"Why, the usual way. Having obtained a motel room with a comfortable bed, you—"

"I am not speaking of the physical manifestations of love, George, but of the inner and spiritual beauty. You might as well expect oil and water to mix, fire and sand to coexist, dolphins to cohabit with deer, as to expect writers and critics to love. Could I refrain from reviewing her books?"

"Of course you can, Lucius. Just ignore them."

"No. Having reviewed *Wash Your Hands in My Blood* I have established reviewing rights, and I must review all her future books including the one she is now writing, a tender tale to be entitled *Hang Me Up by My Intestines*."

"Well, then, if you do review, say something nice. Emphasize the nausea and disgust."

Hazeltine looked at me with loathing. "How can I do that, George? You forget the Critic's Oath as established in ancient Greek times. Translated into English it reads: 'Though the subject is divine, and the outlook wide and vasty, Put starch into your spine, and utter something nasty.' I cannot break that oath, George, though it destroys my love and tears me apart."

I went to see Ms. Lissauer. I did not know her, but I introduced myself as a close friend of Lucius Lamar Hazeltine. That, combined with my air of stately dignity, worked wonders, and in no time she was bedewing my shirt with her tears.

"I love him; I love him," she said, finding a dry spot on my sleeve with which to wipe her eyes.

I said, "Then why not try to write something he would like?"

"How can I?" she said, eyeing me with loathing. "I could not break the Writer's Oath."

"There's a Writer's Oath?"

"It goes back to the ancient Sumerian. Translated into English it states: 'Be always keen and analytic, with the back of your hand to every critic.'"

My heart bled for these two sundered people and I felt that I had to turn to Azazel, whom I proceeded to call from the high-technology continuum in which he lives.

For a wonder, he was in a good mood. His little red face, with its nubbins of horns, smiled at me, and his inch-long tail wobbled to and fro.

"O Wonder of the Cosmos," I said, "You seem happy."

"Indeed, I am," he said, "I have written a zyltchik which has been greeted with universal approbation."

"What is a zyltchik?"

"A witticism. All have laughed. It is a great triumph for me."

"Would that I could report triumphs for two young hearts that are steadily breaking. But, obviously, since your zyltchik met with universal approbation, there are no such things as critics on your world."

"Are there not?" said Azazel, in sudden indignation. "There you reveal your puny ignorance. We have these fossil remnants of Hades among us. It was only last week, in discussing another zyltchik I had perpetrated—I mean, composed—that a critic said, 'Horsabelum desoderatim andeviduali stinko.' Can you credit the ignorance and vile personality of anyone who would say that?"

"What does it mean in English?"

"I wouldn't sully my lips to explain."

He was becoming furious and I could see his willingness to cooperate beginning to disappear, so I hastened to put the situation before him.

He listened closely, and said, "You have this critic and you want me to ameliorate his behavior."

"Yes."

"Impossible. Even I could not do that. A critic is beyond all help, at any level of technology."

"Could you in some way, then, manage to make him something other than a critic?"

"Again impossible. Surely you understand that a critic is totally unable to succeed at any other line of endeavor. If he had a trace of talent at anything, would he choose to be a critic?"

"There is something to that," I said, rubbing my chin.

"However," said Azazel, "let me think. There is a second person involved. A writer."

"Yes," I said, with sudden enthusiasm. "Could you manage to make her write something bland enough to avoid criticism?"

"You know that's impossible. Nothing is so bland, or, for that matter, so good, that a critic will refrain from tearing it to shreds. Where else lies the point of criticism? However—"

"However," I said, tensely.

"If I can't change a critic and can't change a writer, either by itself, I can change the two together. That is—I can turn the critic into a writer and the writer into a critic, by making use of the Law of Professional Conservation, and perhaps each one, having experienced the other side of the fence, so to speak, may then approach each other with newer eyes."

"Wonderful," I said. "I think you have the solution, O Master of the Infinite."

―――

About a week later, I went to see Lucius Hazeltine and, sure enough, the virus was working.

He heaved a sigh in my direction and said, "I have grown tired of being a critic, George. The social obloquy that meets me on all sides; the hatred; the scorn and contumely, wearies me. Even the keen ecstasy of finding new ways of being unfairly nasty and vile in my estimates of literature no longer makes up for it."

"But what will you do instead?" I asked, anxiously.

"I will be a writer."

"But, Lucius, you can't write. You can stumble through critical invective, but that's about all."

"I will write poetry. That's easy."

"Are you sure?"

"Of course. You bung in a rhyme or two and count the feet and if it's modern poetry, it doesn't even have to make sense. For instance, here is a morceau I have just tossed off. I call it 'The Vulture.' It goes:

"He clasps the crag with crooked claws;
Close to the Sun without a pause,
Ringed with the azure world because
He watches for prey from mountain sides,
Then down like a thunderbolt he glides."

I said, thoughtfully, "Lucius, that sounds derivative."

"Derivative? What do you mean?"

"There's a poem entitled 'The Eagle' that starts with 'He clasps the crag with crooked hands.'"

Hazeltine glared. "An eagle? With hands? Anyone knows an eagle doesn't have hands. To be ignorant of so elementary a fact of natural history must make the poet a fool of no common size. Who wrote that poem you mention?"

"It was Alfred, Lord Tennyson, actually."

"Never heard of him," said Hazeltine. (He undoubtedly never had, for, after all, he had been a literary critic.)

"Let me read you some additional pieces," he said. He intoned:

"Listen, my children, and you will find
That I'll tell you a story, if you don't mind,

19

About the Land of the Rising Sun
On the Seventh of December, forty-one,
Almost all who remember are over and done—"

I interrupted. "What do you call this one, Lucius? 'The Daylight Snooze of Kimmel and Short'?"

He stared at me narrowly. "How did you know?"

"A wild guess," I said.

He then went on to recite, "That's my last mother-in-law painted on the wall—", and "You know, we Yanks stormed Anzio, and on the trysting day—"

I had to stop him when he began what would clearly be a long, long ballad. It started:

"It was an ancient sailing man
And he stoppeth one of five.
'If you don't unhand me, graybeard loon,
You won't be long alive.'"

I staggered away. It wasn't as bad as being a critic, but it wasn't much better.

I went to see Ms. Lissauer. I found her in her study, drooping sadly over a manuscript.

"I don't seem to be able to write any longer, George," she murmured softly. "The whole process no longer seems to grab me. My book *Hang Me Up by My Intestines* is doing well despite the cruel and vicious review of it by my beloved Lucius, but this new one palls. It is called *Skin Me to the Bone,* but I can't seem to put my heart into the skinning."

"But what are you going to do instead, Agatha?" I asked.

"I have decided to be a critic. I have sent in my curriculum vitae to the Critics Congregation, including documentary proof that I beat my aged grandmother and that I have stolen milk from babies on numerous occasions. I believe that will qualify me for the profession."

"I'm sure it will. And is it your intention to be a literary critic?"

"Not quite. I am, after all, a writer, and what does any writer know about literature? No, indeed, I am going to be a poetry critic."

"Poetry?"

"Of course. That's easy. The pieces are usually short so you don't get a headache reading them. And if they're modern you don't have to strain to understand them, because they're not supposed to have meaning of any kind. Naturally, I shall find a post with *Booksellers Weekly*, which publishes anonymous reviews. I am certain I can really fulfill myself if no one ever finds out who said the nasty things I plan to say."

"But, Agatha, you probably have not heard of this, but your beloved Lucius is no longer a critic. He is writing poetry."

"Wonderful," said Lissauer. "I will review his books."

"Gently, I hope," I said.

She eyed me with loathing. "Are you mad? And be fired from my post by *Booksellers Weekly?* Never."

I suppose you see the end.

Hazeltine's book of poetry was published under the title of *Fragrant Reminiscences* and was reviewed anonymously by Ms. Lissauer. This time it was Hazeltine who went about the livery stables, testing out horsewhips for the necessary springiness. He stormed the offices of *Booksellers Weekly* and before they could get in a squadron of police to remove him, he had found Ms. Lissauer cowering in a corner.

"Yes, yes," she said, "It was I who wrote the review."

Hazeltine threw away his horsewhip and burst into tears. As they dragged him off, he said, "She well deserves a lashing but I could not bring myself to raise welts on that glorious skin."

But it is still the same. Despite the changeover, they are still critic and writer and their love, which is as deep and as passionate as ever, must remain forever unfulfilled.

I had listened closely to the story and, when it was done, I said, "Let me get this straight, George. Lucius Lamar Hazeltine, who had been a literary critic, is still suffering, is he?"

"He is suffering the agonies of the damned."

"Wonderful. And Agatha Dorothy Lissauer, who became a critic, is also still suffering, is she not?"

"If anything, more than Hazeltine is."

"And they will continue to suffer forever?"

"I am sure of it."

"Well," I said, "no one can ever say that I am a vicious person or that I hold grudges. All who know me speak favorably of my sunny disposition and my ability to forgive and forget. But I do make some exceptions. George, for once you don't have to ask me for anything. Here is twenty dollars. If Azazel has any use for Earthly money, give him half."

IT'S A JOB

I HAD BEEN NOTICING IT ALL THROUGH dinner and by now I had decided it was unmistakable. George had an undeniable look of prosperity about him.

Not much, you understand. It was just that his jacket sleeve looked less frayed, his tie more neatly knotted, his cheeks a little pinker. It was no use actually trying to spot the individual changes that made up the impression. It was the impression as a whole.

Nothing in the world would make George look like anything but a deadbeat, but somehow today the beat seemed to have a wan spark of life in it.

"George," I said, "you haven't done something desperate like getting a job, have you?"

He winced, and took a quick sip of wine. Then he said to me haughtily, "Didn't your mother ever tell you that there are some subjects that aren't proper in civilized discourse? A j—a j—"

"A job," I said, helping out.

"I can say it," he answered with asperity. "I'm just too much of a decent human being to say it in connection with myself."

"Well, then, George, what accounts for your altogether unaccountable air of not being utterly and completely broke?"

"Ah, I see. You are impressed by my devil-may-care impression of munificence. —Actually, I made a small investment that paid off rather handsomely."

"To the extent of your picking up the check that sooner or later will be handed to me?"

"On the other hand," said George, "talking about jobs—I can recall the days when a friend of mine was dying for a job, and would, in fact, have given anything for a job, and couldn't possibly keep one even when he had it."

"I said, George—are you munificent to the extent of your picking up—"

"Why do you insist on interrupting me with aimless chatter when I'm trying to tell you the story of Vainamoinen Glitz?"

George always knows how to stop me cold. "Vainamoinen!" I said. "What kind of name is Vainamoinen? You haven't the faintest idea who Vainamoinen was!"

"Of course I do. I've just told you. He was my friend, Vainamoinen Glitz. Everyone called him Van."

"But that's ridiculous. There's not a person outside Finland who could possibly be called Vainamoinen. Vainamoinen is the Finnish mythic hero; a musician; a magician; a demigod—"

"My Vainamoinen was just a pleasant sort of nebbish, very good-looking the young ladies seemed to think, and as rich as the day was long. Actually, he was Vainamoinen Glitz III."

"You mean his father and grandfather—"

"Yes, that's the assumption. Maybe he had a faint trace of Choctaw blood in him. I think Vainamoinen is a Choctaw word meaning 'brave warrior.' But, talking about Finnish, can we finish with this thing you seem to have over an ordinary Choctaw name, or Chickasaw, and let me go on with the story."

I shrugged.

I see that you are eager [said George] so let me plunge into the story without any further ado.

I had known Van's father well (his name being Vainamoinen Glitz, Jr.) and I had watched with pleasure as Van grew older. He had the pleasant upbringing of a young man in comfortable

circumstances, since his father, having had the newsstand conces-
sion at the Pentagon, was naturally a multimillionaire.

Van was a daring young fellow, too, for I'll never forget his disappointment at having the Vietnam War end just before he reached
draftable age. He was looking forward with such excitement to
entering the National Guard.

But it was not to be. He served his country, instead, by inspecting the various resort areas of our great nation, returning to the city
every once in a while, for as he said, "All that lounging about is
hard work, George, and it's nice to get back to the occasional dinner
with you."

Things might have gone very well with him, for he was becoming one of the nation's leading experts on beaches, nightclubs, theaters, and other important business establishments, and then he met
Dulcinea Greenwich. Now don't start gasping over the first name,
old man. She told me that her father had once read a book called
Don Quixote, but I think she was making that up, because you
know and I know that no one would ever write a book with a silly
name like that. It wouldn't sell.

Van came to me all of a twitter. "George," he said, "I have met
the most wonderful woman in all the world. She is dynamic. She is
strong. She is intelligent."

"Intelligent?" I said. I had seen him through a dozen mild love
affairs and it had never seemed to me that his criterion for feminine
excellence had been intelligence.

"Well," he said, simpering, "she says she's madly in love with
me and if that's not a sign of intelligence, George, what is?"

"Van," I said, "when someone is as good-looking as you are,
and as filthy rich, what's not to love? That's not a sign of intelligence, that's just a sign that she's not dead."

"No," said Van, "she's not that kind of young woman and I
think that cynicism does not become you. It so happens that the
other young women who seemed to me to be attracted to my charm
and insouciance all wanted to marry me and achieve large settle-
ments and double-indemnity insurance policies. Remember?"

"I remember."

"Well, Dulcinea doesn't want anything."

"Not *anything*?" I viewed that statement with the deepest
suspicion.

"Well, one thing."

"Aha."

"It's not what you think. She wants me to get a job."

I won't deny the fact, old man, that I swallowed the wrong way when he said that and it took me some time before I could convince myself I wasn't going to choke to death. Finally, everything stopped swimming before my eyes and I said in a ghastly whisper, "A *job*? Why does she want you to have a job?"

"She thinks," said Van moodily, "that it will make a man of me."

"But you *are* a man. You are even," I said with a sense of awe, for I have always been impressed by those with the talent and cleverness to be born rich, "a wealthy man, and if anything defines a man more securely than pelf, lucre, and a thick wallet, I would like to know what it is."

(I feel strongly about such things, old man, for though my circumstances have cast me into a certain shadow of poverty, I have the heart and soul of as rich a man as any in these United States.)

"She says," said Van, "that I am charming and that she loves me dearly, but I'm an idle wastrel."

"Idle wastrel? With all the work you've been doing on the beaches and resorts?"

"For some reason, she won't count that. She wants me to have a nine-to-five job, however humble, and to hold it for no less than six weeks, thus proving myself to be a go-getter—to use her phrase."

"She must be sick."

"No, George. She is not. She is a creature of high ideals and she has my heart. I will simply get a job and show her that I can go-get as well as any go-getter in the world."

"What kind of a job are you thinking of, Van?"

Van shook his head. "There you have me, George. I have not been trained or educated for anything and I can only hope that some prospective employer will be satisfied with the fact that I know very little—even nothing." He smiled bravely, "I am, of course, an expert and certified beach inspector. Perhaps that will help. Good-bye, George, I'm off to the barricades."

Poor Van. What followed thereafter was pitiful. Pitiful! If I were to give it to you in detail, old man, I could a tale unfold whose lightest word would harrow up thy soul, freeze thy—

(Please don't recite along with me. Has someone been stealing my lines again? —Hamlet's father? Never heard of him.)

In any case, he didn't make it. I didn't follow his case closely, of course, for I am a busy man with a million things to do constantly. The racing form alone—but I digress.

Occasionally, he would invite me to dinner and it was plain that he was sinking under the strain. His tan was fading and he admitted that his polo game was quite off. "When I tell you, George," he said, in a husky whisper, "that in the last month I have fallen off my polo pony twice you will know what I mean. Please don't let it get round."

"But it must get round. Surely the other players would have noticed that you fell off?"

"Polo players never talk about such things, George. It's the code of the pony."

The problem was that infernal matter of a job, of course. He had tried everything, he said. He had obtained a job as champagne taster at his favorite nightclub, got drunk the first night and insulted the boss. He was evicted with extreme prejudice. He offered to show me where he was kicked but I was not interested in the sight.

He got a job as a cashier, but couldn't figure out how to work the register. And he said all those numbers made him numb, which (he thinks) is why they're called numbers. He got a job at a gasoline pump but never figured out how to get the gas cap off the tank. He got a job at the information desk at Bloomingdale's, but quit after one hour in a dudgeon because it seemed the customers expected him to have information. Need I go on?

"It seems," said Van, "that I will never have the girl of my dreams. My life, George," he went on, "will be empty and void of meaning. Inspecting beaches will have no allure. Trying out a new nightclub will result in but hollow gaiety. Of what use is it if I plumb the heights of idle wastreldom, if I lose the woman to whom my soul is indissolubly bound?" And here he wept into his champagne, diluting it in the most appalling fashion.

My heart ached for him, old man. It seemed to me that if he retired into a life of moroseness and sorrow, he would be far less likely to stand me the occasional meal. True altruism, as you know very well, begins at home, so I would have to do something for him.

That meant Azazel. —Have I ever told you about my two-centimeter alien whom I can call upon by means of **arcane methods** known only to myself?

I have? —Surely you jest.

But be that as it may, I called upon Azazel.

Azazel, as you might have expected, was furious. He arrived still shrieking in his counter-soprano and waving his arms madly. Then he looked about, spied me, and said, "You idiot of a grobbledug, is this a time to call me?"

"It is a time I need you, O Marvel of the Universe."

"But I was watching—" He went on to describe the matter in tedious detail. There are apparently beasts on his world with six legs who proceed by leaps and somersaults in random directions and a great deal of money is placed on their progress. The first one to blunder across a finish line wins. Azazel insisted that his steed, whose name was unpronounceable, was on the point of winning.

"If I don't get back to the exact instant at which I left," he screamed, "I will lose seventy dworshaks."

"Of course you will get back to the exact instant. What I am going to ask of you is simplicity itself and will take you only another instant, O Champion of the Cosmos." (He loves being addressed in that fulsome fashion for he is a little creature and on his home planet he is usually referred to with the utmost contempt, I gather.)

I explained the situation. "A job?" he said, "On my world, we have the word *klastron* by which we refer to any demeaning task that must be performed by people of low social status over their objections and against their will."

"Yes," I said, feelingly, "that's what we mean by a 'job.'"

"Poor fellow," said Azazel, dripping a tiny tear that fell upon the table cloth and burnt a tiny hole in it. "And he actually wants one?"

"He needs one if he is to have the girl of his dreams, the woman to whom his soul is indissolubly bound."

"Ah, love, love," said Azazel, dripping another tiny tear, "to what extremities it takes even the wisest being. I remember once, when for the love of a dear zapulnik—who was six feet tall, which created a problem, I can tell you—I challenged her middle-mate to a—But that is neither here nor there. I take it you want me to arrange to have him find a job that he can keep."

"That is right."

"And he has no qualifications?"

"None."

"Then we must work purely emotionally. We must arrange to have an employer who will be perpetually satisfied with this friend of yours, and arrange further to have your friend perpetually satisfied with his job. An intricate affair."

"Not too intricate for the Unpuzzler of the Pulsars."

"No, of course not," said Azazel doubtfully, "and yet this has its difficult points. Since we don't know who the employer might be, I will have to arrange a general field of acquiescence and that's not easy."

I must say, old man, that this was one time when I seemed to lack faith in Azazel. He took a long time, mumbled a great deal, and, although I cannot tell what it is he does when he is engaged in the advanced technology of his own society, it did *seem* to me that he was backing and filling, with much shaking of the head and the making of new starts.

When he finally heaved a tremulous sigh and said, "It is done," he said it in a tone of voice that filled me with doubt. I thanked him effusively, of course, but I didn't entirely believe he had done it.

I blame myself for this, old man. It was my doubt that led to disaster. —No, I am not about to drip a tiny tear into my champagne. And this is not champagne, I might as well remind you. It is cheap white wine.

I put a lot of thought into it, old man. It seemed to me that Azazel was a broken reed and that, besides, I didn't want to see Van get a job. I admit jobs have to be done, but surely not by myself or those I consider my friends and loved ones. So I had an idea.

I sought Van out at his club. "Van," I said, "I have never met this Dulcinea of yours and I would like to."

He looked at me with what I can only describe as an ugly suspicion. "She is too young for you," he said.

"Van," I said, "you wrong me. Women are entirely safe with me. They may beg and they may offer money, as they frequently do, but except out of pure kindness and a view of ameliorating their suffering I assure you I would have nothing to do with them."

My earnestness and my transparent honesty had their effect. "Well, well," he said. "I will introduce you."

He did, eventually, and I got to know her. She was a rather small girl, thin, beautiful figure, dark hair. She had dark eyes that were very keen. She moved quickly and had an air of suppressed energy about her at all times. She was, in fact, quite the opposite of Van, for Van was easygoing and allowed life to drift casually past him. Dulcinea, on the other hand, gave me the definite impression that she seized life by the throat, shook it, and threw it in the direction she wanted it to go.

Frankly, I have never had the impulse to marry, but had I—if one can imagine so ludicrous a possibility—it would never have been Dulcinea. Being near her was like standing too close to a crackling bonfire—it made one uncomfortably warm. Of course, opposites attract and I was perfectly willing to let Van marry Dulcinea. It would after all remove her from circulation and make it more comfortable for other males she might meet.

"I have longed to meet you, Miss Greenwich," I said, in my most courtly manner, pronouncing it 'Gren'ij,' as any civilized person would do.

"It's pronounced 'Green'wich,' and you can call me Dulcie. I take it you are George, a friend Van has told me much of." She gave me an appraising look that seemed to skin me.

"A close friend," I said.

She harumphed, then said, "Well, after he manages this job-thing, I'll be able to get on to other matters. I'll have to, obviously."

I'll tell you frankly I didn't like her tone, but I said, "It is about the job-thing that I wish to talk to you. Why on Earth do you want Van to have a job?"

"Because it is not good for a man to be a gadabout, and to waste his life on trivialities."

"For a *man*?" I said. "Not for a woman?"

She blinked a few times. "A woman should be up and at 'em, also."

"Shouldn't one of a couple be taking care of the house while the other is out there in the jungle?"

"Blatant male chauvinist propaganda."

"Nonsense! I said 'one of a couple.' I didn't specify. It's whichever is best suited for whichever job. I take it you are a feminist."

"Absolutely. I come from a long line of feminists. One of my ancestresses busted General Ambrose Burnside in the snoot for having the nerve to wink at her. She messed up his sideburns, I can tell you."

"Exactly. Then it strikes me that you are far more capable of handling yourself in this cruel world of ours than poor Van is. Van is a soft and gentle human being—"

"Yes, he is," and her voice softened a bit and a look of what was almost human feeling came into her eyes. "He's my little lambsie-pie."

I controlled the shudder and went on smoothly, "Where you are as hard as nails."

"Hard as drop-forged alloy steel, I've always thought."

"Then shouldn't *you* be the one who gets the job?"

"Hmm," she said.

"In fact," I said. "I think you ought to go into politics. We need a hard-hitting, hardheaded, hardfisted, hard-shelled American telling all those shifty swivel-heads what to do."

"Hmm," she said.

"And if you go into politics, what can you better have than a rich husband who can supply the money for all those TV shots? Not that it would be lost money, for once you are elected you will find a thousand ways of earning the money back; some of them nearly ethical."

"Hmm," she said.

"And Van is just the type of mate a politician would need—at the left, one step back. Smiling for the camera, charming the elderly female vote, looking up at you adoringly as you make your speeches. The last thing you would want is to have him take a job. He'll need to use all his time to take up some good cause that will make you look good—like homes for aged polo ponies, where he can teach them all to 'Just say neigh.'"

"Hmm," she said. "There's a great deal in what you say."

"There usually is," I admitted.

"Let me think about it."

"Certainly, but act quickly. Otherwise, Van may get a job and it may spoil him for the exacting task of being First Gentleman."

"First Gentleman." She rolled the phrase over her tongue, then she murmured, "Madam President"—and said, energetically, "I'll see him tonight."

And so she did, and the results were as I had foreseen.

Van phoned me the next day in the greatest excitement. "George," he said, "Dulcinea wishes to marry me. I am not in the least required to get one of those nine-to-five jobs. She says I will

31

certainly have plenty to do when I marry her and she can no longer wait to have her heart's desire fulfilled. —You see, she means me, when she speaks of her heart's desire, of course."

"Undoubtedly," I said. To be sure, it might have been the White House, but I saw no reason to mention that to Van at this happy time in his life.

He was married in less than a month. I was one of the Gentlemen Ushers, and the champagne was superb. When I tell you that I even managed to avoid kissing the bride, you will understand that it was an occasion on which the heavens themselves smiled.

The happy couple went off on a honeymoon, and they then retired to their suburban mansion.

They kept themselves busy, for Dulcinea Glitz, as she now was, did enter politics. I don't know how closely you follow politics, old man, sitting there, as you do, with your nose in your word processor at all times, but in just a few years she blazed her way through the city council, and is now running for the state senate.

I must tell you that I was very proud of myself. For once, I had not depended on Azazel but had done it all myself, and very neatly, too, you will have to admit. It was clear to me that, in this one case, Azazel had failed. There was no strange emotional force field that lured employers into demanding Van's services; no wild yearning for menial position on Van's part. No, he and his loved one simply got married.

All was well.

At least, I thought all was well until I met Van a month or so ago. He had aged considerably. His tan was gone; his hands trembled a little; he walked with a slight stoop; and there was a haunted look in his eyes.

I ignored it all, and said heartily, "Van! Long time no see!"

He turned to look at me and it seemed to take him a while to recognize me. "Is that you, George?"

"None other."

"How are you, George? Meeting you is such delicious pain. It reminds me of the old days; days that are never more to be, alas." And tears coursed down his cheeks.

I was taken aback. "Van!" I said. "What is the matter, old chap? Don't tell me she made you get a job after all!"

"No, no," he said. "Would that she had. I am busy in other ways. I must consult the head gardeners on the matter of the grounds and gardens, busy myself with the cook in preparing menus, go into a huddle with the housekeeper on the parties we must constantly give, hire nursemaids for the twins that dear Dulcie took two days off to have. In general, the work is very, very demanding, but on top of that—"

"Yes?"

"On top of that, she is in politics, you know. Someone apparently suggested it to her once. Blithering, interfering idiot," he said peevishly. "If I could find him, I'd hit him over the noggin with my polo mallet. After all, I have no other use for it these days. You wouldn't know who suggested it, would you, George?"

I said, "I think it must have been her own idea. I can't conceive that anyone would be so foolish as to suggest it to her. —But tell me, what's wrong with her having entered politics?"

"What's wrong? It deprives me of all my individuality. I am constantly being asked by interviewers the extent to which I influence her decisions, whether I actually get to sleep with her, whether it's true that I consult an astrologer to get the proper time for her to make her speeches? I tell you, George, I have no life of my own anymore. Nobody even knows my first name, and why should they? Do you know Mr. Margaret Thatcher's first name? Of course not. I hate it. I hate it. I hate it."

My heart was wrung. "Have you told her this, Van?"

"Frequently. But she says that I am the ideal politician's mate and that someday when she retires from her second term as President, I will be able to visit the beaches and nightclubs again."

"I hate to say this, Van, but have you considered a divorce? She's a politician who can't stand scandal, so she's sure to let you go quietly and probably even let you retain custody of the children. Then you'll be a free man again."

Van nodded his head and said sadly. "I have often thought of this. I would even allow *her* to retain custody of the rotten—of the precious tykes of ours. But I can't, George, I can't."

"Why can't you? I'm sure she'd make no trouble."

"It's not she, George, it's I—I—I—I." He pounded himself on his chest with each *I* till a fit of coughing stopped him.

When he had recovered, he said, "This marriage I view as a job. From the moment Dulcinea and I stood before the minister I thought to myself exultantly, 'This is a job—the job I swore to my Dulcinea I would get and keep.' In fact, I have the feeling that I must *never* give up this job, no matter what, and Dulcinea feels the same. I don't know why. It is a kind of mystical thing. And so you see, I'll never be free. Never."

So there you are. You see the mistake. Azazel's workings *did* do the job. And when I interfered—with the very best motives in the world, I assure you—I arranged a marriage which, under the circumstances, turned out to be the job neither he nor Dulcinea could end, and which he, at least, couldn't bear. It's too bad, but it's just a case of too many cooks spoiling the broth, to coin a phrase.

I shook my head sadly. "You seem to spoil the broth every time, George. What is it with you? —But in any case, as long as you're on the road to prosperity, would you take care of the tip, at least?"

George looked revolted. "When I have just told you a sad story, a terrible tragedy—is that the time when you should be discussing anything as sordid as money?"

He was right, of course, so I lumped the tip in with the rest of the check and paid it. Then I handed him five dollars to show that I was sorry I had hurt his feelings.

Habit is a hard thing to break. It would be very hard for me to stop giving money to George, and much harder *still* for George to stop accepting it.

BABY, IT'S COLD OUTSIDE

GEORGE AND I WERE HAVING LUNCH and the waiter had just placed a bowl of navy-bean soup before him, a beverage of which he is inordinately fond. He inserted some of it into himself, sighed with pleasure, and, looking out the window, said, "There's a hint of snow in the air."

Whereupon I said, "If you call gobs of snow in thick swirls falling from the sky a 'hint' then I suppose you're right."

"I am merely," said George, haughtily, "trying to lend an air of poetry to the otherwise bald statement that it is snowing. However, trying to talk poetry to you is much like trying to talk it to a horse."

"Except that a horse wouldn't pay for this lunch."

"And neither need you, were it not that I am short of funds at the moment."

It was a moment that had lasted, so far, as long as George had, and though it would have been pleasantly unkind to say so, I refrained.

"A sight like this," I said, "fills me with apprehension at the cold weather to come. Still, I can console myself with the thought

35

that it will be over in a matter of a few months and I can then amuse myself by feeling apprehension at the hot weather to come. A periodic change of apprehension, I suspect, is good for one and feeds that necessary feeling of divine discontent."

"I wonder why," said George, "they call discontent divine."

"Because it's discontent with things as they are that has driven humanity into the creation of civilization and culture. Contentment would lead to stagnation and to stultification, as in your case. And yet even you, George, if the stories you inflict on me are true, recognize the divine discontent in others and you then labor to improve their lot. Of course, if those same stories that you continue to inflict on me remain true, it would appear that your interference in the lives of your friends invariably leads to catastrophe."

George reddened. "That's twice in one short statement you've cast doubt on the slices of life which I have favored you with."

"Slices of life that include a two-centimeter extraterrestrial being that you can call up through a space warp and that can do all sorts of things beyond human technology is not something which it is difficult to doubt."

"And I also resent your statement that my good-natured help invariably leads to catastrophe. That is a statement so wide of the truth that I'm sure the angels in heaven are weeping on your behalf at this very moment."

"If they weep, the divine tears are falling on your behalf. You're the one who recounts the tales and describes the catastrophes. I am merely pointing them out."

"The fact is, old man, that I have, on occasion, produced a happy, love-filled marriage, replete with fidelity and morality, something that is entirely my doing. The case I am thinking of is that of Euphrosyne Mellon and her husband, Alexius. I will now tell you their story."

"Actually, I don't want to hear the story."

Euphrosyne Mellon [said George] was Euphrosyne Stump before her marriage and I knew her from a child. She was a shy tot, who, when introduced to those outside her immediate family, would shrink behind the nearest item of furniture and peep out through large and bashful eyes. This shyness of hers was never overcome, and as she grew older, it centered itself on members of the opposite sex.

This grew the more incongruous when, as she grew up, she turned into a miracle of appropriate proportion, possessing the body of a goddess. She was a small goddess, to be sure, only five feet two inches tall, but the young men of the vicinity did not fail to notice the phenomenon.

Many a young man attempted to scrape up a friendship and if they had succeeded then, for all I know, they would have engaged her in deep philosophical discussions. I could never put that to the test, however, nor could she, for they never managed to scrape up the necessary friendship that is the prerequisite for such discussions.

Euphrosyne carefully dressed in such a fashion as to obscure the startling nature of her physical attributes, but found that young men have a sixth sense in those respects. A young man with scarcely enough sense to find an omelet resting on a plate in front of him can nevertheless pierce, in his mind's eye, the layers of burlap with which Euphrosyne swathed herself, to detect the wonders beneath.

I was, of course, her godfather, for, as I have told you on previous occasions, I have been blessed with an inordinate number of beautiful goddaughters, undoubtedly because of my intense virtue and respectability. Even Euphrosyne made an exception of me in what was an otherwise universal suspicion of the motives of the male sex.

She sat on my lap and sobbed into my shoulder while I stroked her golden hair.

"It is simply that I cannot bear to touch any of those creatures," she said, "and I feel that they have that vicious tactile urge. I can't help but notice that they generally wash their hands before they approach me, as though they feel that they will achieve greater success with clean hands."

"And won't they?"

Euphrosyne shuddered. "Filthy hands I could not endure, but clean hands are not much better, Uncle George."

"And yet you sit on my lap, and I am stroking your hair and, I believe, occasionally your shoulder and upper arm."

"That's different, Uncle George. You're *family*."

I continued stroking. Family has its privileges.

Considering her attitude, though, you can well imagine my stupefaction when she brought me the news that she was marrying Alexius Mellon, a young and husky man, of no great poetic gifts—

of no small poetic gifts, either—who made a good living as a traveling salesman.

When she came to me with the great tidings, blushing and simpering, I said, "Considering your views on the male sex, Euphrosyne, how could you bring yourself to agree to marriage?"

"Well," she said shyly, "I guess I'm just a romantic at heart. I know that it's unsafe to let yourself be guided by mercenorotic motives. They do say that 'cash is blind' and that seduced by it you make terrible mistakes. However, I've also heard that 'cash conquers all,' and I believe it now. I tried to keep away from Alexius and to lock him out, but everyone says that 'cash laughs at locksmiths,' and so it proved. And—well, I guess I'm just a silly girl but, after trying so hard all my life to keep away from men, I just woke up one morning, thought of Alexius and realized that I was helpless—I had fallen in cash. I went around all that day singing, 'Cash is the sweetest thing,' and when Alexius proposed again, I said, 'Yes, dear, we will get married and I promise to "cash, honor, and obey".'"

I smiled and wished her all possible good luck, but when she had gone, I shook my head sadly. I had seen enough of the world to know that the golden glow of cash can make for a splendid honeymoon, but that when the serious tasks of life make themselves felt, cash alone is not enough. I mournfully foresaw disillusionment for my sweet silly little goddaughter, who had read too many tales of cash and romance.

And so it turned out. She had not been married more than six or eight months, when she came to me, with a white, pinched look about her. "Greetings, Euphrosyne," I said, heartily, "and how is dear Alexius?"

She looked about as though to be sure of not being overheard, and said, "Away on one of his business trips, thank goodness." Her lips quivered and, finally, with a sad wail, she threw herself at me.

"What is it, my dear?" I said, resuming the stroking ploy that I always found gave so much pleasure—and perhaps to her as well.

"It's Alexius. For a while, cash was enough. We spent freely and we enjoyed ourselves. It seemed we didn't have a care in the world, and then, somehow, he began to change. He began to hint that marriage entailed—love. I tried to laugh it off and said, gaily, 'Cashiers live on cash alone.' As the weeks passed, however, I found he was growing more insistent, and it dawned on me that I had married a secret lovaholic.

"It was like a disease, Uncle George. Until last week, we had been sleeping in twin beds, one on one side of the room, one on the other, with a heavy piece of furniture in between—like any normal pair of newlyweds would. And then I suddenly found a—a—a double bed in the room. He said that twin beds tended to estrange a couple. And now, Uncle George, I can't even call my bed my own, and when he gets into my bed, his hand touches mine sometimes. In fact, it keeps crawling toward me. I can't imagine what sick cravings may be overcoming him. Would you know, Uncle George?"

"Do you think, Euphrosyne dear, that you might grow to like the touch of his hand?"

"Never. He seems to be so warm all the time, and I'm always delightfully cool. I don't want all that male heat. I told him so and he said that I was a cold—Well, I can't tell you the other word but it begins with a 'bi' and it ends with a 'tch.'"

"I think," I said, "I can puzzle it out."

"Do you think, Uncle George, that he is no longer in cash with me? After all, you can't call your cashmate, with whom you've been spending together for half a year, a cold you-know-what and still be in cash."

"There, there, Euphrosyne. How long will Alexius be away?"

"It's a long trip. He's got to tour the southwest. He may not be back for a month."

"Leave it to me, then, dear, and I will think of something to do."

"I know you will," she said, her charming little face looking up at me trustingly, "You're *family*."

It seemed to me it was a case for Azazel and I called him up. He appeared on the usual shelf I had fixed up for him at eye level. He was, as usual, unprepared for the call-up, and, as usual, he caught my eye without warning and let out his usual piercing squeak. He claims he always reacts in that fashion when he comes unexpectedly face-to-face with a horrible monster, though why he should squeak when he sees me, he has never explained.

He seemed a little redder than usual, as though he had been engaged in some exertion, and he did have an object in his tiny hand that looked like a BB shot. Even as he squeaked at the sight of me, he was still lifting and lowering it rhythmically.

He said, "Do you realize that you have interrupted me in my setting-up exercises?"

"Sorry!"

"And what good does that do? Now I'm going to have to miss my exercises for today. Just skip them. How I am to keep in shape I simply don't know."

"Why do you have to miss them, O Grand and Exalted Ruler of the Universe? Can't you go back to the instant at which you left and continue with your exercises?"

"No, that's too complicated, and I don't need your foolish advice. I'll just skip them. But let me ask you a question—"

"Yes, Your Puissance?"

"So far, you have interrupted me in games of chance—when I was about to win. You have also interrupted me when I was in the process of receiving various honors, when I was taking showers, when I was engaged in complicated rituals with certain fair members of my species. How is it that not until now have you interrupted me at my daily exercises? If you must interrupt me, *that* is the time to do so. Make sure you do it again."

And he put down the BB shot and kicked it to one side. I gathered he was not fond of his daily exercises.

"What is it you want this time?" he asked sourly.

I told him the tale of Euphrosyne and Alexius Mellon, and he made little tch-ing noises with his tongue. "The old, old story," he said. "Even on our world, the misguided follies of youth create untold unhappiness. —But it seems to me that this Euph—Euph—or whatever her name is, need only join with her mate in his vile and perverted desires."

"But that's what's wrong, O One of Infinite Might, she is a pure and unsullied damsel."

"Come, come, you have just committed an oxymoron. At least, you have if the damsels on your world are anything like the damsels on my world. I have encountered, in my time, an incredible collection of cold zybbuls—and by zybbuls, I am referring to female domestic animals—"

"I know what you mean, Overpowering One, but what do we do about Euphrosyne?"

"Actually, it strikes me as simple. Since she objects to male warmth—Can you bring me a photograph of her or an article of clothing—something I can focus my energies on?"

I had, as good fortune would have it, one of her more revealing photographs, at which Azazel made a dismal face. It didn't take him long, however, to do whatever he had to do, and then he departed. I noticed that he left his BB shot behind him. As a matter of fact, I have the BB shot in my pocket and I will show it to you as proof of Azazel's existence. —Well, I don't know what you would consider "real" evidence, to use your phrase, but if you don't want to look at it, I will continue.

Two weeks later, I met Euphrosyne again. She looked more miserable than ever and I feared that, whatever it was that Azazel had done, he had only made things worse. And Azazel never consents to modify anything he has done.

"Has Alexius come home yet?" I asked.

"He'll be home on Sunday," she said listlessly. "Uncle George, has it seemed to you to be cold lately?"

"Not unseasonably so, my dear."

"Are you sure? I feel it so, for some reason. I just sit around all day shivering. Underneath this heavy overcoat, I've got my warmest suit and I've got nice warm underwear under that and I've even got woolen socks over my panty hose, and heavy shoes over that, and I'm *still* cold."

"Perhaps you're undernourished. A nice big bowl of navy bean soup would warm you up miraculously. And then, if I were you, I would get into bed. Turn on the heater in the room, and pile on the blankets and you will be as warm as a beach on a south Pacific isle."

"I don't know," she said, wrinkling her adorable nose and shaking her head. "It's when I'm in bed that I feel coldest. My hands and feet especially seem lumps of ice. When Alexius gets back, he won't want to get into bed with me, I'm so cold. That will be one good thing," she added darkly. "He's going to find out I'm really a cold what-he-said."

Two more weeks passed and there was a knock on my door; a happy knock if ever I heard one; the rat-tat-tat of a blissful knuckle. I was engaged in some complicated mathematical maneuvering in connection with some equine statistics, as I recall, and I was not very pleased at the interruption, but when I opened the door, in whirled Euphrosyne, virtually dancing.

I gaped. I said, "What it is, Euphrosyne?" And, trying to account for her ecstasy, I added, "Has Alexius left all his cash with you and run away?"

"No, no, Uncle George, of course not. Alexius has been home for a week, that dear good man."

"Dear, good man? Do you mean he has gotten over his lovaholic tendencies and has returned to the blissful enjoyment of cash?"

"I don't know what you're talking about, Uncle George," she said, her little chin held high. "All I know is that the day he came home, I got onto my side of the bed and I was colder than ever. I was blue and shivering. And then he got into bed on his side and it seemed to me that I could feel his warmth at a distance. I don't know how he managed it, but his body seemed to exude a delightful heat that just washed over me. Oh, it was bliss.

"Naturally, I just moved toward the warmth. He was like a magnet and I was an iron filing. I felt myself slide toward him and, in fact, I slammed into him and threw my poor cold arms about him. He let out a fearsome shriek at the touch of my cold hands and feet, but I wasn't going to let him go. I held on more tightly than ever.

"He turned around to face me and said, 'You poor thing. You're so cold.' And he put his sweet, warm hands on my icy back and passed them up and down. I could feel the warmth of his hands through my nightgown, up and down, up and down. Uncle George, I just slept in his arms, happily. I never had a better night, and in the morning I hated to have him get out of bed. I'm afraid he had to fight me off. 'Don't go,' I said, 'I'll get cold.' But he had to go.

"And it's been like that every night. Such happiness. In the warm arms of my warm Alexius, Uncle George, it seems to me that even cash has lost its importance. There's something so cold about cash."

I said, "Hush, child," for I found that shocking.

"No, I mean it," she said.

"Tell me, dear," I said, "with all that hugging and touching and warming, did you—" I paused, unable to find words for the shameful thoughts that crossed my mind. After all, I am old enough to have plumbed the wickedness of the world.

"Yes, I did," she said, proudly, "and I don't think that there's anything wrong with it. Oh, moralists can talk all they want about cash being the greatest of God's gifts to men, and they can say that 'love is the root of all evil,' but I say that love is the warmest thing."

"What will you do in the summer?" I challenged her.

"So I'll sweat a little," she said, and I knew she was lost beyond all redemption.

I never knew a marriage as happy as that of Euphrosyne and Alexius Mellon. They were warm every night, sweating a little in the summer, and they had two children eventually.

And Euphrosyne changed completely. She was no longer in the least afraid of men, or suspicious of their motives. In fact, she welcomed their motives and took to speaking in a very depreciating manner of any of them who seemed imbued with an Old World courtesy.

She dressed in such a way as to attract the attention of the males and did, indeed, attract them in large numbers.

She confided in me, later on, that out of sheer curiosity, she had attempted to warm herself on one or another of them, but after the fifteenth or sixteenth attempt—she admitted she had lost count—she had given up. None of them had the heavenly warmth of Alexius.

She is a little petulant about the matter, and complains that love, unlike cash, should be shared; and that love, unlike cash, can only be increased by giving freely. She kept on saying that even though I reminded her that cash, shrewdly invested, would bring in large profits.

And so she remains with Alexius and if that is not a happy ending, what is?

"It sounds to me, George," I said, "as though Euphrosyne is probably very unhappy at not getting any pleasure out of illicit relationships and finds herself monogamous as a matter of force through Azazel's interference, rather than of choice."

"As I said," said George, "she *is* a little petulant at the failure of her experiments, but what of that? A little unhappiness is a trifling payment for the achievement of morality. And," he added, "when the folly of love lifts from her wearied body, which it does, now and then, there's still cash, always cash, always cash. As, for instance, when I tell you that I can use a five-dollar bill for a few days."

The few days have also lasted all of George's life, but I gave him the five dollars, anyway.

THE TIME TRAVELER

"ACTUALLY, I KNOW SOMEONE MUCH like you," said George to me as we sat in the lobby of the Café des Modistes, after having consumed a more or less gracious repast.

I was rather enjoying the opportunity to do nothing, in defiance of the deadlines that awaited me at home, and I should have let it go, but I couldn't. I have a profound appreciation of the uniqueness of my character. "What do you mean?" I said. "There is no one like me."

"Well," admitted George, "he doesn't write as much as you do. No one does. But that's only because he has *some* regard for the quality of what he writes and is not of the opinion that his lightest typographical error is deathless prose. Still, he *does* write, or rather *did* write, for some years ago, he died and passed on to that special spot in purgatory reserved for writers, in which inspiration strikes continually, but there are no typewriters and no paper."

"I yield to you in your knowledge of purgatory, George," I said, stiffly, "since you embody it in your person, but why does this writer-acquaintance of yours remind you of me, aside from simply being a writer?"

"The reason the resemblance burst in upon my inward eye, old friend, is that, while having achieved worldly success and wealth, as you have, he also complained continually and bitterly of being underappreciated."

I frowned. "I do *not* complain of being underappreciated."

"Do you not? I have just spent a tedious lunch listening to you complain at not receiving your full and just deserts, by which, I suspect, you do not mean horse-whipping."

"George, you know very well that I was merely complaining about some of the reviews I have received lately; reviews written by small-minded envious writers-manqué—"

"I have often wondered: What is a writer-manqué?"

"A failed writer or, in other words, a reviewer."

"There you have it, then. Your comments reminded me of my old friend, now no longer with us, Fortescue Quackenbrane Flubb."

"Fortescue Quackenbrane Flubb?" I said, rather stunned.

"Yes. Old Quackbrain, we used to call him."

"And what did he call you?"

"A variety of names I no longer remember," said George. "We were friends from youth, because we had gone to the same high school. He had been some years ahead of me, but we met at meetings of the alumni association."

"Really, George? Somehow I had never suspected you of a high-school education."

"Yes, indeed, we went to Aaron Burr High School, old Quackbrain and I. Many's the time he and I sang the old alma mater song together, while tears of nostalgia ran down our cheeks. Ah, golden high-school days!"

And, with his voice rising into a non-musical quaver, he sang:

> *"When the Sun shines on our high school,*
> *With its golden hue;*
> *There, above our loved Old Cesspool,*
> *Waves the black and blue."*

"Old Cesspool?" I said.

"A term of affection. Yale is known as 'Old Eli,' and the University of Mississippi is 'Ol' Miss' and Aaron Burr High School—"

"Is Old Cesspool."

"Exactly."

"And what is 'black and blue?'"

"Our school colors," said George, "but I am sure you want to hear the story of Fortescue Quackenbrane Flubb."

"There's nothing I want to hear less," I said.

Fortescue Quackenbrane Flubb [said George] was, in middle life, a happy man; or, at least, he should have been a happy man, for he was blessed with all anyone could reasonably want.

He had had a long career as a successful writer, turning out books that sold well and were popular and, despite that, books that were spoken of highly by those writers-manqué who call themselves reviewers.

I can see from your face, old man, that you are about to ask me how it is possible for a man to be a successful writer, and to have a name like Fortescue Quackenbrane Flubb—and yet remain completely unknown to you. I might answer that this is evidence of your total self-absorption, but I will not, for there is another explanation. Like all writers of even a minimum of sensibility, old Quackbrain used a pseudonym. Like any writer with a modicum of feeling, he didn't want anyone to know how he made his living. I know that you use your own name, but you have no shame!

Quackbrain's pseudonym, of course, would be well known to you, but he had made me promise, once, to keep it an inviolate secret even after he had passed on to his typewriterless purgatoriality and I, of course, must honor that promise.

Yet old Quackbrain was not a happy man.

As a fellow alumnus of dear old Burr, he confided in me. "Of what use is it, George, that money pours in on me in a never-stinting spate? Of what use is it that my fame is worldwide? Of what use is it that I am treated with the utmost consideration by all and sundry."

"Quackbrain," I said solemnly, "I believe that there is good use in all this."

"Bah," he said, "possibly in a worldly sense; possibly in a mere material sense. Yet it leaves the soul untouched."

"Why?" I asked.

"Because," and here he struck his chest a resounding thump, "the burning memories of youthful snubs and spurnings remain unavenged and, indeed, forever unavengeable."

I was thunderstruck. "Surely, you did not receive youthful snubs and spurnings?"

"Did I not? At Old Cesspool itself. At Aaron Burr High School."

"But what happened?" I said, scarcely able to credit my ears.

"It was in 1934," he said, "I was a junior then and beginning to feel the divine flow of inspiration within me. I knew that someday I would be a great writer and so I signed up for a special writing class that old man Yussif Newberry was giving. Do you remember Yussif Newberry, George?"

"Do you mean Old Snarley Face Newberry?"

"The very same. It was his notion that by calling together such a class, he would have an untapped well of talent from which he could draw written gems that would fill the school's literary semiannual magazine. Do you remember the magazine, George?"

I shuddered, and old Quackbrain said, "I see you do. We were assigned to write essays as a preliminary measure of our ability and, as I recall, I wrote a paean to spring, breathlessly eloquent, and poetic besides.

"When Snarley Face called on volunteers to read their products, my hand went up proudly at once, and he called me to the head of the class. I clutched my manuscript in a hand which, I recall, was perspiring with excitement, and I read my effusion in a ringing voice. I anticipated going through all fifteen pages to gathering excitement in the audience and ending it to the swelling sound of cheers and applause. I anticipated wrongly. Within a page and a half I was interrupted by Newberry. 'This,' he said, enunciating clearly, 'is the veriest crap, unfit for anything but fertilizer, and only dubiously so even for that.'

"Upon this, the class of young sycophants broke into uproarious laughter and I was forced to sit down without completing my reading. Nor was that all. Newberry seized every chance thereafter to humiliate me. Nothing that I wrote pleased him, and he made his displeasure disgustingly public, and always to the delight of the class that, in this way, made me its butt.

"At last, as the final task assigned us that term, we were each required to write a story, or a poem or an essay designed to be submitted for publication in the literary semiannual. I wrote a lighthearted essay filled with sparkling wit and humor, and imagine my pleased surprise when Newberry accepted it.

"Naturally, I felt it only just and wise to seek out old Snarley Face after class and congratulate him on his acumen. 'I am glad, sir,' I said, 'that you will have achieved a better product than usual through the use of my essay in the literary semiannual.'

"And he said to me, baring his yellow fangs in a most unpleasant manner, 'I took it, F. Q. Flubb, only because it was the only submission that made any attempt whatever, however unsuccessfully, to be funny. Its enforced acceptance, Flubb, is the last straw and I will not give this class again.'

"Nor did he, and, though forty years have passed, the memory of my treatment in that class at Old Cesspool remains green. The scars remain fresh, George, and I can never erase them."

I said, "But Quackbrain, think of how that old beloved son of an unidentified father must have felt as you rose to literary fame. Indeed, the manner in which you soared to nearly the top of the literary world must have embittered him far more than his old snubs and spurnings could possibly have embittered you."

"What do you mean, 'to *nearly* the top'—but never mind. You have clearly not kept up with the later history of the school. The miserable miscreant who gave that class died about five years after I attended it, doing so, it is clear, in an obvious effort to avoid witnessing the triumph of the downtrodden, since the lightnings of fame did not begin to flicker about my brow until three years after his death, and so here I am, forever in frustration over the fact that I cannot snap my fingers scornfully under the snub nose of the master snubber. But what would you? Even the gods cannot change the past."

"I wonder," I said softly.

"Eh?"

"Nothing. Nothing."

But, of course, I was thinking of Azazel, my two-centimeter friend from another World, or possibly Universe, or possibly Continuum, whose technological expertise is so far beyond our own as to seem a kind of magic. [Oh, did someone named Clarke say something like that. Well, since I never heard of him, he can be of no importance whatever.]

Azazel was asleep when my calling routine fetched him from his own World, or possibly Universe, or possibly Continuum, and, of course, I won't give you details of the routine. A coarse mind such as yours would be irretrievably damaged if it tried to encompass the subtleties of the endorcism. I'm only thinking of you, old friend.

I waited patiently for Azazel to wake up, for he is inclined to be a bit testy if aroused, and a testy Azazel is a dangerous Azazel for all his tiny size. So there was nothing to do but to watch his arms and legs move through complicated evolutions I could make nothing of. Presumably, he was dreaming something and reacting to the dream.

As the motions became violent, his eyes opened and he sat up with what seemed a start. "I thought so," he moaned (a high-pitched sibilant moan like a tiny steam whistle), "It was only a dream."

"What was, O Wonder of the Universe?"

"My assignation with the fair Zibbulk. Will it never become reality? Of course," he added sadly, "she is something of your size and so she refuses to take me seriously."

"Can't you make yourself larger, O Miracle of the Ages?"

"Of course," he said, with a tiny snarl, "but then my substance becomes thin, smoky and wraithlike and, when I try to embrace her, she feels nothing. I don't know why it is, but fair females like to feel *something* under such conditions. Still, enough of the poetic out-pourings of my personal tragedy. What do you want this time, you miserable piece of trumpery?"

"Time travel, O Astounder of Astrality."

"Time travel," shrieked Azazel. "That is impossible."

"Is it? I am no physicist, Great One, but scientists on this world speak of faster-than-light travel and of wormholes."

"They may, for all I care, speak of molasses and of humming-birds, but time travel is theoretically impossible. Forget it."

"Very well," I sighed, "but that means that old Quackbrain will spend his last few remaining years unable to avenge the snubs and spurnings he has received from villains in the past, villains who did not perceive, let alone appreciate, his great talents."

At this Azazel's face turned from its normal beet-red color to something more approaching the delicate pink of a watermelon's interior. "Snubs and spurnings?" he said. "Ah, how well I know the spurns that patient merit of th'unworthy takes. You have a friend, then, who suffers as I have suffered."

"No one," I said cautiously, "can suffer as your mighty spirit has suffered, O Solace of the Impoverished, but he has suffered somewhat and still suffers."

"How sad. And he wishes to go back in time in order to avenge his patient merit on th'unworthy."

"Exactly, but you said time travel is impossible."

"And so it is. However, I can adjust minds. If you have, or can get something that has been in much contact with him, I can so arrange the workings of his mind that it will *seem* to him that he has gone into the past and met face to face with his ancient tormenters, and he can then do as he wishes."

"Excellent," I said. "As it happens, I have here a ten-dollar bill which I borrowed out of his wallet on the occasion of our last meeting and I am quite sure that it has been in intimate contact with him for at least a month, for old Quackbrain is anything but a Quick-buck."

And so it was, for I met Quackbrain about a month later, and he pulled me to one side.

"George," he said, "last night I had the most amazing dream. At least, I *think* it was a dream, for if it were anything else, I would be going mad. It seemed so *real* it was as though I had stepped back in time. Forty years back."

"Back in time, eh?"

"That's what it seemed like, George. It was as though I were a time traveler."

"Tell me about it, Quackbrain."

"I dreamed I was back at Old Cesspool. I mean *old* Old Cesspool. Not the way it is today, broken down and lost in the inner city, but as it was forty years ago when it was a respectable antique building, aged only by age. I could walk through the corridors and see the classes, the high schoolers at work. There was the faint aura of Depression. Do you remember the Great Depression, George?"

"Of course I do."

"I read the notices on the bulletin board. I looked over the latest edition of the school paper. No one stopped me. No one noticed me. It was as though I didn't exist to them, and I realized that I was my present-day self wandering in an earlier time. And suddenly I further realized that somewhere in the building was Yussif Newberry, still alive. I realized at that moment that I had been brought to Old

Cesspool for a purpose. I had a briefcase in my hands and I searched its contents and a great gladness came over me for I had with me all the proofs I needed.

"I pounded up the stairs to the third floor, where his office was to be found. Do you remember his office, George, and the musty smell of stale books that existed within it? That smell was still there after forty years, or, rather, I had gone back forty years and found it where it had always been. I was afraid that Old Snarly Face might be in class, but my dream brought me back at the right time. He was having a free hour and was engaged in marking papers.

"He looked up as I entered. *He* saw me. *He* took notice of me. He was meant to.

"He said, 'Who are you?'

"I said, 'Prepare for astonishment, Yussif Newberry, for I am none other than Fortescue Quackenbrane Flubb.'

"He frowned. 'You mean you are the aged father of that grubby nincompoop I had in my class last year?'

"'No I am *not* the aged father of that grubby nincompoop. Beware, Newberry, for I am that grubby nincompoop himself. I come from forty years in the future to confront you, you cowardly torturer of my youthful self.'

"'From forty years in the future, eh? I must admit that the passage of time has not improved you. I would have placed the chance of your looking worse than you look now as trifling, but I see you have managed.'

"'Newberry,' I thundered, 'Prepare to suffer. Do you know what I have become in forty years?'

"'Yes,' he said calmly, 'you have become a remarkably ugly man in late middle age. I suppose it was unavoidable but I can almost bring myself to be sorry for you.'

"'I have become more than that, Yussif Newberry. I have become one of the great literary figures of the United States. I have here, for your selection, a copy of my entry in *Who's Who in America*. Note the number of my published books and note further, Newberry, that nowhere in these august volumes is the despised name of Yussif Newberry mentioned. I have here, in addition, Yussif Newberry, a sampling of reviews of my latest works. Read them and note particularly what it says of my talent and my sterling writing ability. I have here, even more, a profile in the *New Yorker* magazine that makes much of me. And now, Yussif Newberry, think of all the callous and wicked things you said of me and of my writing last year in class, and hang your head in bitter shame, Yussif Newberry!'

"'I suppose,' said Newberry, 'this is a dream.'

"'It is probably a dream,' I said, 'but if so, it is my dream, and what I have here to show you is the truth as it shall be forty years from now. Is not your head bowed in deep contrition, Yussif Newberry?'

"'No,' said Newberry, 'I am not responsible for the future. All I can say is that last year in my class everything you wrote was crap and it will stay crap not only forty years from now but to the last syllable of recorded time. Now get out of here and let me mark my papers.'

"And with that, the dream ended. What do you think of it, George?"

"It must have been realistic."

"Indeed. Indeed. But that's not what I mean. Can you imagine that teacher-insult to the human condition, upon learning of my greatness, still clinging to his position. No shame. No despair. He still maintained that my juvenilia was crap and moved not one centimeter from that position. My heart, George, is broken. It was a far, far worse thing I did than I have ever done. It is a far, far worse rest that I go to than I have ever known."

He drifted away, old man, a shattered and broken hulk. It was not long afterward that he died.

George ended his story and wiped his eyes with the five-dollar bill I had given him for the purpose. It was not as absorbent as a handkerchief would have been, but he insists that he finds the tactile sensation of the bill to be superior.

I said, "I suppose it is useless to ask, George, that your stories make sense, but I find I must point out that this was not a true travel in time, according to your own account, but only an imaginary one. It was, indeed, a vision induced by Azazel's manipulation of Flubb's brain. In that case, Flubb was in control of it, or should have been. Why did he not have Yussif Newberry crawling at his feet in a hopeless plea for forgiveness?"

"That," said George, "is precisely what I asked Azazel on another occasion. Azazel said that poor Quackbrain, whatever his prejudice in his own favor, was enough of a literary craftsman to know, at least in his unconscious, that some of his writing *was* crap and that Newberry was correct. Being honest, he had to face that."

George thought a moment or two and then added, "I suppose he's not much like you after all."

WINE IS A MOCKER

GEORGE HAD ORDERED A GLASS OF white wine with which to begin his dinner, and I had ordered a Virgin Mary, which is as close as I care to come to vinous revelry.

I sipped at my spiced tomato juice gently and became aware that George was staring at his bijou goblet with disgust. It was quite empty and I had not seen him down it. He can be extraordinarily deft at times.

"What's the matter, George?" I asked.

He sighed heavily. "In the old days," he said, "you could get a huge tankard of hearty ale for a penny."

"In what old days, George? Are we talking about the Middle Ages?"

"In the *old* days," repeated George. "Now, for just enough weak wine to cast a mist on your upper lip, you have to break into your little boy's piggy bank—if you have one."

"What piggy bank are you discussing? It's not even costing you that medieval penny you've just mentioned. And if you didn't have enough, order another. I'm good for it."

"I wouldn't dream of doing it," said George haughtily. "Ordinarily. But since you suggest it, and I would like to oblige you—" He tapped the rim of his empty glass and the waiter hastened to bring him another.

"Wine," he said, staring at his second goblet, "is a mocker. The Bible says that. Either Moses or Beelzebub said it."

"Actually," I said, "you'll find it in Proverbs 20:1, where it says, 'Wine is a mocker, strong drink is raging: and whoever is deceived thereby is not wise.' The book is attributed, by tradition, to King Solomon."

He stared at me with massive indignation. "Why on Earth do you insist in indulging in your pseudo-erudition? It gets you condemned on all sides. As I was about to say, you'll find the statement either in Habbakuk or Malachi. I suppose you're not going to argue about its being in the Bible."

"Not at all."

"There you are, then. I mentioned the fact that wine is a mocker because I was thinking of my friend, Cambyses Green."

"Cambyses?"

"He was named for some ancient oriental potentate."

"I know that," I said. "The son of Cyrus the Great of Persia. But how did he come—"

"Let us order our dinner," said George, "and I will tell you the story of Cambyses Green."

My friend, Cambyses Green [said George], who was named in honor of some ancient oriental potentate, was very nearly the most charming, the most pleasant person you could ever expect to meet. He had a never-ending fund of droll stories that he could tell in a fascinating manner. He was utterly at ease with strangers and could win them over at once. He was suave and charming toward young women, all of whom were fascinated with him, though he reserved his love, with all the ardor that Eros could bestow on him, for Valencia Judd, a young woman of surpassing beauty and intelligence.

It was Valencia who came to me on one occasion, her light blonde hair disheveled, her small tip-tilted nose just slightly reddened, as though she had been weeping, and a little handkerchief, suspiciously moist, clutched in her left hand. Her name was not really Valencia, you know. That was actually a shortened version of her true name, which was Benevolencia, from which you can judge the sweetness of her disposition and the warmth of her heart.

She said, "Oh, Uncle George," and she paused to gurgle a bit, as the words stuck in her throat.

I was not her uncle in the genetic sense, but if she considered me an uncle, I was bound to consider her my niece, and with the natural affection I would have for any incredibly beautiful young woman bearing such a relationship, I put my arm about her waist, and let her weep softly on my shoulder, while I soothed her with a gentle kiss or two.

"It's Cambyses," she said, at last.

"Surely," I said, a nameless fear tugging at my chest, "he has not forgotten himself and made any suggestions—"

"Oh, no," she said, her large, blue eyes opening wide. "*I* make all the suggestions. It's just that—well, he is *so* nice."

"Of course, and handsome and intelligent and charming and with a keen sense of humor—"

"Oh, yes, Uncle George, oh, yes. All that and more."

"In that case, dear little Valencia, what is it that is making you weep? An overdose of joy?"

"Not really. You see, Uncle George, I don't know if you've ever noticed it, but Cambyses is always just a little bit drunk."

"Is he?" I looked blank. I had always been with him under convivial conditions, at which times he *was* drunk, but then so was everybody. Even I, myself, having had a very few drinks, was usually in a rather pleasant humor, as any barmaid would be willing to testify. "Surely, on those occasions, when he—"

"No, Uncle George," she said, gently. "There are no occasions when it is not so. He is *always* just a little bit drunk." She sighed. "And, of course, when I say 'a little bit drunk,' I mean he is quite drunk. In fact, mostly stinking drunk."

"I cannot believe it."

"Just the same, I cannot endure it. Do you think, Uncle George, since you are such an impressive figure of rectitude and dignity, that you could perhaps speak to Cambyses and persuade him that wine is a mocker and that he should drink fresh, wholesome water, with perhaps an occasional Perrier at times of great hilarity."

"Granted," I said, dubiously, "that I am a model of rectitude and dignity, I don't know if I can persuade Cambyses—"

At this point, Valencia's mouth opened, her handkerchief moved to her eyes and I know she was a microsecond removed from howling her grief. So I said, "But I will try, little one. I will do my best."

I did see Cambyses in consequence. It was the first time I had ever visited him at his home. In fact, it was the first time I had ever seen him alone and without the presence of a roystering throng, all of whom were steadily consuming spirituous liquor of varying degrees of potency.

I suppose I had, therefore, an instinctive expectation that I would meet up with a grave and serious Cambyses, for it is not for nothing that those who are grave and serious are characterized by the adjective "sober."

But I was quite wrong. It was the same merry Cambyses I was accustomed to. As I stepped into his room, he laughed loudly and clapped me on the shoulder by way of a hearty greeting.

"My pal," he said. "My buddy. What are you doing without a drink in your hand? You look naked. Come, let me correct that vile omission."

And he forced a small whiskey on me. It was a little early for such dissipation but it would have been unkind of me to refuse. I tossed it off and, as I did so, I thought of all the times when he had stood me a drink, and of all those other times when he had refused to let me stand him a drink but had stood me another. He was, if you like, one of nature's noblemen in that respect.

He was also, now that Valencia had opened my eyes, one of nature's drunks. Although it was early afternoon and he was alone, there was a distinct weave to his steps, a pronounced glaze to his eyes, a definite vagueness to his smile, and an emphatic touch of alcoholic fragrance in the air—especially when he exhaled.

I said, "Cambyses, my friend, I come to you on behalf of that excellent young creature, Valencia Judd."

He said, "Nature's noblewoman; a beautiful and virtuous goddess. I drink to her."

"No," I said, urgently, "don't drink to her. That is the root of the problem. She has the feeling you drink to her too often and to everything else, indiscriminately, as well. She wishes you to cease."

He stared at me owlishly. "She has never said so to me."

"I suspect that, cowed by your manifold good qualities, she has hesitated to hurt your feelings by pointing out your one small fault, your one tiny misdemeanor, your one minuscule flaw—the fact that you are a drunken bum."

"Just because I take a tiny sip of something for medicinal purposes on rare occasions?"

"The sips are not tiny, Cambyses, nor the occasions rare, nor the reasons medicinal, though the rest of your statement I accept. Therefore, though Valencia did not say so directly, she wishes you to understand that lips that touch liquor are likely to touch hers only at infrequent intervals."

"But it's too late, George, old boy, old friend. My lips touch liquor. I can't deny it."

"They are pickled in it, Cambyses. Can you not cease? Can you not turn away from this dreadful habit and bathe in the pure sun of sobriety as you once did?"

He frowned thoughtfully. "When did I once do?"

"Start now."

He poured himself another drink, and put it to his lips. "George," he said, "have you ever thought what a stinking, miserable hellhole the world is?"

"Frequently," I said.

"Have you never wanted to change it into a fine, warm, delightful paradise?"

"Often," I said.

"I've done it. I've discovered the secret. A few drinks, the merest imbibing of the friendly warmth of gin, or rum, or brandy or—or any of a number of drinks of the sort—and the grim misery of this Earth, melts and dissolves. Tears are changed to laughter, sour looks to smiles, the welkin rings with song. Come, come, am I to give up all this?"

"Some of it. When Valencia is looking, at least."

"I cannot. Not even for Valencia. My duty is to humanity and to the world. Can I allow society to sink back into the foulness that would characterize it were it not for the alchemy of alcohol?"

"But the alchemy you speak of is subjective. It shows its effect only in your mind. It has no real existence."

"George," said Cambyses, solemnly, "you are a dear and beloved friend, so I cannot order you out of my house. But I intend to do it anyway. Out of my house!"

———

As you know, old man, if I have a failing it is that of having an incredibly soft heart. I would never consent to these meals I consume at your expense, for instance, were I not concerned over your obvious need for stimulating company. It means that I must suffer yours, but what of that?

In any case, my heart was aching for Valencia and I felt it was a case for Azazel, my two-centimeter friend from another plane of existence.

This being —Oh, have I told you about him? —Very well, there is no need to sigh melodramatically.

For once, Azazel was not annoyed at being called up. He was delighted. At least, he said he was.

He was dancing around, making peculiar gestures with his tiny hands, the details of which I could not make out. "How triply fortunate for him that you called me here," he said in his squeaky little voice. "I would have sepotulated him. I would have flaxated his modinem. I would have—"

"You would have done this to whom?" I asked with mild interest. "And for what reason?"

Azazel said, with an attempt at dignity quite incompatible with his squeaky voice and tiny size, "He addressed me in terms no gentlebeing would use to another, the big sasquam."

I let him cool down. Being a small object on his own world as on ours, he was forever being stepped on and tripped over, which was a good thing, for it was his forever bruised ego that made him willing to help me. He had a great need to demonstrate his powers.

I said, "A friend of mine is an alcoholic."

"Ah," said Azazel. "He creeps into holes with alcos. What are alcos?"

"No, no. Alcohol is an organic fluid that acts as a stimulant in small doses, but as a mental disorienter in large. My friend is incapable of refraining from large doses."

For a moment, Azazel looked puzzled. Then, "Ah, you mean a 'phosphotonic.'"

"A phosphotonic?" I said, rather puzzled, I admit.

Azazel explained. "People on my world enjoy phosphatones of one sort or another. We sniff phosphine, drink a variety of phosphate solutions, lap up phosphopyruvic acid and so on." Azazel shuddered. "Carried to excess it is a vile habit, but I have found that a little bit of phosphorylized ammonia taken after meals is an excellent digestive aid. Hence our proverb, 'Take a little phospham for your stomach's sake.'" Azazel rubbed his BB-shaped abdomen and licked his red lips with a small red tongue.

I said, "The question is: how to cure my alcoholic friend and induce him to lay off the sauce?"

"Lay off the—"

"I mean cease drinking in and out of season."

"That is easy," said Azazel. "It is child's play to a being of my technological attainments. I need merely to alter the taste centers of his brain as to make alcohol taste to him like something vile—excrement, perhaps."

"No," I said. "Absolutely not. That is going too far. A rational amount of alcoholic intake, such as the amount in which I indulge myself, scarcely a quart a day, is invigorating and no one should be deprived of that. In the excellence of your wisdom, O Mighty Vastness, think of something else."

"Well," said Azazel, "is there any way in which drinking alcohol can be made into a virtue? Are there drinkers who are admired?"

"There are connoisseurs," I said, after some thought. "There are people who are very knowledgeable about drinks, and can distinguish those of high quality. They are usually treated with great admiration."

"Your friend is not one of these? He does not distinguish between high quality and low?"

"Good lord, no. He'll drink bathtub gin, hair tonic, shoe polish, antifreeze. It is astonishing that nothing seems to kill him outright."

"Well, there you are, then, I shall so alter the sense receptors of his brain that he will be able to distinguish between any two varieties, however closely allied, and tell the superior. He will no longer be considered an alcoholic to be despised but a connoisseur to be admired. —Actually, I have this connoisseurish quality with regard to our own phosphatones and have frequently struck large assemblages with awe at my ability—"

He went on and on in excruciating detail, but I listened, if not gladly, then with patience, so eager was I to help Cambyses.

I visited Cambyses some time afterward when I thought that he had gotten over the spleen with which he had ordered me from his digs. I found I had nothing to fear. Alcoholics are merry spirits who never remember the evanescent angers and petulances of the past—or anything else, either.

Not that Cambyses looked much like a merry spirit. He sat on the floor surrounded by a sea of shotglasses, filled with liquids of different appearances. On his face was a look of settled melancholy.

I said, in alarm, "Cambyses, what is wrong?"

"I scarcely know," said Cambyses, "but I have apparently become aware of the shortcomings of these items. Here, George, try this."

It was a tawny port of considerable power, as a slight sip showed me. I said, "Very good, old man."

He said, "Very good? Are you serious? It is deficient in fruitiness!"

"I hadn't noticed," I said.

"You wouldn't," he said, insultingly. "Nor is it as mellow as it should be. You weren't aware of an inappropriate sharpness?"

"Not at all."

Cambyses closed his eyes and shook his head as though overcome with faintness at having witnessed my obtuseness. He said, "About the best thing I could find in my collection is this one. Try this."

It was a cherry Heering of surpassing excellence. I almost cried aloud at the magnificence of its bouquet and the delicacy of its taste. "Magnificent," I said in awe.

"Barely tolerable," he said. "I admit the idiots meant well, but somewhere in the preparation, the fluid passed over a rusty nailhead. There is a not-quite-overpowering but definitely unpleasant metallic taste to it."

"I noticed no such thing," I said indignantly.

"That's because you wouldn't notice a unicorn if it jabbed you in your fat behind," he replied coarsely.

I could no longer fail to notice the ill nature of his taunts and these forced me to observe a characteristic I had never before associated with my young friend.

"Cambyses," I said, "surely you are sober."

He looked up at me with a snarl. "What do you expect? I have nothing here I can bear to drink. It is all dishwater and poison."

It was strange, I acknowledged to myself in the months that followed. Azazel had not so reoriented Cambyses' sense perceptions so to make all alcoholic drinks taste like excrement. Azazel had instead simply given Cambyses a sense of discrimination of superlative delicacy and in his search for an unattainable ideal, Cambyses acted as though any drink that fell short of that ideal (that is, *all* of them) tasted like excrement.

Cambyses became not merely sober, he became a very model of sobriety. He walked stiffly upright, cultivated an austere glance, went to bed early, woke early, adopted habits of distressing regularity and was stern to the point of captiousness toward anyone who deviated from the paths of rigid virtue in the slightest. To him, all normal human behavior resembled drinks of insufficient fruitiness and metallic taste.

My dear young niece, Valencia, was woebegone. She was wrenching at a sopping wet handkerchief, and her face was blotched.

"Cambyses is, as you wished," I pointed out, "sober."

"Cold sober," she said. "Frigidly sober. Liquid-air sober. Yes, that is as it should be." She blubbered a bit, then seized hold of her emotions and said, "His post in his father's financial firm, until now a sinecure, has become a showcase for his talents. He is known as the 'tyrannosaur of Wall Street.' He is widely admired as the epitome of American financial enterprise, and crowds gather to watch him grind the faces of widows and orphans. The deftness with which he does it elicits unbounded applause and has won him a citation from the secretary of the Treasury."

"How proud you must be," I said.

"Proud, indeed. His merciless virtue is admired by all, and his eloquent denunciation of lying, theft, and connivery, except when these characteristics are necessary for the gathering of corporate profits, are cheered to the echo. And yet—"

"And yet?"

"He has grown cold to me, Uncle George."

"Cold? Surely you jest. You are as virtuous as he."

"Oh, every bit," she admitted. "I am a solid mass of virtue. And yet—for some reason—I no longer seem to satisfy him."

I went to see Cambyses. It was not easy. So attentive was he now to business that he found twelve hours a day insufficient to the dedication he brought to his task of bilking the public by overcharging the

Department of Defense for toothpicks and bottlecaps. He was therefore surrounded by secretaries, assistants, and aides-de-camp whom it took all my skill and address to evade.

I finally made my way into his large office, and found him scowling at me. He had aged quite a bit, for the essence of sobriety that now consumed him had etched vertical furrows in his cheeks and turned those once bright and sparkling eyes into the hard opacity of marble.

He said, "What in Tophet do you want, George?"

"I come, my friend," I said, "on behalf of your loved one, Valencia?"

"My what one, who?"

I had to admit that was a bad sign. "Valencia," I said. "Blonde little girl so high, beautiful, virtuous, and made to be loved."

"Oh, yes." Cambyses picked up a glass of water from his desk, frowned at it and put it back. "I seem to remember her. She won't do, George."

"Why ever not? She has been acclaimed as utterly lovable by some of the finest experts in the field."

"Finest experts, bah! Incompetent bunglers! George, that woman makes use of perfume that would sicken a muskrat. Toward the end of the day, despite the perfume, I detect an unpleasant body odor. Her breath is frequently appallingly rancid. She has a tendency to eat Swiss cheese, sardines, and other items that linger on her tongue and teeth. Am I expected to bathe myself in this foul effluvium? For that matter, George, you yourself have neglected to bathe this morning, I perceive."

"No such thing, Cambyses," I replied hotly. "I bathed."

"In that case, stand closer to the soap next time," he said. "You needn't tell Valencia the details if you think it will offend her—as it certainly offends me. But you may tell her that if she ever sees me, she must remain downwind."

"This is ridiculous, Cambyses," I said. "Valencia is a dainty and sweet-smelling young lady. You will not find anything better."

"No," said Cambyses, his face growing grimmer. "I expect not. This is a filthy and rancid world. I am astonished that people do not notice."

"Has it occurred to you that you, yourself, might be imperfect in this regard."

He lifted one wrist and sniffed at it. "No," he said, "it has not."

"That can only be because your senses are saturated with your own odor. To others, you are probably offensive."

"To others? What on earth do I care about others?"

Which, I had to admit to myself, was an unanswerable point.

Cambyses lifted the glass of water again, sipped at it, made an appalling face, and said, "I can detect at least five organic chemicals of noisome taste that have been added to this water. Even bottled spring water has a siliceous tang owing to the traces of glass that it dissolves."

I sighed and left. The case was hopeless. Azazel, in giving him a nice discrimination of the senses, had overdone it.

I tried to break the news to Valencia gently. She blubbered, squealed and keened dreadfully. It took me three days and nights to console her, and it was a difficult task, for some of my spring had been sprung in recent years and you can't imagine how much consolation that woman needed.

As for Cambyses, the last I heard of him, he was searching the world for a place to live where the air and water were sufficiently pure for his refined palate, for a cook who could meet his exacting needs and, most of all, a young woman who would not offend his delicate nose. He is as rich as you would expect a defense contracter to be—his low-quality, high-cost equipment is the pride of the armed forces of our glorious nation—but I suspect he's not happy.

George heaved a vinous sigh of commiseration and tossed off his fifth goblet of white wine.

I was furious. I said, "I thought you said wine is a mocker."

"So it is. Not its presence, of course, but its absence."

"I deny that." I had rarely been so annoyed with the man. "I am always prepared for the peculiar attitude toward life that these very dubious reminiscences of yours portray, but I draw the line at this one. I deny that a sober man, simply because he is sober, develops all the evil characteristics you ascribe to this Cambyses you speak of."

"You do?" said George, sounding astonished. "What possible evidence can you have to the contrary?"

"Well, for one thing, I am a teetotaler."

"I rest my case," said George.

THE MAD SCIENTIST

GEORGE AND I GENERALLY MEET AT some neutral spot—in a restaurant or on a park bench, for instance. The reason is simple: my wife won't have him in our apartment because she thinks he's a deadbeat—and I agree. In addition, though, she's immune to his charm and I, for some reason I can't fathom, am not.

However, my dear wife was out for the day and George knew that, so he dropped around in the afternoon. I couldn't very well turn him from my door so I invited him in with what enthusiasm I could muster. That wasn't much because I had a deadline staring me in the face and a set of galleys that had to be read.

"I hope you don't mind," I said. "I have to finish this thing. Why not help yourself to a book and read for a while?"

I didn't really think he would. He glared at me for a moment, then pointing to the galleys, said, "How long have you been making your living that way?"

"Fifty years," I mumbled.

He said, "Isn't that enough? Why don't you quit?"

"Because," I said, speaking very distinctly, "I have to earn

67

enough money to support those of my friends who constantly devour their meals at my expense."

I meant it to sting, but George is immune to such things. He said, "I should think your brain would shrivel to a peanut, spending fifty years writing stories about mad scientists."

I was the one who was stung. I said, rather sharply, "I don't write stories about mad scientists. No one in science fiction above the comic-strip level does it. Mad scientist stories were written back in Neanderthal times; they are not written now."

"Why not?"

"Because, George, they're old hat. And on top of that, the madness of scientists is a base canard accepted only by the hopelessly banal and cliché-ridden. There are no mad scientists. Some may be genially eccentric, perhaps, but never mad."

"Really," said George. "I knew a mad scientist once. Martinus Augustus Dander. Even his initials were mad. Ever hear of him?"

"Never," I said, and fixed my eyes firmly on my galleys.

"I didn't say he was certifiable," said George, totally ignoring my galleys, "but any dull, respectable, uninteresting person—you, for instance—would consider him mad. I will tell you his story—"

"Later," I said, a note of pleading entering my voice.

I see that despite your amateurish attempt to appear busy you are all agog to hear the tale [said George], so I will not tantalize you with delay, but get right to it.

My good friend, Martinus Augustus Dander, was a physicist. He had gained his Ph.D. in physics at Mudlark University in Tennessee, and at the time that all this took place he was professor of physics at the Flatbush Correspondence School of the Physical Sciences.

I used to have lunch with him at the school cafeteria, which was located on the corner of Drexel and Avenue D near a falafel push-cart. As we sat on the stoop and ate our falafels, or occasionally a knish, he would pour out his soul to me.

He was a brilliant physicist, but a bitter man. My own knowledge of physics stops short about the time of Newton G. Descartes so I can't judge his brilliance as a matter of firsthand knowledge, but he told me he was brilliant, and surely a brilliant physicist can recognize brilliance when he sees it.

His bitterness arose from the fact that he was not taken seriously. He would say to me, "George, in the world of physics, every-thing depends on your connections. If I had a degree from Harvard and taught at Yale, or at MIT, or at CalTech, or even at Columbia, the world would hang on my every word. But I must admit that a Ph.D. from doughty old Mudlark and a professorial seat at Flatbush CSPS carries a somewhat lesser weight."

"I take it Flatbush isn't part of the Ivy League."

"You are quite right," said Martinus. "It is *not* part of the Ivy League. What's worse, it does not have a football team. But then," he added defensively, "neither does Columbia, and yet I am ignored. *Physical Reviews* will not publish my research papers. They are brilliant, revolutionary, cosmically significant," (it was at this point that his eyes got that peculiar glint that would lead prosaic people like yourself to consider him mad) "but they are rejected not only by *PR* but by the *American Journal of Cosmology, the Connecticut Bulletin of Particle Interactions,* and even the *Latvian Society of Impermissible Thought.*"

"That's too bad," I said, wondering if he would be willing to pay for an additional yam knish, which this particular pushcart produced à la française. "Have you tried a vanity press?"

"I admit," he said, "that I sometimes feel desperate, but I have my pride, George, and never will I pay to have my world-shaking theories published."

"What, incidentally," I asked, with faint curiosity, "*is* your world-shaking theory?"

He glanced furtively from side to side as though to make sure that no colleague was within earshot. Fortunately, the only people present were some seedy individuals exploring the contents of neighboring trash cans, and a keen glance seemed to convince him that none of these were members of the Flatbush CSPS faculty.

He said, "I can't give you the details, of course, since I must maintain my priority. After all, my academic confreres, while souls of integrity in most ways, will, without hesitation, steal any man's intellectual property. I will, therefore, omit the mathematics and merely hint at the results. You know, I presume, that sufficient energy sufficiently concentrated, will bring about the production of an electron and a positron or, in a more general sense, any paired particle and antiparticle."

I nodded sagely. I had, after all, inadvertently glanced over one of *your* science essays at one time, old man, and had gathered something of the sort.

69

Dander went on. "The particle and antiparticle curve off in response to an electromagnetic field, one to the left and one to the right, and if they are in a good vacuum, they separate indefinitely without reconversion into energy, since in that vacuum they do not interact with anything."

"Ah," I said, following the little fellows off into the vacuum in my mind's eye. "Very true."

He said, "But the equations governing this action work in either direction, as I can prove by a very subtle line of argument. In other words, it is possible to create a particle-antiparticle pair, well separated, in a vacuum—without any energy input, of course, since in the forward motion they produce energy. In other words, we produce unlimited energy out of the vacuum, fulfilling the dreams of every human being who has ever longed for Aladdin's lamp. Indeed, I can only assume that the genies who filled medieval Arabic legendry knew of my theory and applied it."

—Please, old man, don't interrupt me with pompous outcries to the effect that this is impossible because it would require a reversal of time or the violation of both the first and second laws of thermodynamics. I am merely reporting what Dander told me, and I do so without elaborate editorialization.

Now to get back to my story—and, yes, my feathers *are* ruffled—

Upon hearing what Dander had to say, I commented thoughtfully, "But, Martinus, my friend, what you are suggesting would imply either that time is reversed or that both the first and second laws of thermodynamics are violated."

To which he replied that, on the subatomic level, time *can* be reversed, and that the laws of thermodynamics are statistical rules that do not apply to individual subatomic particles.

"In that case, my friend," said I, "why do you not tell the world of this great discovery of yours?"

"Indeed?" said Dander, sneering elaborately. "Just like that? What do you suppose would happen if I buttonholed a fellow physicist and told him what I have just told you. He would babble of time reversal and thermodynamic laws as you do, and rush off. No! What I need is to publish my theory in full detail in a prestige-laden journal of hoary scientific repute. Then people will pay attention."

"In that case, why don't you publish—"

He did not allow me to finish, "Because what stuffy, flannel-brained editor or referee would accept any paper I write that is in the least bit unusual? Do you know that James P. Joule could not get his paper on conservation of energy printed in a scientific journal because he was a brewer? Do you know that Oliver Heaviside could not persuade anyone to pay attention to his important papers because he was selftaught and used unconventional mathematical symbolism? And you expect that I, a member of the lowly Flatbush CSPS, can get *my* paper printed."

"Too bad," I said, with a manly sympathy.

"Too bad?" he said, throwing off my arm, which was resting on his shoulder soothingly. "Is that all you can say? Do you realize that if I could only get my paper printed, people who studied it would see exactly what I mean and would greet it as the greatest elaboration and application of quantum theory ever advanced? Do you realize that I would surely receive a Nobel Prize, and that I would be canonized right alongside of Albert Einstein. And only because no one in the scientific establishment has the courage and the wit to recognize genius, I am doomed to lie in an unmarked grave—unwept—unhonored—and unsung."

That touched me, old man, although I admit that I hadn't the faintest idea why Dander objected to being unsung. What good it would do his dead body to have a rock group caterwaul over his fresh-turned grave, I can't imagine.

I said, "You know, Martinus, I can do something for you."

"Oh," he said, with a faint touch of bitterness in his voice. "You are perhaps a second cousin of the editor of *Physical Reviews;* or your sister is, perhaps, his mistress; or you are, perhaps, privy to the exact manner in which he succeeded to his post, following the suspicious—"

I raised an austere hand. "I have my methods," I said. "I promise I will get your paper published."

And I did, for it so happens, I know how to contact a two-centimeter extraterrestrial being, whom I call Azazel, and whose advanced technology makes it possible for him—

[Oh, you *have* heard of him. Is it possible that I have warned you before of the dire consequences to yourself were he to hear you add your fatuous *ad nauseam* to your statement?]

In any case I contacted him and he arrived in my apartment in his usual high state of dudgeon. He is, of course, a small being compared to the human beings of our planet and he is, in point of fact, even smaller compared to the intelligences on his own world, all of whom, I have gathered, have long curved, sharp horns as opposed to the little nubbins sported, to his incredible embarrassment, by Azazel. It is to the unhappiness arising from his size and his pigmyish equipment that I attribute his fiery temper. A person of my broad understanding can sympathize with his situation, and even approve of it, since his frustrations are useful to me. After all, he grants my requests only because it is his chance to shine as a being of accomplishment, something that never happens on his own world.

In this case, though, his fury vanished as soon as I had explained the situation.

He said thoughtfully, in his high-pitched squeak. "Poor fellow. He finds himself at odds with editors, does he?"

"I'm afraid so," I said.

"I am not surprised," said Azazel. "Editors are fiends, one and all, and it is a worthy task to get even with them after being at odds with them. It would be a happier, a purer, a more fragrant world," his voice rose into a sudden passionate outbreak, "if every editor were buried under a huge heap of stinking maradram, though that, of course, would make the smell worse."

I said, "How is it you know so much about editors?"

"Why," he said, "I once wrote a tender little short story, fragrant with true love and redolent of sacrifice, and an incredibly stupid—" He broke off. "Do you mean to say that on this backward mudball, you have editors of the same sort we have on our own advanced world?"

"Apparently," I said.

Azazel shook his head. "Truly, in fundamentals, all intelligent societies are alike. We may differ in all superficialities, such as biological makeup, mental attitudes, moral sensibilities, but in the true basics—the characteristics of editors—we are alike."

(Yes, old man, I know that you have no trouble with editors, but that's because you grovel.)

"Is there anything you can do, O Mighty One and Universal Power, to correct the situation," I asked.

Azazel thought. "I must have some indication of the psychic makeup of some particular editor. I presume your friend has a—you should excuse the expression—rejection slip from some editor."

"I am convinced of that, Great One."

"The wording and aura of that slip would give me the information I need. A slight adjustment of that aura, a drop of the milk of human kindness, a soupçon of intelligence, a trace of tolerance—We can't expect to make a moral beacon of an editor, to be sure, but we can mitigate the evil just sufficiently—"

Well, it is not my intention to go into the nitty-gritty of the techniques of Azazel; it would be dangerous to do so in any case.

Suffice it to say, I had obtained a rejection slip from Professor Dander by a clever piece of strategy that involved picking the lock of his office and going through his files. I then persuaded him to resubmit his paper to the journal from whose august offices the rejection slip had come.

In fact, old man, I used a little trick I had once picked up from you. I said, "Dander, my friend, send this paper back to that black-hearted incompetent and write a covering letter that reads as follows, 'I have made all the changes suggested by the referee and it is incredible the extent to which these have improved the paper. I am grateful to all of you for your help.'"

Dander objected feebly at first, pointing out that he had made no changes and that the statement was not, therefore, an objective description of the actual circumstances. I explained to him, however, that what he needed was a publication and not a Boy Scout badge.

He thought about that for a while, and then said, "You're correct. A Boy Scout badge would be most inappropriate since I never actually qualified for Scouthood. I flunked tree identification."

Off went the paper and two months later, it was published. You have no idea how happy Martinus Augustus Dander was. We bought enough skewered meat at the sidewalk cafeteria to blister our stomachs and then downed it in drink after drink of orange crush à la ptomaine.

[Please stop nodding your head, old man, and reaching for your dreary galleys. I have not finished the story.]

It was about that time I spent a winter with my friend who owned a house in the country; the one whom I taught to walk on snow. I believe I told you the story. For that reason I did not see Professor Dander for some three or four months.

I sought him out at once on my return, however, for I was certain that by now he had completed preliminary negotiations with some Japanese firm for manufacturing energy out of nothing, and that he was rolling in pelf of large denominations. I was certain he would be in no mood to skimp and that a dinner at Burger King was well within the realm of practicality. I had even brought a bottle of my own special ketchup mix in anticipation.

I found him in his office staring blankly at the wall. He had a three-day growth of beard, and his suit looked as though he had slept in it for three nights although he himself looked as though he had not slept at all for four. It was a paradox I did not attempt to unravel.

I said, "Professor Dander, what has happened?"

He looked up at me, with lackluster eyes. They focussed only slowly and a look of near-comprehension entered them by microscopic stages. "George?" he said.

"The same," I assured him.

"It didn't work, George," he said, feebly. "You failed me."

"Failed you. In what way?"

"The paper. It was published. Everyone read it. Each person who read it found a mathematical error in it. Each person who read it found a *different* mathematical error. You deceived me, George. You said you would solve my problem and you didn't. There's only one thing I can do now, George. I added up the food bill at the street-corner cafeteria. You owe me $116.50 in pizza slices alone, George."

I was horrified. Once my friends start adding up bills, who can tell where it would end? Even you might bestir yourself, despite the difficulties you have in doing sums.

I said, "Professor Dander. I did not deceive you. I told you I would see to it that you had your paper published, and that I did. I promised nothing more than that. It never occurred to me to guarantee your mathematics. How could you expect me to know that your mathematics had fallen short?"

"It didn't." A certain indignant energy crept into his voice. "It did not fall short."

"But those professors who found errors?"

"Fools, one and all. They know no mathematics."

"But each one found a different mistake."

"Exactly." His voice was almost normal now and his eyes were beginning to glitter. "I should have seen this before. They're incompetent. They *must* be incompetent. If they knew their mathematics, they would all have found the *same* mistake."

And then the glitter faded and an air of hopelessness pervaded him again. "But what's the use?" he said. "They've destroyed my reputation. I've been made a laughing stock. Unless—Unless—"

He sat up suddenly and seized my hand, "Unless I can *show* them."

"How do you expect to show them, Professor?"

"So far I have only a theory, a line of argument, an intricate mathematical demonstration. That is something one can argue with, and supposedly disprove. But if I can actually produce my particles and antiparticles. If I can do it in significant quantities and create substantial amounts of energy out of nothing—"

"Yes, but can you?"

"There must be some way. I'll have to think—think—" He bent his head between his two fists. "Think," he muttered. "Think."

Then he looked up at me, eyes narrowed. "After all, it's been done before."

"It has?"

"Absolutely. I'm convinced of it. Eighty years ago, some Russian must have worked out a method for obtaining energy from a vacuum. Einstein had just established the quantum theory in 1905 by his work on the photoelectric effect, and from that it followed—"

I won't deny that I was skeptical of this. "What was the name of the Russian?"

"How should I know?" said Dander, indignantly. "But he must have created a mass of particles here on Earth and an equal mass of antiparticles in space beyond the atmosphere, just as a demonstration. They curved toward each other and met in the atmosphere. That was in 1908 in Siberia near the Tunguska River. It's called the Tunguska Event. No one was able to figure out what had happened. Knocked down every tree for forty miles but left no crater. But *we* know what happened, don't we?"

He had gotten quite excited and had gotten to his feet. He was hopping about and rubbing his hands. He was babbling in his enthusiasm, saying, "The Russian, whoever he was, deliberately experimented in the middle of Siberia to avoid damage and he was undoubtedly killed in the explosion. Nowadays, though, we have ways of conducting experiments with radio signals at long distances."

"Dander," I said, quite shocked. "Surely, you don't intend to conduct dangerous experiments."

"Oh, don't I, though?" he said, and an expression of pure evil came over his face. That's when the madness truly began to show. Remember that I told you he was a mad scientist.

"I will show them," he shrieked. "I will show them *all*. They will see whether energy can be obtained from a vacuum or not. I shall create an explosion that will shake Earth to its foundations. Laugh at *me*, will they?"

Then he suddenly turned on me, "Get out, you! Get out! I know very well you are trying to steal my ideas, but you won't. I will cut your heart out and mince it to mush." He snatched at some sharp-edged instrument on his desk and rushed at me, continuing to babble.

Well, old man, let it never be said of me that I did not know when I wasn't wanted. I left with the dignity that becomes me so well—running slightly, of course.

I never saw Dander again and he is no longer at the Flatbush CSPS.

And that's my story of the mad scientist.

I stared at George's face, with its look of bland innocence.

I said, "When did all this happen, George?"

"Several years ago."

"Of course, you have a reprint of Professor Dander's paper?"

"No, old man, as a matter of fact, I haven't."

"A reference, perhaps, to the journal in which it was published."

"I haven't the faintest idea, old man. I don't interest myself in such trivia."

"I don't believe you for a minute, George. When you tell me that this mad scientist of yours is somewhere attempting to arrange a huge collision of matter and antimatter, I tell you it's all nonsense."

"For your own peace of mind," said George, calmly, "you had better continue to think so. Nevertheless, somewhere in this world, Dander is busily working. From his last incoherent remarks, I gather he was planning to create a Tunguska event, long distance, over the lower Potomac. He pointed out that next to the middle of Siberia, or possibly the Gobi desert, Washington, D.C. was the most dispensable place on Earth. Of course, its destruction will convince what's left of the government that the Soviets have struck and they will retaliate at once so that the resulting thermonuclear war will destroy the Earth. —I wonder, therefore, if you could lend me fifty dollars till the first of the month, old sport?"

"Why should I?"

"Because if Dander succeeds, money will have lost all value and you will have lost nothing. Or to put it another way, you will have lost everything, so what's another fifty?"

"Yes, but what if Dander doesn't succeed?"

"In that case, in your relief at knowing that all humanity will survive, will you be so small-minded as to cavil at a mere fifty dollars?"

I gave him the fifty.

THE FABLE
OF THE
THREE
PRINCES

THERE WAS A KING ONCE NAMED Hilderic who ruled over a very small kingdom known as Micrometrica. It was not a rich kingdom or a powerful one, but it was a happy one, because Hilderic was a good sort of king who loved his people and was loved by them.

Because Micrometrica was so small and poor, Hilderic did not try to conquer other kingdoms, and because it was so small and poor other kingdoms did not think it worthwhile to conquer it. As a result, all was peaceful and pleasant in Micrometrica.

Of course, King Hilderic didn't like to be poor. The palace was quite small, and he had to help in the garden while his wife, Queen Ermentrude, had to help in the kitchen. This made them both unhappy, but they did have an ample supply of one thing—sons.

One day, it so happened, the queen had had a child for the first time. All the kingdom would have been extremely happy, except that she overdid it. She had triplets. Three boys.

"Dear, dear," said King Hilderic, thoughtfully. "With triplets, how will we ever decide which one shall succeed to the throne?"

"Perhaps," said Queen Ermentrude, who looked at the three

new babies with love and pride, "we can allow all three to rule when the time comes."

But King Hilderic shook his head. "I don't think so, my love. The kingdom is scarcely large enough for one ruler. All the other kingdoms will laugh if it has three. Besides, what if the three should disagree? Our people would be so unhappy with quarreling monarchs."

"Well," said the queen, "we'll decide when they grow up."

The three babies grew up tall and strong and handsome, and the royal parents loved them all equally. They saw to it that all three boys studied hard, so that each one might be perfectly fit to be a king when the time came.

Though all did very well in their studies, it soon became clear that the sons were not identical triplets. Their appearances and tastes were different.

One of the three princes was larger and stronger than either of the other two. He came to be called Primus, which, in the ancient, sacred language of the kingdom, meant "number one."

When he was not at his studies, Prince Primus exercised and developed his muscles. He could lift heavy weights, bend thick iron bars, and crack a coconut in his bare hands.

Everyone in the kingdom admired his strength and thought they would feel safe if only he were the king when the time came for it.

Another son was not quite as tall or as strong as Prince Primus, and so he came to be called Secundus, which, in that same ancient, sacred language meant "number two."

His muscles didn't bulge as those of Prince Primus did, but when he was not at his studies, he practiced with weapons of war. Prince Secundus could throw his spear farther and shoot an arrow straighter than anyone in the kingdom. No one could stand against him in a sword fight, and he rode a horse to perfection.

Everyone in the kingdom admired his skill and thought they would feel safe if he were the king, too.

The remaining son was reasonably tall and strong, but he was not quite as tall and strong as his two brothers, so he was named Tertius, which meant "number three."

Prince Tertius was even better at his studies than his two brothers, but he was not interested in lifting weights or throwing spears. When he was not studying, he wrote love poems and would sing them in a very pleasant voice. He also read a great many books.

The young ladies of the kingdom thought the poetry of Prince Tertius was beautiful. Everyone else, however, wasn't sure it would be safe to have a poet as king. They were glad there were two stronger princes to choose from.

The three princes were quite friendly with each other, fortunately, and as they grew older, they decided that they would not fight or quarrel over who was to be the king someday. In fact, they loved their father and wanted him to stay king for many years.

"Still," said Prince Primus, "Our Royal Father is getting old, and we must come to some decision. Since we are all the same age there's no use trying to select the oldest. However, I am the largest and strongest. There's that to consider."

"Yes," said Prince Secundus, "but I am the most skilled warrior. I don't want to make a fuss about that, but it is important."

"I think," said Prince Tertius, "we ought to let Dad and Mom make the decision."

Prince Primus frowned. "I don't think you ought to call Our Royal Parents 'Dad and Mom.'"

"But that's who they are," said Prince Tertius.

"That is not the point," said Prince Secundus. "There is their dignity to think of. If I were king someday, I should certainly expect you to refer to me as 'My Royal Brother.' I should be very hurt if you were to call me 'buddy' or 'pal.'"

"That is very true," said Prince Primus. "If I were king, I would despise being called 'Primey.'"

"In that case," said Tertius, who never liked to quarrel, "why don't we ask Our Royal Parents what we ought to do? After all, they are the monarchs, and we should obey their wishes."

"Very well," said the other two, and all three rushed to the royal throne room.

King Hilderic thought about it. Being a good king, he wanted to do what was best for his little country. He wasn't at all sure that the country would be well off under a very strong king, or a very warlike king, or even a very poetic king.

What the country needed, he thought, was a very *rich* king, one who could spend money to make the country happier and more prosperous.

Finally, he sighed, and said, "There's no way I can choose among you. I will have to send you on a hard and dangerous quest to get money—a great deal of money. I don't want to make it seem that money is so terribly important, but, you know, we *do* need it quite badly. Therefore the one who brings back the most money will be king."

Queen Ermentrude looked very disturbed. "But, Father—" (She never called him "Your Majesty" unless courtiers were about, and the kingdom was so poor there weren't many of those.) "But, Father," she said, "what if our dear princes should be hurt in the course of the quest?"

"We can only hope they won't be hurt, Mother, but we need money, you see, and Emperor Maximian of Allemania has a great deal of money. He is probably the richest monarch in the world."

Prince Primus said, "That may be so, My Royal Father, but the emperor won't give us money just because we ask for it."

Prince Secundus said, "In fact, no one will give us money just because we ask for it."

Prince Tertius said, "I don't think princes ought to ask for money in any case."

"Well, my princes," said the King, "it is not a matter of asking for money. The emperor Maximian, it seems, has a daughter named Meliversa. She is an only child."

He put on a large pair of spectacles and pulled a stiff sheet of parchment from a drawer in the royal desk.

He said, "I received this notice by courier two days ago, and I have been studying it ever since. It has been distributed to all the kings in the world, and it is really very kind of the emperor to remember me, since I am king of so small and poor a country."

He cleared his throat. "It says here," he said, glancing over the parchment very carefully, "that the imperial princess is as beautiful as the day; tall, slender, and very well educated."

Prince Primus said, "It's a little troublesome to have a princess well educated. She may talk too much."

"But we needn't listen to her," said Prince Secundus.

Prince Tertius said, "But My Royal Father, what has the imperial princess got to do with the matter of obtaining money?"

"Well, my young princes," said the King, "anyone who is a

royal prince, and who can prove he is one by presenting his birth certificate, will be allowed to demonstrate his abilities. If these should please the imperial princess Meliversa so that she wishes to marry the prince, he will be named successor to the throne and given a large allowance. Then, eventually, he will become emperor. If it is one of you, why then he will also become king of this country in time; and with the wealth of the empire to dispose of, he will make Micrometrica very prosperous."

Prince Primus said, "The princess Meliversa could never resist my muscles, My Royal Father."

Prince Secundus said, "Or my horsemanship, if it comes to that."

Prince Tertius said, "I wonder if she likes poetry. . . ."

King Hilderic said, "There is one catch, though. I have educated you boys in economics, sociology, and other subjects a king must know. Meliversa, however, has been educated in sorcery. If any prince tries to win her heart and fails, she will turn him into a statue. She says she needs a great many statues for the promenade in her park."

Queen Ermentrude said, "I knew it," and began to weep.

"Don't weep, My Royal Mother," said Prince Tertius, who loved her dearly. "I'm sure it isn't legal to turn princes into statues."

"Not ordinarily." said the king, "but it is part of the agreement. Besides, it is difficult to argue law with an imperial princess. So if you princes don't want to take the chance, I certainly won't blame you. . . . It's just that we need money so badly."

Prince Primus said, "I am not afraid. She will never be able to resist me."

"Or me," said Prince Secundus.

Prince Tertius looked thoughtful and said nothing.

The three princes made ready at once for the long journey. Their clothing was rather faded and out of fashion, and their horses were old, but that was all they could manage.

"Farewell, My Royal Parents," said Prince Primus. "I shall not fail you."

"I hope not," said King Hilderic doubtfully, while Queen Ermentrude wept quietly in the background.

"I shall not fail you either, My Royal Parents," said Prince Secundus.

Prince Tertius waited for the other two to start on the way, and then he said, "Good-bye, Mom and Dad. I will do my best."

"Good-bye, son," said King Hilderic, who had a lump in his throat.

Queen Ermentrude hugged Prince Tertius, who then galloped after his two brothers.

It took the three princes a long time to reach the chief city of the empire. Their horses were very tired by then, and their clothes were quite worn out. They had also used up their money and had had to borrow from the treasurers of the kingdoms through which they passed.

"So far," said Prince Tertius sadly, "we've piled up a considerable debt, which makes our kingdom worse off than ever."

"After I've won the princess," said Prince Primus, "I will pay the debt three times over."

"I will pay it five times over," said Prince Secundus.

Prince Tertius said, "That's *if* one of us wins."

"How can we lose?" asked Princes Primus and Secundus together.

And indeed, when they arrived in the capital, they were greeted with kindness. They were given fresh horses and beautiful new clothing of the richest description, and were shown to a lavish suite in the largest and most beautiful palace they had ever imagined. Many servants were at their call, and all served them with the greatest politeness.

The three princes were very pleased with their treatment.

Prince Primus said, "The emperor must know what a wonderful family we come from. Our ancestors have been kings for many generations."

"Yes," said Prince Tertius, "but they have all been poor kings. I wonder if the emperor Maximian knows that."

"He must," said Prince Secundus. "Emperors know everything. Otherwise, how could they be emperors?"

The second assistant serving maid was at that moment bringing in fresh towels so that the princes might take their baths in preparation for a great feast that night.

Prince Primus said at once, "You! Serving maid!"

The serving maid trembled at being addressed by a prince, and curtsied very low. "Yes, Your Highness."

"Is the emperor a wise emperor?"

The serving maid said, "Oh, Your Highness, the entire empire marvels at his wisdom."

Prince Secundus said, "Would he care whether the princes who visit him are rich or poor?"

"Oh, no, Your Highness," said the serving maid. "He is so wealthy that money means nothing to him. He is concerned only with the happiness of his daughter. If she asks to marry a certain prince, that prince will become heir to the kingdom even if he doesn't possess a single penny."

Prince Primus and Prince Secundus smiled and nodded to each other as though to say: We knew it all along.

Prince Tertius smiled at the serving maid and said, "And what about the princess, my dear? Is she as pretty as you are?"

The serving maid turned very pink and her mouth fell open. She seemed quite unable to speak.

Prince Primus said to his brother in a low voice, "Don't call her 'my dear.' It unsettles servants to be addressed so by a prince."

Prince Secundus said to his brother in an even lower voice, "How can a serving maid be pretty? A serving maid is just a serving maid."

Prince Tertius said, "Just the same, I would like an answer to my question."

The serving maid, who was really quite pretty even though she was a serving maid (but most princes wouldn't have noticed that), said, "Your Royal Highness must be joking. The princess is taller than I am and far more beautiful. She is as beautiful as the sun."

"Ah," said Prince Primus. "A rich princess who is as beautiful as the sun is someone to be interested in."

Prince Secundus said, "It would be quite a pleasure to have a rich princess like that about one's palace."

Prince Tertius said, "She might be too bright to look at, if she is as beautiful as the sun."

The serving maid said, "But she is haughty."

Prince Primus said, at once, "A serving maid may not speak unless she is spoken to."

Prince Secundus said, severely, "This comes of saying 'my dear' to serving maids."

But Prince Tertius said, "Is she *very* haughty, my dear?"

"*Very* haughty, Your Highness," said the serving maid, trembling at the haughty stares of the other two brothers. "There have been a number of princes who have already applied for her hand, but she would have none of them."

"Of course not," said Prince Primus. "They were probably pipsqueaks who couldn't bend an iron bar an inch. Why should she be interested in them?"

"Probably," said Prince Secundus, "they couldn't even lift a sword, let alone fight with one. She wouldn't be interested in them."

"Perhaps," said Prince Tertius, "we ought to ask the serving maid what became of the princes who didn't please the princess."

The serving maid's eyes dropped, and she said sadly, "They were all turned into statues, Your Highness. Handsome statues, for they were all young and handsome princes."

Prince Tertius shook his head. "I had hoped the emperor was only joking, but he must have really meant what he said on the parchment. Are there many of those statues?"

"There are about a dozen on each side of the garden path along which the princess walks each morning, Your Highness. She never looks at them, for she is as hard-hearted as she is beautiful."

"Pooh," said Prince Primus. "It doesn't matter that she is hard-hearted, as long as she is rich. And beautiful, too, of course. I shall soften her heart. . . . Now be off with you at once, serving maid."

The serving maid curtsied deeply and left the room, taking backward steps, for it would have been very impolite for her to turn her back on three princes.

That night there was a great feast, and the three princes were the guests of honor.

The emperor, seated on a splendid throne at the head of the table, greeted them. Next to him was the princess Meliversa, and she was indeed as beautiful as the sun. Her hair was long and the color of corn silk. Her eyes were blue and reminded everyone of the sky on a bright spring day. Her features were perfectly regular and her skin was flawless.

But her eyes were empty, and her face was expressionless.

She did not smile when Prince Primus was introduced to her. She looked at him proudly and said, "What kingdom are you from?"

He said, "I am from Micrometrica, Your Imperial Highness."

The princess said, with contempt, "I know all the kingdoms of Earth, and Micrometrica is the smallest of them." And she looked away from him.

Prince Primus backed away from her and took his seat at the

table. He whispered to Prince Tertius, "She will grow interested once I show her what I can do."

Prince Secundus was introduced to her, and she said, "You are also from Micrometrica, I imagine."

"Yes, Your Imperial Highness. Prince Primus is my brother."

"Micrometrica is also the poorest kingdom on Earth. If you and your brother must share its wealth, you must be poor indeed." And she looked away from him.

Prince Secundus backed away from her and took his seat at the table. He whispered to Prince Tertius, "She will forget our poverty when I show her what I can do."

Prince Tertius was introduced to her, and she said, "Still another from Micrometrica?"

"We are triplets, Your Imperial Highness," said Prince Tertius, "though not identical ones. And what we have, we share."

"But you have nothing to share."

"We have no money and no power," said Prince Tertius, "but we and our kingdom are happy. And when happiness is shared, it increases."

"I have never noticed that," said the princess, and she looked away from him.

Prince Tertius backed away from her and took his seat at the table. He whispered to his brothers, "She is rich, and our country needs money. But her beauty is ice-cold and her wealth does not bring her happiness."

The next morning, Prince Primus made ready to put on a demonstration of his abilities for the princess. He had dressed in a fine pair of athletic shorts supplied by the emperor, and he made his magnificent muscles ripple as he stood before the mirror. He was quite satisfied with his appearance.

At that moment, however, there was a timid knock on the door, and when Prince Primus called, "Enter," the second assistant serving maid came in with a bowl of apples.

"What is this?" demanded Prince Primus.

The serving maid said, "I thought you might wish some refreshment before undertaking your task, Your Highness."

"Nonsense," said Prince Primus. "I have all the refreshment I need. Take away those silly apples."

"I also wonder, Your Highness," said the serving maid, blushing at her own daring in continuing to speak to him, "if you ought to undertake the task."

"Why not?" said Prince Primus, flexing his arms and smiling at himself in the mirror. "Do you think I am not manly enough?"

The serving maid said, "You are certainly manly enough for anyone in the world but the princess. She is so hard to please, and it would be a shame that such a fine prince as Your Highness should be made into a marble statue."

Prince Primus laughed, scornfully. "She cannot be so hard to please that *I* do not please her—and that is enough talk. You must only speak when spoken to, serving maid. Get out at once."

And the serving maid got out at once, though she curtsied first.

Prince Primus stepped out into the large arena. Before him were the stands, covered by a beautiful silk canopy. The emperor was seated in the center, and at his right was the imperial princess Meliversa. The officials of the court were in the stands too, as were many a young gentleman and young lady. In one corner were Prince Secundus and Prince Tertius.

Prince Primus faced the stands, and around him was all the equipment he needed.

He turned, to begin with, to a large stack of barbells. The lighter ones he tossed aside lightly, even though an ordinary man might have had trouble lifting them.

Then he lifted the heavier ones, seizing them with both hands and bringing them up to his shoulders with a jerk, and then, more slowly, lifting them high in the air.

All the courtiers broke into applause when he managed to lift the heaviest weight that had been supplied. No other person had ever been known to lift that weight.

Finally, he bent an iron bar by placing it behind his neck and pulling the ends forward till they met in front of him. He then pulled the ends apart again, lifted the bar over his head, and threw it to one side.

Whatever he did brought round after round of applause from the courtiers. Even the emperor nodded approvingly. The princess, however, did not applaud; nor did she nod.

The emperor bent toward his daughter and said, "Really, my dear, this prince is quite the strongest man I have ever seen. It would be a pretty good thing to make him heir to the throne."

The princess said coldly, "It would be a pretty good thing to make him a strong man at the circus, My Imperial Father, but he is quite unsuitable for marriage to me. After all, do I have a set of weights in my chamber, or iron bars that need bending? I would quickly grow weary of watching him flex his arms, and if he tried to embrace me, he would break my ribs."

She rose in her seat, and at once everyone was quiet.

"Prince Primus," she said, in her beautiful voice.

Prince Primus folded his arms and listened confidently.

The princess said, "You are the strongest man I have ever seen, and I thank you for your efforts to please me. However, I do not wish you for my husband. You know the penalty."

She made a mystic pass with her hands (for she was a very well educated princess indeed), and there was a bright flash of light. The courtiers had covered their eyes, for they knew what to expect; but Prince Secundus and Prince Tertius were not prepared, and they were blinded for a moment by the flash.

When they recovered, they saw a statue being loaded into a cart so that it might be transported to the avenue in the garden along which the princess took her morning walk.

The statue was that of Prince Primus, arms folded, expression handsome and proud.

Prince Tertius was sad that evening. He had never lost a brother before, and he found he didn't like it.

He said to Prince Secundus, "I don't think Our Royal Father is going to like it either. And as for Our Royal Mother, she's going to hate it. How are we going to tell them?"

Prince Secundus said, "After I win the princess's hand, I may perhaps be able to persuade her to try to find a way to restore Our Royal Brother. After all, someone as well-educated as she ought to be able to think of a way of doing so."

"But how will you be able to win her hand? She seems to have a heart of stone. Cold stone."

"Not at all," said Prince Secundus. "It's just that she wasn't interested in useless strength and muscles. What good is it to lift weights? Now *I* am a warrior. I can fight and handle weapons. That is a useful occupation."

"I hope so," said Prince Tertius, "but you will be taking a great chance. Still, the princess is rich, and we *do* need the money."

———

The next morning, Prince Secundus was arraying himself in gleaming armor when the second assistant serving maid staggered in, carrying an enormous sword for him. She was bowed down by its weight, and when she tried to curtsy, she dropped it with a loud clang.

Prince Secundus said, with annoyance, "You are very clumsy."

"I beg your pardon, Your Highness," she said humbly, curtsying again, "but are you really going to undertake the task for the princess?"

"Certainly I am, but what business is that of yours, serving maid?"

"None at all, Your Highness," admitted the serving maid, "but the princess is so hard-hearted and so difficult to please. I do not want to see you turned into a statue, like your brother."

"I will not be turned into a statue," said Prince Secundus, "because the princess will be fascinated with me. And now, serving-maid, leave my presence at once. I cannot bear anyone as impertinent as you are."

The serving maid curtsied and left.

Prince Secundus stepped out into the arena, and at once there was applause from all the courtiers. The armor that had been given him by the emperor was beautiful and shiny, and fit him very well. His shield was pure white, his sword was of the best steel, his spear was perfectly balanced, and his helmet covered his face and gave him a ferocious appearance.

He threw his spear, and it flew the length of the arena and impaled itself in the center of a target.

Prince Secundus then challenged anyone at all to a swordfight. A large man in armor came into the arena, and for long minutes the two fought, sword clashing on shield. But Prince Secundus could strike twice for every once that his opponent could, and as the other tired, Prince Secundus seemed to grow stronger. Soon enough, the opponent raised his hands in surrender, and Prince Secundus was the victor. The applause was deafening.

Finally, Prince Secundus removed his helmet and armor and mounted a horse. With one hand only, he controlled the horse perfectly, making it rear on its hind legs, leap, and dance. It was a remarkable performance, and the audience went wild.

"Really, my dear," said the emperor, as he bent toward his daughter, "this prince is an excellent warrior. He could lead my armies into battle and defeat all my enemies. Surely he must please you."

The princess's haughty face was cold, and she said, "He might make an excellent general if he also knew how to handle an army, but of what use would he be as a husband? There are no armed men in my chamber for him to fight, no horses for him to ride, no targets for him to shoot at. And if he forgot himself, he might throw his spear at me, since weapons are his greatest love and talent."

She rose in her seat, and at once everyone was quiet. She said, "Prince Secundus, you are the greatest warrior I have ever seen, and I thank you for your efforts to please me. However, I do not wish you for my husband. You know the penalty."

She made the same mystic pass as before. This time Prince Tertius knew enough to cover his eyes. When he took his hand away, there was another statue: that of a graceful, handsome prince with one hand raised as though it had just hurled a spear. Prince Tertius knew that he had lost a second brother.

Prince Tertius sat alone in the suite the next morning. He hadn't slept all night, and to tell the truth, he didn't know what to do.

He said to himself, "If I go home now, everyone will say I am a coward. Besides, how can I go home now and break the news to Dad? And dear Mom will weep for the rest of her life. As for me, I have lost two brothers who were good brothers to me, even if they were a little conceited and headstrong."

And now the second assistant serving maid edged her way into the room. She had nothing in her hands.

Prince Tertius said, "Are you bringing me something, my dear?"

She curtsied very nervously and said, "No, Your Highness. Do not be angry with me, for I have only come to tell you that I asked both your brothers not to attempt the task, but they would not listen."

Prince Tertius sighed. "They were both very willful, I know. You mustn't blame yourself that they did not listen to you. And certainly I am not angry with you."

"Then, Your Highness, would *you* listen to me if I ask you not to attempt the task? You are not a great strongman or a great warrior. How can you win the cold, hard princess if your brothers could not?"

Prince Tertius said, "I know that all I can do is write a little poetry and sing a bit, but perhaps the princess might like that."

"She is very hard to please, Your Highness," said the serving maid, shuddering at her impudence in arguing with a prince. "If you are made into a statue too, your parents will be left entirely without children, and they will have no heir to the throne."

Prince Tertius sighed again. "You are perfectly correct, little serving maid. You have a kind heart and a thoughtful mind. But you see, our kingdom is so poor that Dad has to help in the garden and Mom has to help in the kitchen. If I could marry the princess, I would become so rich that I could make Mom and Dad and the whole kingdom happy. . . . So I think I *must* try to please the princess. Perhaps if I use my very best poems and sing them as sweetly as I can, she will be pleased."

Tears rolled down the serving maid's cheeks. "Oh, how I wish she would, but she is so hard-hearted. If only she had *my* heart inside her, it would be different."

"Well then, my dear," said Prince Tertius, "let me test your heart. I will sing you some of my songs, and you can tell me if *you* like them. If you do, perhaps the princess will like them too."

The serving maid was horrified, "Oh, Your Highness. You mustn't do that. Your songs are made to be sung to a princess, not to a simple serving maid. How can you judge a princess by a serving maid?"

"In that case," said Prince Tertius, "let us forget the princess, and I will ask only what the serving maid thinks."

Prince Tertius tuned his lyre, one that was his own and that he had brought with him. Then, in a very soft and melodious voice, he sang a sad song of love denied. And when the serving maid seemed to melt away in tears at the sadness, he sang a happy song of love attained, so that the tears vanished and she clapped her hands and laughed.

"Did you like them?" said Prince Tertius.

"Oh, yes," said the serving maid. "The songs were beautiful, and your voice made me feel as though I were in heaven."

Prince Tertius smiled. "Thank you, my lady." He bent and

kissed her hand, and the serving maid turned red with confusion and quickly put the hand he had kissed behind her back.

But just then there was a loud knock on the door, and there entered a chamberlain, a high court official, who bowed to Prince Tertius (but not very deeply) and said, "Your Highness, the imperial princess Meliversa wishes to know why you have not appeared in the arena."

He looked hard at the second assistant serving maid as he said this, and the terrified young woman left the room hurriedly.

Prince Tertius said, "I do not know whether I will undertake the task. I am considering it."

The chamberlain bowed even less deeply than before and said, "I will inform the princess of what you have said. Please remain in this room until she decides what is to be done."

Prince Tertius waited in the room and wondered if the princess would turn him into a statue at once for hesitating over the task.

He was still wondering about it when the princess Meliversa entered the room. She did not knock. Imperial princesses never knock.

She said, "My chamberlain tells me that you might not under-take the task."

Prince Tertius said, "Your Imperial Highness may not like my poetry or my voice. It is all I have to offer."

"But if I do like them, what then?"

"In that case, I wonder if I wish to have as my wife someone who is so cold and hard-hearted, she is willing to turn brave, good princes into statues."

"Am I not beautiful, Prince?"

"It is an outside beauty, Imperial Princess."

"Am I not rich, Prince?"

"Only in money, Imperial Princess."

"Are you not poor, Prince?"

"Only in money, Imperial Princess, and I am used to it, actually, as are my parents and my kingdom."

"Do you not wish to be rich, Prince, by marrying me?"

"I think not, Imperial Princess. I am, after all, not for sale."

"And yet my chamberlain, on the other side of your door, heard you singing to a low-born serving maid."

"That is true, but the serving maid was tender-hearted and loving, and I wanted to sing to her. A tender and loving heart is, after all, the beauty and wealth I really want. If she will have me, then I will marry her, and someday, when I am king in my father's place, the low-born serving maid will be my queen."

At that, the princess smiled. She was even more beautiful when she smiled. "Now," she said, "you will see the use of a good education."

She made a motion with her hand, muttered two or three words, and with that she grew foggy in appearance, shrunk a little, changed a little—and Prince Tertius found himself looking at the second assistant serving maid.

He said, in amazement, "Which are you, the imperial princess or the serving maid?"

She said, "I am both, Prince Tertius. It was in the form of a serving maid that I set myself the task of finding a suitable husband. Of what use was it to me what princes might do to win the hand of a beautiful and rich princess, not caring that she was cold and cruel. What I wanted was someone who would be kind and loving to a gentle, tenderhearted girl, even if she was not as beautiful as the sun or richer than gold. You have passed that test."

Again she changed and was the princess again, but a smiling, warm princess.

"Will you have me as wife now, Prince Tertius?"

And Prince Tertius said, "If you will remain always in your heart the gentle, loving woman I came to love, then I will marry you."

And with that all the princes who had been statues were suddenly brought back to warm flesh and blood again.

Prince Tertius and Princess Meliversa were married two months later, after the king and queen of Micrometrica were brought to the Imperial City by the very fastest coaches. They were as happy as anyone can imagine.

Prince Primus and Prince Secundus were also as happy as anyone can imagine, for they were alive again instead of being frozen in cold stone. They kept saying, "The serving maid? We would never have imagined such a thing!"

Naturally, Prince Tertius was happy too, but the imperial

princess was happiest of all. After all, she had been afraid that even with all her education she would never find anyone who would turn away from mere beauty and money, and love her for herself alone.

MARCH AGAINST THE FOE

"TELL ME, GEORGE, HAVE YOU EVER thought of getting a job?" I asked.

We had finished dinner and were walking through the mellow twilight along the edge of the park. I had asked the question idly. I knew he never had.

But he did shudder and a look of nameless horror passed across his face, as though he had suddenly found himself gazing into a pit of writhing vipers.

"That is no question," he said, hollowly, "to ask a gentleman who is placidly digesting one of your less-than-scrumptious dinners."

"Why not?" I was annoyed enough at his description of the lavish meal I had provided him to pursue the subject. "Uncounted millions of human beings work for a living."

"Yes," said George. "Exactly. So they do. And I believe I am quite right to choose not to be one of their number." He heaved a sigh that seemed to come from the profoundest depths of his being. "Have I never told you the tale of Cuthbert Cantrip Culloden?"

"No, George, you haven't, and I am grateful for it. Thank you."

George seated himself at a park bench that had just been vacated by a New York gentleman of the hippy persuasion and said, "I will now tell you the tale of Cuthbert Cantrip Culloden."

Desperately, I tried to fend it off. "Culloden," I said, "is an interesting name. At the Battle of Culloden in 1745—"

Cuthbert Cantrip Culloden [said George] had been a classmate of mine at the old university. He was not a remarkable fellow and not one of his names lent themselves to the easy informality of a short-ened nickname. It was, of course, impossible to call him Cuth or Cant or Rip or Cull or Loden, and we ended up—

Why, yes, now that you mention it, it might have been possible to call him Bert, but we never thought of that. It's just as well, too, for I had a better solution to the problem. I called him "Cussword," which, as a reasonable facsimile of his first name, was at once adopted by all and sundry.

That seemed to induce a certain gratitude in him. At least, he called me several cusswords in return.

These things build a friendship you know and all through our years at the university we remained close. And when we graduated we swore that we would remain friends through all eventualities and that, without fail, on the anniversary of our graduation we would get together, he and I, and have a drink to our old fellowship.

What do you mean, and did I? Without fail, old man. I never once failed to miss it. And I believe he never failed to miss it, either. Ah, college days.

You can imagine my surprise, then, when one day some fifteen years after graduation, I came across old Cussword, in a bar on which I was, in those days, bestowing my custom. The meeting was a beneficent one for I was busily engaged in an intricate financial deal that was failing to extend my credit for one more drink, when an arm threw itself around my shoulder, and a voice said in my ear, "This one's on me, old buddy."

And it was Cussword.

Nothing could have been more gratifying than his kindly offer, and in no time at all we were engaged in those reminiscences that are the bane and dread of all college reunions. He dredged up names and events that I preferred not to remember, and I was careful to do the same for him. And all the time I watched him narrowly.

Cussword had shown no promise at the university of ever becoming prosperous unless he met a woman of sufficiently uncertain age and looks and sufficiently certain wealth. Casual questioning, however, convinced me that he had been as unsuccessful in this laudable search as I had been.

And yet there was an undefinable air of prosperity about him. The fact that he had paid for several drinks meant nothing, for anyone can have a little money in his pocket at some particular time. Rather, Cussword had a feeling to him, a kind of self-confidence that came from more than the immediate supply of coins. He exuded the kind of aura that someone would if he had a source of additional coins that he could draw on at will.

It was difficult to believe, but I felt that I was right. "Cussword," I said, with a certain awe and revulsion in my voice, "can it be that you have a *job?*"

He had the grace to redden, but Cussword was a man of integrity who would not lie without good reason, or, anyway, fair reason. "Yes, George," he said, "I have a job."

His redness deepened. "In fact, George, I'm a vice president."

I stared my disbelief. "Of what?"

"I'm Vice President in Charge of Corporate Enthusiasm at B & G."

"What's B & G?"

Cussword told me and I continued to find everything hard to believe. "Are you trying to tell me that B & G stands for 'Bunk and Garbage'?"

"Not at all," said Cussword, with annoyance. "You're completely missing the pronunciation, George. It is not for nothing we used to call you Tin-Ear. The firm was founded by Morris U. Bunque and Charles F. Gabbage. Bunque is of an old English family and it comes from an old Teutonic word referring to oratorical expertise. Gabbage is of Dutch origin and is the term used in a regional dialect there to represent a rich fertilizing mixture. For some reason, though, the firm feels that 'Bunque and Gabbage' lends itself to misapprehension and 'B & G' is the term generally used."

"Very sensible," I said, "and what kind of business is B & G involved in?"

"Why, there, George," said Cussword, "you have me. I do not know. It is not my department. I am concerned only with Corporate Enthusiasm." He ordered another drink for each of us, which was a kindly thought, and said, "Let me explain Corporate

Enthusiasm to you, George, for in your happy state of unemployment you, perhaps, are unaware of the complexities of modern business."

"Indeed, I am," I said, repressing a slight shudder.

"The worst problem that corporations face these days is employee disloyalty. You may think that the average employee would be intent on having the business he works for succeed, but this is not so. The average employee," and here Cussword began ticking off his fingers, "demands regular pay increases, job security, medical insurance, long paid vacations, and various other items that must all eat into the profits well earned by Bunque and Gabbage.

"When it is explained to said employees that all these demands would cut into the large annual pensions paid to Bunque, Gabbage, and several relatives; that private golf courses and yachts are expensive to maintain and cannot be properly taken care of if money is to be wasted on employees, an ugly spirit of dissatisfaction arises, which goes to the heart of Bunque and Gabbage.

"They have decided, therefore, to cultivate a spirit of pride in B & G, an exciting feeling of working for a great corporation and putting to one side petty considerations of salary. After all, you remember the football team at the old university."

"Very well," I said.

"And you remember the pride we had in it. No one had to pay us to be proud. We would have scorned money—unless it was quite a lot. Remember that time when the team actually won a game."

"Oh, yes."

"Well, that's the spirit that was wanted at B & G. Someone at the firm happened to know me as a writer of inspirational songs at church functions and outdoor barbecues, and so they came to me to create the necessary corporation enthusiasm."

"And you've written songs for the firm."

"Quite a few. My best so far is a spirited marching song that goes" [and here he sang it in a ready tenor that drew disapproving glances from every person in the bar]

"Ever onward, B & G, we march against the foe!
Forward, forward, B & G, the lily banners go!
Always there's a little bit to spare for thee and me,
And always there's a great deal more to give to B & G."

"Hmm," I said. "Very stirring. But why the lily banners? Do you have lily banners?"

"The words don't matter," said Cussword, "It's the spirit that counts. Besides we *will* have lily banners. I'm designing a corporation flag right now that will have a fleur-de-lis design. The French, I understand, are no longer using it, and it's silly to waste it."

"But what about the little bit for thee and me and the great deal more for B & G. Is that fair?"

"Absolutely fair. Bunque and Gabbage need the money much more than the unimportant people who work for them. You have never seen their mansions. It costs a fortune to heat them."

"Yes, but do the employees think that's fair?"

Cussword looked annoyed. "There you have put your finger on a sore point, George. The employees do *not* think that's fair. I have held seminars on the subject, complete with slides of Bunque and Gabbage's personal properties and home movies of their darling children and I can't seem to rouse any decent set of Corporate Enthusiasm. In point of fact, I have been as good as told by Bunque, and also by Gabbage, that if I can't show results in two weeks, I will be fired."

That bothered me, as you can well imagine, old man. Not only was Cussword an old school chum, but he had just bought me several drinks and had never mentioned a word concerning repayment. It seemed a small thing to me to try to return the favor by means of Azazel.

Azazel was, as usual, in a state of violent protest, once I had managed to drag him out through the space warp, or whatever it was that connected his world and ours.

Since he was red to begin with, he could not turn red with fury, but his two-centimeter body twitched uncontrollably, and his long spiked tail lashed back and forth. Even the small nubbins of his horns seemed to swell slightly.

"What is this?" he said. "It was only two months ago that you called me last. Am I to be at your beck and call every moment of the day and night? Am I to have no private life?"

I had no choice but to placate him. "Please, Coordinator of the Universe. There is no power anywhere in the cosmos that can do what you can do. When one is the best there is, one must expect to be called upon."

"Well, that's true enough," said Azazel, grudgingly. "But what in juguwolen do you want now?" He was sufficiently mollified to apologize at once for using that vile term. I didn't know what it meant, but when he said it his tale briefly turned blue, so it must have been powerful indeed.

I explained to him the fix in which poor Cussword had found himself.

"And you say he was a schoolmate of yours? —Ah, college days. I remember an old professor I once had, a vicious grumchik, who was supposed to teach us neuroadjustometrics but spent all his time drinking phosphoamitol and showing up for lectures unable to speak, let alone teach."

"I had a vicious grumchik, too, O Master of the Infinite. Several, in fact."

"Poor fellow," said Azazel, wiping his tiny eyes. "Well, we will have to do something. Do you have anything belonging to him?"

"Well, yes," I said. "I managed to abstract the school pin from his lapel."

"Ah. There is, of course, no use in trying to adjust the minds of the callous and cold-blooded employees of that marvelous firm that employs him. I will instead so adjust your friend's mind as to make his views irresistible."

"Can that be done?" I asked, rather foolishly.

"Watch and see, Miserable Remnant of a Fetid Planet," he answered.

I did watch, and I did see.

Before the two weeks were up, Cussword was calling at my humble abode, face distorted into a broad grin.

"George," he said, "meeting you in the bar was a stroke of luck or something because everything has suddenly changed, and I am no longer in danger of being fired. It can't be anything you said, because, as I recall, you didn't say anything sensible at all, so it must have been the mere fact that I unconsciously compared myself to you. There I was, a vibrant, handsome vice president; and there you were, a cadging bum—a description I use without any intent to insult you, George—and the contrast was such that I just went out and licked the world."

I will not deny that I was taken aback, but he went right on without noticing how far aback I had been taken.

He said, "The entire body of employees, at 8:50 A.M., every work morning, sings 'Ever onward, B & G' with unexampled enthusiasm. You should see, George, with what vim and vitality they march against the foe. As soon as I have the lily banners, they will wave them with enthusiasm.

"We will have parades. Everyone will wear the B & G uniform, complete with a B & G sash in different colors and designs to show the level of employment. We will march down the main street to the town square singing songs, and I have written two more."

I said, "Two more," rather dumfounded at his daring.

"Yes," he said, "one for Bunque and one for Gabbage. The one for Bunque goes as follows:"

"Cheer, cheer for Morris U. Bunque
Without his wisdom, we would be sunk.
Watch him with his genial smile
That's just like a crocodile."

"Crocodile? Is that the *mot juste*?"

"Why, yes. He has long been known affectionately as 'Old Crocodile' and he's rather proud of that."

"What about the one for Gabbage?"

"That goes like this."

"O, whom do we love? Yes, whom do we love?
It's Charles F. G-A-B-B-A-G-E.
We are below and he is above
Hurrah for him and also B & G."

"The trouble is," said Cussword, "that Gabbage is difficult to rhyme. The only rhyme I could think of was cabbage, which is what he smells like, but I didn't think it wise to say so. So instead I spelled out his name. Ingenious, don't you think?"

"I suppose one could call it that," I said, dubiously.

"Well, I have no time to talk further, George. I just wanted to give you the great news. I've got to go back now and organize a snake dance for the five-o'clock whistle, one expressing the great joy every employee has had at the opportunity of working for B & G all day."

"But, Cussword, are you implying that the employees are no longer interested in pay increases and all the rest?"

"You don't hear a word of it anymore. It's all fun and games now. It's all joy and hilarity. And it's my job to make sure that every moment of every day is filled with Corporate Enthusiasm. I am sure that before long I will be made a partner in the firm."

And so it went, old man. B & G became the center of an amazing joy. It was written up in *Fortune,* in *Time* and in *Corporations Illustrated.* In the last case, Cussword's face appeared on the cover.

And that's the story, old man.

"That's the story, George?" I said, with astonishment. "But it ends happily. Why has that soured you on the prospects of employment?"

George rose from the park bench, and said, "I left out the last little bit, inadvertently, old man. Cussword was a resounding success. You couldn't imagine a greater one. But B & G wasn't. As a matter of fact, it went bankrupt."

"Bankrupt? Why?"

"Well, everyone was having so much fun, and there was so much singing and parading and going around in uniforms that no one did any work, apparently, and the firm just collapsed."

"Too bad."

"Yes. Poor Cussword is an exemplification of the uncertainties of the corporate life. Although an enormous success, was he made a partner in the firm? No. His job simply vanished and he has been unemployed ever since. And you ask me if I have ever thought of getting a job. Why? To fail even in the midst of success? Never! Why only last week, old Cussword asked me to lend him five dollars and I couldn't. Of course, old man, if you gave me ten, I could give him half and you would be killing two birds with one stone."

I passed over the ten and said, "I suppose it would be too much to expect that I would really be killing the two of you."

George looked at the ten-dollar bill, contemptuously, and said, "Well, you won't be killing us with kindness."

"Wait, George," I called out, as he began to walk away. "What kind of business was B & G involved in?"

"I never found out," called back George. "Neither did old Cuss-word."

NORTH-WESTWARD

THOMAS TRUMBULL SAID TO EMMANUEL Rubin in a low voice, "Where the devil have you been? I've been trying to reach you for a week."

Rubin's eyes flashed behind the thick lenses of his spectacles, and his sparse beard bristled. "I was away at the Berkshires for a week. I was *not* aware I had to apply for permission to you for that."

"I wanted to speak to you."

"Then speak to me now. Here I am. That is, supposing you can think of something intelligent to say."

Trumbull looked about hastily. The Black Widowers had gathered for the monthly banquet at the Milano, and Trumbull had managed to arrive on time because he was the host.

He said, "Keep your voice down, for God's sake, Manny. I can't speak freely now. It's about," his voice dropped to a mere mouthing, "my guest."

"Well, what about him?" Rubin glanced in the direction of the tall, distinguished-looking elderly man who was conversing with Geoffrey Avalon in the far corner. The guest was a good two

107

inches taller than Avalon, who was usually the tallest person at the gathering. Rubin, who was ten inches shorter than Avalon, grinned.

"I think it does Jeff good to have to look up now and then," he said.

"Listen to me, will you?" said Trumbull. "I've talked to the others, and you were the only one I was really worried about and the only one I couldn't reach."

"But what are you worried about? Get to the point."

"It's my guest. He's peculiar."

"If he's your guest—"

"Sh! He's an interesting guy, and he's not nuts, but you may consider him peculiar and I don't want you to mock him. You just let him be peculiar and accept it."

"How is he peculiar?"

"He has an idée fixe, if you know what that means."

Rubin looked revolted. "Can you tell me why it's so necessary for an American with a stumbling knowledge of English to say 'idée fixe' when the English phrase 'fixed idea' does just as well?"

"He has a fixed idea, then. It will come out because he can't keep it in. Please don't make fun of it, or of him. *Please* accept him on his own terms."

"This violates the whole principle of the grilling, Tom."

"It just bends it a little. I'm asking you to be polite, that's all. Everyone else has agreed."

Rubin's eyes narrowed. "I'll try, but so help me, Tom, if this is some sort of gag—if I'm being set up for something—I'll stand on a stool if I have to, and I'll punch you right in the eye."

"There's no gag involved."

Rubin wandered over to where Mario Gonzalo was putting the finishing touches on his caricature of the guest. Not much of a caricature at that. He was turning out a Gibson man, a collar ad.

Rubin looked at it, then turned to look at the guest. He said, "You're leaving out the lines, Mario."

"Caricature," said Gonzalo, "is the art of truthful exaggeration, Manny. When a guy looks that good at his age, you don't spoil the effect by sticking in lines."

"What's his name?"

"I don't know. Tom didn't give it. He says we ought to wait for the grilling to ask."

Roger Halsted ambled over, drink in hand, and said in a low voice, "Tom was looking for you all week, Manny."

"He told me. And he found me right here."

"Did he explain what he wanted?"

"He didn't *explain* it. He just asked me to be nice."

"Are you going to?"

"I will, until I get the idea that this is a joke at my expense. After which—"

"No, he's serious."

Henry, that quiet bit of waiter perfection, said in his soft, carrying voice, "Gentlemen, dinner is served."

And they all sat down to their crableg cocktails.

James Drake had stubbed out his cigarette since, by general vote, there was to be no smoking during the actual meal, and handed the ashtray to Henry.

He said, "Henry's announcement just now interrupted our guest in some comments he was making about Superman, which I'd like him to repeat, if he doesn't mind."

The guest nodded his head in a stately gesture of gratitude and, having finished an appreciative mouthful of veal marengo, said, "What I was saying was that Superman was a travesty of an ancient and honorable tradition. There has always been a branch of literature concerning itself with heroes; human beings of superior strength and courage. Heroes, however, should be supernormal but not supernatural."

"As a matter of fact," said Avalon, in his startling baritone, "I agree. There have always been characters like Hercules, Achilles, Gilgamesh, Rustam—"

"We get the idea, Jeff," said Rubin, balefully.

Avalon went on, smoothly, "Even half a century ago, we had the development of Conan by Robert Howard, as a modern legend. These were all far stronger than we puny fellows are, but they were not godlike. They could be hurt, wounded, even killed. They usually were, in the end."

"In the *Iliad*," said Rubin, perfectly willing, as always, to start an argument, "the gods could be wounded. Ares and Aphrodite were each wounded by Diomedes."

"Homer can be allowed liberties," put in the guest. "But compare, say, Hercules with Superman. Superman has X-ray eyes, he can fly through space without protection, he can move faster than light. None of this would be true of Hercules. But with Superman's abilities, where is the excitement, where's the suspense? Then, too, where's the fairness? He fights off human crooks who are less to him than a ladybug would be to me. How much pride can I take in flipping a ladybug off my wrist?"

Drake said, "One trouble with these heroes, though, is that they're musclebound at the temples. Take Siegfried. If he had an atom of intelligence, he took care never to show it. For that matter, Hercules was not remarkable for the ability to think, either."

"On the other hand," said Halsted, "Prince Valiant had brains, and so, especially, did Odysseus."

"Rare exceptions," said Drake.

Rubin turned to the guest and said, "You seem very interested in storybook heroes."

"Yes, I am," said the guest, quietly. "It's almost an *idée fixe* with me." He smiled with obvious self-deprecation. "I keep talking about them all the time, it seems."

It was soon after that that Henry brought on the baked Alaska.

Trumbull tapped his water glass with his spoon at about the time that Henry was carefully supplying the brandy. Trumbull had waited well past the coffee, as though reluctant to start the grilling, and even now the tinkle of metal against glass seemed less authoritative than customary.

Trumbull said, "It is time we begin the grilling of our guest, and I would like to suggest that Manny Rubin do the honors."

Rubin favored Trumbull with a hard stare, then said to the guest, "Sir, it is usual to ask our guest to begin by justifying his existence, but against all custom, Tom has not introduced you by name. May I, therefore, ask you what your name is?"

"Certainly," said the guest. "My name is Bruce Wayne."

Rubin turned immediately toward Trumbull, who made an unobtrusive, but clear, quieting gesture with his hands.

Rubin took a deep breath and managed a smile. "Well, Mr. Wayne, since we were speaking of heroes, I can't resist asking you if you are ever kidded about being the comic-strip hero, Batman. Bruce Wayne is Batman's real name, as you probably know."

"I do know," said Wayne, "because I *am* Batman."

There was a general stir at the table at this, and even the ordinarily imperturbable Henry raised his eyebrows. Wayne was apparently accustomed to this reaction, for he sipped at his brandy without reacting.

Rubin cast another quick glance at Trumbull, then said carefully, "I suppose that, in saying this, you imply that you are, in one way or another, to be identified with the comicstrip character, and not with something else named Batman, as, for instance, an officer's orderly in the British army."

"You're right," said Wayne. "I'm referring to the comic-strip character. Of course," and he smiled gently, "I'm not trying to convince you I am literally the comic-strip Batman, cape, bat symbol, and all. As you see, I am a three-dimensional living human being, and I assure you I am aware of that. However, I *inspired* the existence of the comic-strip character Batman."

"And how did that come about?" asked Rubin.

"In the past, when I was considerably younger than I am now—"

"How old are you now?" asked Halsted, suddenly.

Wayne smiled. "Tom has told me I must answer all questions truthfully, so I will tell you, though I'd prefer not to. I am seventy-three years old."

Halsted said, "You don't look it, Mr. Wayne. You could pass for fifty."

"Thank you. I try to keep fit."

Rubin said, with a trace of impatience, "Would you get back to my question, Mr. Wayne? Do you want it repeated?"

"No, my memory manages to limp along satisfactorily. When I was considerably younger than I am now, I was of some help to various law enforcement agencies. At that time, there was money to be had in these comic strips about heroes, and a friend of mine suggested that I serve as a model for one. Batman was invented with a great many of my characteristics and much of my history.

"It was, of course, distinctly romanticized. I do not go about with a cape and never have done so, or had a helicopter of my own, but I did insist that Batman be given no supernatural powers but be restricted to entirely human abilities. I admit they do stretch it a bit sometimes. Even the villains Batman faces, although they are invariably grotesque, are exaggerations of people with whom I had problems in the past and whom I helped put out of circulation."

Avalon said, "I see why Superman annoys you, then. There was a television Batman for two seasons. What about that?"

"I remember it well. Especially Julie Newmar playing Cat-woman. I would have liked to have met her as an opponent in real life. The program was played for laughs, you know, and good-natured fun."

"Well," said Drake, looking about the table and carefully lighting a cigarette now that the meal was over (and cupping it in his hand in the obvious belief that that would trap the smoke), "you seem to have had an amusing life. Are you the multimillionaire that the comic-strip Batman is?"

"As a matter of fact," said Wayne, "I'm very well off. My house in the suburbs is elaborate, and I even have an adjoining museum, but you know, we're all human. I have my problems."

"Married? Children?" asked Avalon.

"No, there I also resemble my alter ego—or he resembles me. I have never been married and have no children. Those are not my problems. I have a butler who tends to my household needs, along with some other servants who are of comparatively trivial importance."

"In the comic strip," said Gonzalo, "your butler is your friend and confidant. Right?"

"Well—yes." And he sighed.

Rubin looked thoughtful, and said, "Tell us about the museum, Mr. Wayne. What kind of museum is it? A headquarters for science and criminology?"

"Oh, no. The comic strip continues successfully, but my own day as an active upholder of the law is over. My museum consists of curios. There have been a great many objects made that have been based on the Batman cartoon and his paraphernalia. I have, I believe, at least one of every single piece ever made in that fashion, Batman notepaper, large-scale models of the Batmobile, figurines of every important character in the strip, copies of every magazine issue featuring the character, cassettes of all the television shows, and so on.

"It pleases me to have all this. After all, I am sure the strip will survive me, and it will be the part of me that will be best remembered after my death. I don't have children to revere my memory and I have done nothing very much in my real life to make me part of history. These evidences of my fictional life are the best I can do to bring myself a little nearer to immortality."

Rubin said, "I see. Now I'm going to ask a question that may cause you to feel a little uncomfortable, but you must answer. You said—oh, for God's sake, Tom, this is a legitimate question. Why don't you let me ask it before you start jumping."

Trumbull, looking both abashed and troubled, sank back in his chair.

Rubin said, "A little while ago, Mr. Wayne, you said that you too have your problems and, almost immediately afterward, when you mentioned your butler, you looked distinctly uncomfortable. Are you having trouble with your butler? —What are you laughing at, Tom?"

"Nothing," said Trumbull, chuckling.

Wayne said, "He's laughing because he bet me five dollars that if I just answered any questions about me, and did so naturally and truthfully, the Black Widowers would have this out of me within twenty minutes, and he's won."

"I take it, then, that Tom Trumbull knows about this."

"Yes, I do," said Trumbull, "but I'm dealing myself out of this one for that reason. The rest of you handle it."

"I would suggest," interposed Avalon, "that Tom and Manny both quiet down and that we ask Mr. Wayne to tell us his troubles with his butler."

"My butler's name," began Wayne, "is Cecil Pennyworth—"

"Don't you mean Alfred Pennyworth?" put in Halsted.

"No interruptions," said Trumbull, clinking his water glass.

Wayne said, "That's all right, Tom. I don't mind being interrupted. Alfred Pennyworth was indeed my butler originally, and with his permission, his name was used in the strip. However, he was older than I, and in the course of time, he died. Characters do not necessarily age and die in comic strips, but real life is rather different, you know. My present butler is Alfred's nephew."

"Is he a worthy substitute?" asked Drake softly.

"No one could ever replace Alfred, of course, but Cecil has given satisfaction—" Here Wayne frowned. "—in all but one respect, and there my problem rests.

"You must understand that I sometimes attend conventions that are devoted to comic-strip heroes. I don't make a big issue of my being Batman, and I don't put on a cape or anything like that, although the publishers sometimes hire actors to do so.

"What I do is set up an exhibition of my Batman memorabilia.

Sometimes my publishers set up the more conventional items for sale, not so much for the money that is taken in as for the publicity, since it keeps the thought of Batman alive in the minds of people. I have nothing to do with the commercial aspect. What I do is exhibit a selection of some of the more unusual curios that are *not* for sale. I allow them to be seen and studied, while I give a little lecture on the subject. That has its publicity value, too.

"Needless to say, it is necessary to keep a sharp eye on all the exhibits. Most of them have no intrinsic value to speak of, but they are enormously valuable to me and sometimes, I'm afraid, to the fans. While the vast majority of them wouldn't think of appropriating any of the items, there are bound to be occasional individuals who, out of a natural dishonesty or, more likely, an irresistible desire, would try to make off with one or more items. We have to watch for that.

"I am even the target for more desperate felons. On two different occasions there have been attempts to break into my museum; attempts that, I am glad to say, were foiled by our rather sophisticated security system. I see you are smiling, Mr. Avalon, but actually my memorabilia, however trivial they might seem, could be disposed of quietly for a considerable sum of money.

"One item I have *does,* in fact, have a sizable intrinsic value. It is a Batman ring in which the bat symbol is cut out of an emerald. I was given it under circumstances that, if I may say so, reflected well on the real Batman—myself—and it has always been much dearer to me for that reason than because of the value of the emerald itself. It is the *pièce de résistance* of my collection and I put it on display only very occasionally.

"A year or so ago, though, I had promised to appear at a convention in Minneapolis, and I did not quite feel up to going. As you see, I am getting on in age, and for all my fitness program, my health and my sense of well-being are not what they once were.

"I therefore asked Cecil Pennyworth to attend the convention as my substitute. On occasion I have asked him to fill in for me, though, till then, not at a major convention. I had promised an interesting display, but I had to cut that to Cecil's measure. I chose small items that could all be packed systematically—so they could be quickly checked to make sure the display was intact—in a single good-size suitcase. I sent Cecil off with the usual unnecessary admonition to keep a close watch on everything.

"He called me from Minneapolis to assure me of his safe arrival and, again, a few hours later, to apprise me of the fact that an attempt had been made to switch suitcases."

"And failed, I hope," I said.

"He assured me that he had the right suitcase and that the display was safe and intact, but he asked me if I really felt he should display the ring. You see, since I was sending only small items, I felt that I was, in a way, cheating my public, and I therefore included my ring so that at least they could see this rarest and most valuable of all my curios. I told Cecil, therefore, that he should certainly display the ring, but keep the sharpest of eyes upon it.

"I heard from him again two mornings later, when the convention was drawing to a close. He was breathless and sounded strained.

"'Everything is safe, Mr. Wayne,' he said, 'but I think I am being followed. I can duck them, though. I'm going northwest, and I'll see you soon.'

"I said, rather alarmed, 'Are you in danger?'

"He only said, 'I must go now,' and hung up.

"I was galvanized into activity—it's the Batman in me, I suppose. I threw off all trace of my indisposition and made ready for action. It seemed to me that I knew what was happening. Cecil was being tracked by someone intent on that suitcase, and he was not himself a strong person of the heroic mold. It seemed to him, therefore, that he ought to do the unexpected. Instead of returning to New York, he would try to elude those who were after him, and quietly head off in another direction altogether. Once he had gotten away from his pursuers, he could then return to New York in safety.

"What's more, I knew where he was going. I have several homes over the United States, which is the privilege of one who, like myself, is quite well off. One of my homes is a small and unobtrusive place in North Dakota, where I sometimes go when I feel the need to isolate myself from the too-unbearable insinuations of the world into my private life.

"It made good sense to go there. No one but Cecil and me and some legal representatives knows that the house in question belongs to me. If he got there safely, he could feel secure. He knew that to indicate to me that he was going northwestward would have complete meaning to me, and would mean nothing to anyone who might overhear him. That was clever. He had to hang up quickly because, I presume, he was aware of enemies in the vicinity. He had said, 'I'll see you soon,' by which, it seemed to me, he was begging me to go to my North Dakota home to join him. Clearly, he wanted me to take over the responsibility of defense. As I said, he was not the heroic type.

"He had called me in the morning, and before night fell, I was at my North Dakota house. I remember being grateful that it was early fall. I would have hated to have to go there with two feet of snow on the ground and the temperature forty below."

Rubin, who was listening intently, said, "I suppose that your butler, in weather like that, would have chosen some other place as a hideout. He would have told you he was going southeastward and you would have gone to your home in Florida, if you have one."

"I have a home in Georgia," said Wayne, "but you are correct otherwise. I suppose that is what he would have done. In any case, when I arrived in North Dakota, I found that Cecil was not yet there. I got in touch with the people who care for the place in my absence (and who know me only as a 'Mr. Smith'), and they assured me that nobody, to their knowledge, had arrived. There were no signs of any very recent occupancy, so he could not have arrived and been waylaid in the house. Of course, he might have been interrupted en route.

"I spent the night in the house, a very wakeful night as you can imagine, and an uncomfortable one. In the morning, when he still had not arrived, I called the police. There were no reports of any accidents to planes, trains, buses, or cars that could have possibly applied to Cecil.

"I decided to wait another day or so. It was possible, after all, that he might have taken a circuitous route or paused on the way, 'holed up,' one might say, to mislead his pursuers, and would soon take up the trip again. In short, he might arrive a day late, or even two days late.

"On the third morning, however, I could wait no more. I was certain, by then, that something was very wrong. I called my New York home, feeling he might have left a message there, and was rather berating myself for not having made the call earlier for that purpose; or, if no message had been received, to have left the number at which I could be reached when the message came.

"At any rate, on the third morning I called, and it was Cecil who answered. I was thunderstruck. He had arrived on the afternoon of the day I had left. I simply said I would be home that night and, of course, I was. So you see my difficulty, gentlemen."

There was a short silence at the rather abrupt ending to the story, and then Rubin said, "I take it that Cecil was perfectly safe and sound."

"Oh, yes, indeed. I asked him about the pursuers, and he smiled faintly and said, 'I believe I eluded them, Mr. Wayne. Or I may even have been entirely mistaken and they did not really exist. At least, I wasn't bothered at all on my way home.'"

"So that he got home safely?"

"Yes, Mr. Rubin."

"And the exhibition curios were intact?"

"Entirely."

"Even the ring, Mr. Wayne?"

"Absolutely."

Rubin threw himself back in the chair with an annoyed expression on his face, "Then, no, I don't see your difficulty."

"But why did he tell me he was going northwestward? He told me that distinctly. There is no question of my having misheard."

Halsted said, "Well, he thought he was being followed, so he told you he was going to the North Dakota place. Then he decided that either he had gotten away from the pursuers, or that they didn't exist, and he thereupon switched his plans, and went straight to New York without having time to call you again and warn you of that."

"Don't you think, in that case," said Wayne, with some heat, "he might have apologized to me? After all, he had misled me, sent me on an unnecessary chase into North Dakota, subjected me to a little over two days of uncertainty during which I not only feared for my collection, but also felt that he might be lying dead or badly injured somewhere. All this was the result of his having told me, falsely, that he was heading northwestward. And then, having arrived in New York, he might have known, since I wasn't home, that I had flown to the North Dakota house to be with him, and he might have had the kindness to call me there and tell me he was safe. He knew the North Dakota number. But he didn't call me, and he didn't apologize to me or excuse himself when I got home."

"Are you sure he knew that you were in North Dakota?" asked Halsted.

"Of course I'm sure he knew. For one thing, I told him. I had to account for the fact that I had been away from home for three days. I said, 'Sorry I wasn't home when you arrived, Cecil. I had to make a quick and unexpected trip to North Dakota.' It would have taken a heart of forged steel not to have winced at that, and not to have begun apologizing, but it didn't seem to bother him at all."

There was another pause at this point, and then Avalon cleared his throat in a deep rumble and said, "Mr. Wayne, you know your butler better than any of us do. How do you account for this behavior?"

"The logical feeling is that it was just callousness," said Wayne, "but I don't know him as a callous man. I have evolved the following thought, though: What if he had been tempted by the ring and the other curios himself? What if it was his plan to dispose of them for his own benefit? He could tell me that he was being pursued, and that would send me off on my foolish mission to North Dakota so that he would have a period of time to put away his ill-gotten gains somewhere and pretend he had been robbed. See?"

Rubin said, "Do you know Cecil to be a dishonest man?

"I wouldn't have said so, but anyone can yield to temptation."

"Granted. But if he did, he resisted. You have everything. He didn't steal anything."

"That's true, but his telling me he was going northwestward and then never explaining why he had changed his mind tells me that he was up to skulduggery. Just because he was too fainthearted to go through with it this time doesn't excuse him. He might be bolder the next time."

Rubin said, "Have you asked him to explain the northwestward business?"

Wayne hesitated. "I don't like to. Suppose there is some explanation. The fact that I would ask him about it would indicate that I didn't trust him, and that would spoil our relationship. My having waited so long makes it worse. If I ask now, it would mean I have brooded about it all year, and I'm sure he would resign in resentment. On the other hand, I can't think what explanation he might have, and my not asking him leaves me unable to relax in his presence. I find I am always keyed up and waiting for him to try again."

Rubin said, "Then it seems that if you don't ask him, but convince yourself he's guilty, your relationship is ruined. And if you do ask him and he convinces you he's innocent, your relationship is ruined. What if you don't ask him, but convince yourself he is innocent?"

"That would be fine," said Wayne, "but how? I would love to do so. When I think of my long and close association with Alfred Pennyworth, Cecil's uncle, I feel I owe something to the nephew—but I must have an explanation and I don't dare to ask for it."

Drake said, "Since Tom Trumbull knows about all this—What do you say about it, Tom?"

Wayne interposed. "Tom says I should forget all about it."

Trumbull said, "That's right. Cecil might have been so ashamed of his needless panic that he just can't talk about it."

"But he *did* talk about it," said Wayne, heatedly. "He casually admitted that he might have been mistaken about being pursued, and did so as soon as I got home. Why didn't he apologize to me and express regret for the trouble he had put me to?"

"Maybe *that's* what he can't talk about," said Trumbull.

"Ridiculous. What do I do? Wait for a deathbed confession? He's twenty-two years younger than I am, and he'll outlive me."

"Then," said Avalon, "if we're to clear the air between you, we must find some natural explanation that would account for his having told you he was heading northwestward and that would also account for his having failed to express regret over the trouble he put you to."

"Exactly," said Wayne, "but to explain both at once is impossible. I defy you to."

The silence that followed endured for quite a while until Rubin said, "And you won't accept embarrassment as an explanation for his failure to express regret?"

"Of course not."

"And you won't ask him?"

"No, I won't," said Wayne, biting off the remark with decision.

"And you find having him in your employ under present conditions is wearisome and nervewracking."

"Yes, I do."

"But you don't want to fire him, either."

"No. For old Alfred's sake, I don't."

"In that case," said Rubin, gloomily, "you have painted yourself into a corner, Mr. Wayne. I don't see how you can get out of it."

"I still say," growled Trumbull, "that you ought to forget about it, Bruce. Pretend it never happened."

"That's more than I can do," said Wayne, frowning.

"Then Manny is right," said Trumbull. "You can't get out of the hole you're in."

Rubin looked about the table. "Tom and I say Wayne can't get out of this impasse. What about the rest of you?"

Avalon said, "What if a third party—"

"No," said Wayne instantly. "I won't have anyone else discussing this with Cecil. This is strictly between him and me."

Avalon shook his head. "Then I'm stuck, too."

"It would appear," said Rubin, looking about the table, "that none of the Black Widowers can help you."

"None of the Black Widowers seated at the table," said Gonzalo, "but we haven't asked Henry yet. He's our waiter, Mr. Wayne, and you'd be surprised at his ability to work things out—Henry!"

"Yes, Mr. Gonzalo," said Henry, from his quiet post at the sideboard.

"You heard everything. What do you think Mr. Wayne ought to do?"

"I agree with Mr. Trumbull, sir. I think that Mr. Wayne should forget the matter."

Wayne rolled his eyes upward and shook his head firmly.

"However," Henry went on, "I have a specific reason for suggesting it, one that perhaps Mr. Wayne will agree with."

"Good," said Gonzalo. "What is it, Henry?"

"I couldn't help but notice, sir, that all of you, in referring to what Mr. Pennyworth said on the phone, mentioned that he said he was going northwestward. That, however, isn't quite so. When Mr. Wayne first mentioned the phone conversation, he quoted Mr. Pennyworth as saying, 'I'm going northwest.' Is that correct?"

Wayne said, "Yes, as a matter of fact, that is what he said, but does it matter? What is the difference between 'northwestward' and 'northwest'?"

"A huge difference, Mr. Wayne. To go 'northwestward' can only mean traveling in a particular direction, but to go 'northwest' need not mean that at all."

"Of course it needs to mean that."

"No, sir. I beg your pardon, Mr. Wayne, but 'to go northwest'

120

could mean one's intention to take a plane belonging to Northwest Airlines, one of our larger plane lines."

The pause that followed was electric. Then Wayne whispered, "Good Lord!"

"Yes, sir. And in that case, everything explains itself. Mr. Pennyworth may have been mistaken about being followed, but, even if he thought he was, he was not sufficiently worried over the situation to follow any circuitous route. He told you he was taking a Northwest airplane, speaking of the matter elliptically, as many people do, and assuming you would understand.

"Despite the name of the plane line, which may have been more accurate at its start, Northwest Airlines serves the United States generally and you can take one of its planes from Minneapolis to New York, traveling eastward. I'm sure that but for the coincidence that you had a home in North Dakota, you might have interpreted Mr. Pennyworth's remark correctly.

"Mr. Pennyworth, under the impression he had told you he was flying to New York, said he would see you soon—meaning, in New York. And he hung up suddenly probably because his flight announced that it was ready for boarding."

"Good Lord!" said Wayne, again.

"Exactly, sir. Then when Mr. Pennyworth got home and found you had been to North Dakota, he could honestly see no connection between that and anything he might have done, so that it never occurred to him to apologize for his actions. He couldn't have asked you why you had gone to North Dakota; as a servant, it wasn't his place to. Had you explained of your own accord, he would have understood the confusion and would undoubtedly have apologized for contributing to it. But you remained silent."

"Good Lord!" said Wayne, a third time. Then, energetically, "I have spent over a year making myself miserable over nothing at all. There's no question about it. Batman has made a terrible mistake."

"Batman," said Henry, "has, as you yourself have pointed out, the great advantage, and the occasional disadvantage, of being only human."

PRINCE DELIGHTFUL AND THE FLAMELESS DRAGON

KING MARCUS AND HIS COMFORTABLE consort, Queen Ermentrude, were going to have a baby. At least the queen was, but the king was a very interested bystander. They were both in their late thirties and had more or less given up hope of having one, and had even discussed adoption, but had to give that up, too, when it turned out that no foundlings of royal birth were available. Of course, anything less than royal birth was unthinkable.

But then, as so often happens, just talking about adoption resulted in a physiological stirring and before you could count the taxes wrung out of ten peasants, the queen was whispering the glad tidings to the king. His eyes opened wide and he said, "Now how on Earth did that happen?" and the Queen said, rather tartly, that if he didn't know, no one did.

As the time approached (and for some reason no one can understand, it takes a queen just as long to have a baby once it gets started as it would a milkmaid) the problem of the christening arose.

The queen, who was feeling very uncomfortable by now and was wishing it was all over, said, "I do hope it will be a boy and that he will have all the characteristics expected of a respectable prince, because, my dear, I really don't think I can go through this a second time."

"We will make sure, my royal love. We will invite every fairy in the kingdom to the christening and, of course, they will ensure that he will be brave, handsome and everything else that is good and wonderful."

"Are you sure?" said Queen Ermentrude. "I was speaking to the sorcerer yesterday and *he* said that actually it is all a matter of genes."

King Marcus frowned. "Do you mean a child of mine will have to wear barbarian pantaloons?"

"No, dear, not jeans. *Genes.* They're pronounced the same but if you listen closely you will hear that it isn't a *j*, but a soft *g*."

"What are soft-*g* genes?"

"I don't know, but we all have them, you see."

"Well," said the king, quite irritated, "I don't believe in this superstitious nonsense of having something we don't know or understand. We know and understand these fairy godmothers and that's what it's going to be."

"Very well, my dear," said the Queen, "but I hope you don't leave one out."

The King laughed. "Do you think I'm crazy?"

Both Marcus and Ermentrude had heard many stories of fairy godmothers not being invited to christenings. Invariably, they turned out to be particularly malevolent and, of course, they would show up anyway and make life very hard for the poor infant. You would think royalty would know better than to omit a malevolent fairy, but it happened amazingly often.

This was not going to happen to King Marcus and Queen Ermentrude, however. They consulted the Fairy Directory and made certain that the royal scribe indited an invitation to each and every one.

And that was a mistake, for it meant that an invitation went out to the fairy, Misaprop, and if the royal couple had known just a little more about it, they would certainly have omitted her. To be sure, she was the nicest and sweetest fairy godmother anyone could imagine, so that leaving her out would not have disturbed her at all. And if she were invited, she was the life and soul of the party, always laughing, always telling jokes, always singing songs. You might wonder therefore what could possibly be wrong either way. Well, once she attended a christening, she *would* insist on giving the baby a present, and that's where the trouble came in.

She didn't mean to do it, you know, but she *always* managed to get the spell wrong.

And that's the way it was. Fairy after fairy approached the crib in which the new young prince was lying. (It was indeed a prince and after he was born, Queen Ermentrude said very plainly—once she managed to get her breath back—that there would be no more.) One after another bestowed gifts on him—charm, a stately carriage, a luminous intelligence, a sense of humor, and so on and so on.

And then along came the fairy, Misaprop, and waved her wand over him and said the mystic words that would make him the most graceful prince who ever lived.

—The only thing was that she dropped her wand just before she got to the crib, and she was so flustered (heaven only knows why, for she was always dropping her wand) that she picked it up by the wrong end, and you know what that means.

One of the other fairies stepped forward and said, "Misaprop, dear, you're holding your wand—" but it was too late. Misaprop had pronounced the spell, waving the butt of the wand over the baby prince's dear little head and, of course, a characteristic that was precisely the opposite of what Misaprop intended flowed out over that head like a drunken halo.

It didn't take the royal parents long to find out that something had gone wrong. The prince was three years old before he could walk more than two cubits without falling down. He couldn't pick up anything at all without dropping it a few times first. And he was always in the way. The royal butler was forever tripping over him and always did so when he was carrying the best wine. The little prince just never got it through his head that he ought to get out of the way of people.

No one ever lost their temper with him, though, because he had all the gifts that the other fairies had given him. He was of a sunny temperament, understood what everyone said to him, was obedient, clever, sweet and all that was delightful—except for his gracelessness.

It's not surprising, then, that he had been named Prince Delightful by his delighted parents, and that's what he was to everyone. Even while he was breaking every priceless piece of crockery that he could place his hands on, everyone found him delightful.

The fairy, Misaprop, was consulted, you may be sure, and the queen asked very politely (one must always be polite to a fairy as some of them are dreadfully short-tempered) what had gone wrong.

Misaprop turned quite red and said, "There, now, I must have managed to get the wrong end of the wand in my hand."

"Well, then, dear," said Queen Ermentrude, coaxingly, "can't you put the right end of the wand in your hand and try again?"

"I'd love to," said Misaprop. "I would do it at once, but it is quite against the fairy rules to try to cancel one's own spell after it has been made in good faith."

"If you don't," said the queen, "you will leave us in a dreadful position."

"If I do," said Misaprop, "I will be expelled from the Fairies Union," and of course there was no answer to that.

Things continued to get worse. When Prince Delightful was thirteen, he was placed in the hands of a dancing master, for one of the prime duties of a prince was to attend the royal balls. There he would be expected to dance with the ladies of the court and to be perfect at gavottes, minuets, and all the other latest steps.

It was just hopeless. Prince Delightful would have been better off dancing on his hands. Whenever he was expected to extend his right foot, he would extend his left and vice versa. Whenever he bowed, his head would hit that of his partner. When he whirled, he invariably staggered into someone else. And he simply could not keep time.

The dancing masters, fearing to offend a royal personage, invariably told the prince's parents that he danced like an angel, but of course, they could see he danced precisely as if he were a tipsy sailor.

It was even worse when he had to learn to handle arms. At swordplay, the cleverest footwork of an opponent could not prevent him from striking the prince with his épée. At wrestling, even when his opponent tried manfully to hold him upright, Prince Delightful managed to step on his shoelaces and fall down.

King Marcus was quite in despair. "My dear," he said to

Queen Ermentrude, "our beloved son, Prince Delightful, will be twenty tomorrow, but we can't give a ball to celebrate it, because he can't dance. We can't hold a tournament because he can't fight. Indeed, I don't even dare hold a procession for he is liable to fall down."

"He might ride a horse," said Queen Ermentrude, doubtfully.

"You do well to say that doubtfully, my dear, for you must have seen him on a horse."

"I have," admitted the queen.

"You know that he jounces up and down, in no way keeping time with the horse's natural movements."

The queen sighed. "What are we to do?"

"What can we do? We must send him out to seek his fortune."

"Oh, no," said the queen. "Not our only son."

"What do you mean, not our only son. The usual practice, I've always understood, is for kings to have three sons, and to send out all three, one after the other. We'll be sending out only one—because you always refused to have any more."

The queen burst into tears at once. "That's a cruel thing to say," she said. "You wouldn't say it if *you* had to have them. I'd like to see you have a baby, if you think it's so much fun. I'd like to see any man—"

King Marcus said, hastily, "Now don't weep, my dear. That was thoughtless of me and I didn't mean it. But just the same, we do have to send out Delightful. It's customary."

"He'll get hurt. He can't help it. He's just not graceful, because that stupid Misaprop—"

"Quiet," said the king, quickly, "she might be flying about, invisibly, and she might hear you. Besides even if Delightful is graceless, he has all the other virtues, and they may suffice. He may go out and slay a dragon and marry a beautiful princess; then defeat an enemy army for his father-in-law and gain that kingdom as well as ours. He'll become a great king and conqueror. If you read history, you'd see that it happens all the time."

"But where will all this take place? There are no dragons about here that I know of. There haven't been for years."

"Of course not. Princes have been very busy slaying them so that dragons are now an endangered species. In fact, there's some talk of having all the kingdoms get together and forbid any further killing of dragons."

"That will be a fine thing for virgins," said the queen indignantly. "That's all they eat."

"I know. The Virgins Union is fighting the movement vigorously. I understand they are sending out appeals for funds under the slogan, 'Would you rather have a dragon or a virgin at your beck and call?' I suppose princes can slay basilisks, chimeras, and hydras instead, but those are all endangered species, too. We live in hard times—just the same, there's hope. I've had the sorcerer check the want ads in the *Dragon-Slayers Gazette*. The kingdom of Poictesme has a dragon they want slain, and the advertisement includes a miniature of his daughter. She seems quite beautiful but the dragon is apparently a large brute and the princes are rather shying away from the task."

"If he's a large brute then I *certainly* won't think of allowing Delightful to risk his life—"

"But, my dear, I've already consulted Delightful. Graceless he may be but he is as brave as a lion—a large-size one, too—and he was very impressed by the measurements of the young lady, something the king of Poictesme had thoughtfully included in his ad."

"I'll just never see him again," wailed the queen. "And I'm sure that hussy of a princess has silicone implants."

Still, though queens may weep, princes must do their duty.

The prince packed his saddlebags, took an ample supply of gold pieces, and studied the route to Poictesme on the map that the sorcerer had supplied, one that showed all the major highways. He took a pair of twelve-foot lances with him, and his trusty sword, and a suit of armor that the sorcerer said was light and would not rust, since it was formed of a magic metal named aluminum.

He took off, and the king and queen waved at him for as long as they could see him. There were quite a few bystanders along the road, too, to cheer their Prince and to make an occasional bet as to whether he would fall off his horse while he was still in eyeshot. — He did, once or twice.

It took Delightful the standard time to make the trip from his father's kingdom to Poictesme—a year and a day.

Actually that was the time it took to reach the palace of King Faraday of Poictesme. He had reached the border of the kingdom some weeks earlier.

He was met by an old chamberlain who studied his ID card most carefully, looked up the location of his kingdom in a well-thumbed atlas and called up the Princes Register for a credit rating. It all seemed to go well for the chamberlain nodded sourly and said, "You seem to be okay."

"Fine," said Prince Delightful, stumbling over a small projection on the smooth floor. "Do I take a number?"

"A number? Why do you want a number, Highness?"

"So I'll know my turn—when I may ride out to slay the dragon."

"Oh, you may do that any time. You're the only foreign prince on the premises at the moment. We've had quite a shortage."

"A deadly dragon, eh?"

"Who can say? The poltroons barely come within sight when they turn and leave hastily. Not one has had the decency to get himself killed before leaving."

The Prince clicked his tongue. It always depressed him to be made aware of the decay of good manners. "It will be different with me. I shall pause only to meet the king and obtain his blessing and to take a gander at—to greet the gracious princess. What's her name, by the way? It wasn't included in the advertisement."

"Laurelene, Highness."

"To greet the gracious Princess Laurelene. Is my future mother-in-law, the queen, alive?"

"Yes, but she has retired to a nunnery."

"Ah, that's probably good all around, except perhaps for the nunnery."

"The nunnery has indeed been complaining, Highness."

King Faraday greeted Prince Delightful with the deepest skepticism, especially after the prince had leaned on his spear, allowing it to slip out from under him.

"Are you sure you know how to kill a dragon?" asked the king.

"With this spear," said Prince Delightful, flourishing it a little overenthusiastically, so that it flew out the window breaking a stained-glass panel.

"It goes by itself, I see," said King Faraday, with another dose of skepticism, and sent a menial out after it.

Princess Laurelene absorbed Prince Delightful's looks and muscles and smiled most fetchingly. "Just don't get killed yourself,

Prince, while you're slaying the dragon," she said. "You'd be no good to me dead."

"You're the best reason I have ever met for staying alive," said Prince Delightful, flourishing his hat as he bowed and catching its feather in the king's eye.

The next morning, he received directions from King Faraday's sorcerer, who also had a map. He then set out, waving jauntily at the king and his daughter.

The king waved back and said, morosely, "He *may* kill the dragon with his self-flying spear, or with his even more deadly hat."

"Think, Father," said Laurelene, who was as beautiful as the day and who had long blond hair that she barely had to touch up, "if he slays the dragon, all the virgins in the kingdom will be safe once more."

"And you, in addition," said King Faraday.

Whereupon Laurelene, with a roguish smile, said, "Now Father, what would Prince Delightful think if he heard you say that?" and she stamped on the old man's foot.

Prince Delightful followed the indicated course for a week and a day and found himself in the depths of a dark forest.

He began to suspect he might be in the vicinity of the dragon when his horse's ears began to prick upward and his horse's nostrils flared.

His own ears began to prick upward as he heard the sound of rusty snoring, precisely like the sound described in his *Dragon-Hunter's Handbook*. It had a deep sound, one that seemed to presage a large beast.

Furthermore, the prince's own nostrils flared as he detected the unmistakable smell of dragon musk. Not a pleasant odor.

Prince Delightful paused to consider strategy. From the snoring, it was obvious that the dragon was asleep, and according to the *Handbook,* its sleep was deep and it was difficult to disturb. That made sense since dragons had no natural enemies except princes and could usually sleep securely.

It seemed only fair to begin by pricking the beast with his spear until he woke it up. He could then fight it fair and square, wakefulness to wakefulness.

On the other hand, thought Prince Delightful, was that truly fair?

After all, the dragon was much larger and stronger than the prince was even if the princely horse were counted in. And the dragon could fly. And it could breathe flame.

Was that fair? No, thought Prince Delightful.

Did the dragon worry about that? No, thought Prince Delightful.

Since the prince had studied logic under the sorcerer, he concluded quite correctly that the balance would be somewhat restored if the dragon were asleep. If it slept, it could not fly or breathe flame, but it would still be far larger and stronger than the prince, so it would still have the advantage on its own side.

Prince Delightful urged his horse forward until it entered a clearing in which he could clearly see the sleeping dragon. It was large indeed. It was nearly a hundred feet long and was covered with tough scales that, the *Handbook* told him, could not be pierced by an ordinary spear. The thing to do was to aim at an eye which, fortunately, was closed.

Prince Delightful leveled his spear and slapped his spurs against his horse's flank. The loyal horse now charged forward, and the prince kept his own eye firmly on the closed eye of the monster.

Unfortunately, though the prince's eye remained firm and steady and true, his spear did not. The effort to keep both objects, eye and spear, aimed correctly was too great for the prince's inherent clumsiness and the spear dipped. It struck against the ground and the prince pole-vaulted high in the air.

The pole wrenched itself out of his hand and the prince came down on something hard and scaly. Instinctively, he clutched it in a death grip and found himself hugging the dragon's neck just behind its head.

The shock woke the dragon and its head lifted twenty feet into the air. Prince Delightful shouted involuntarily, "Hey! Hey!"

The dragon struggled to its feet, and the head shot up another ten feet. The horse, noting that its master was gone, wisely decided to go home. It turned and fled, and Prince Delightful felt deserted.

The dragon turned its head, looking apparently for whatever it was that had made the sound, and was now resting as a small weight upon its neck, but, of course, it could see nothing. There was no way it could turn its head through an angle of a hundred eighty degrees.

Finally, it said, in a deep bass rumble, "Hey, is anybody dere?"

Prince Delightful's eyes opened wide. None of the vast literature on dragons that he had read in the course of his princely education had stated that dragons could speak—and in what was definitely a lower-class accent.

He said, "Why, it is I. It is Prince Delightful."

"Well, whatcha doin' up dere. Get off, will ya. Get out of my scales."

"I don't like to, if it means you're going to eat me."

"I ain't gonna eat you. In the foist place, I ain't hungry. In the second place, what makes ya think ya taste good. Get down and let's talk. Ya ain't got no spear, have ya?"

"I'm afraid it's lost."

"Aw right, den. Get down and tawk like a civilized dragon."

The great head and neck lowered slowly and when it was down against the ground, Prince Delightful cautiously slipped off. There was a small rip in his doublet where it had caught on the rough edge of a scale.

He backed off into the woods. "You're sure now you're not going to attack me?"

"Cawse not. I said I wouldn't. I give you my woid. A dragon's woid is his bond. Not like you lousy princes. Why do you come bothering us for? One of you guys killed my sister. Another killed my father. What do we do to you?"

"Well, you do eat virgins, you know."

"Dat's a lie. I wouldn't touch a voigin. They always smell from cheap poifume. When I was little I licked one in the face. Yech. Powder. Voigins ain't edible."

"But then, what do you eat?"

"Nuttin' much. I eat grass and fruit and nuts and roots, maybe once in a while a bunny rabbit or a kitty cat. And den you guys come after us with spears and swords and horses and we ain't done nothin'."

"But everyone says you eat virgins."

"Dat's just de voigins trying to make demselves important. Boy, dat makes me mad."

"Wait a minute," said Prince Delightful in alarm. "Don't start spouting flame."

"Who, me?" The dragon's lower lip thrust outward and a tear the size of a pint container glinted in its eye. "I can't spout flame. I'm prob'ly the only dragon that can't spout flame."

"Oh? Why not?"

The dragon heaved a large sigh and a somewhat fetid odor filled the air. Prince Delightful held his nose but the dragon didn't seem to notice.

It said, "Mine is a sad story."

"May I hear it, uh, sir? What's your name, by the way?"

"My name? Boinard, but you can call me Boinie. That's when the trouble started. At my christening."

"At your christening?" said Prince Delightful, forcefully. "What an odd coincidence. That's when my trouble started, too."

"Yeah, but what's trouble to a prince? Now you listen to me. My old man and my old lady, dey wanted I should get a good start in life with Boinard, a lucky name in my family, so dey invited every fairy in dis kingdom to the christening. And what do yuh know, a foreign fairy from somewhere else came, also."

"A foreign fairy?"

"Yeah. A nice old dame, my folks told me, but not all dere, you know what I mean? A regular klutz."

"Was her name Misaprop?"

"Yeah, dat was huh name. Howja know?"

"That same fairy was at *my* christening."

"And did she mess yuh up?"

"Very much so."

"Gee, it makes us kind of pals. Shake, pal."

The dragon's gigantic paw extended itself out to Prince Delightful and swallowed up his small hand.

The dragon said, "You know what she did to me?"

"No."

"After all de other fairies made me big and strong and good-looking with nice scales, she came along to give me a good strong flame-throwing mout' only she got it all bollixed up. No flames."

"But I don't understand. If you don't have any flames, Bernie, why don't any of the other knights want to attack you? I'm told they all go away quickly when they meet up with you."

"Dat's the sad part. Nobody wants to hang around me. Not even lady dragons. Looka me. I'm big and strong and beautiful, an' I ain't had a dame look at me for seventy-five years."

"Why not?"

"Well, when I get mad or when I get passionate, if you know what I mean, I don't shoot out flame, I shoot out somepin' else."

"What?"

"You wanna see?"

"It won't hurt me, will it?"

"Cawse not. Just lemme think about de situation, so I get mad."

The dragon brooded a bit, then said, "Now!" It opened its mouth and exhaled and Prince Delightful dropped to the ground immediately, his hands over his nose. What had come out was the worst, the foulest, the most noxious odor he had ever smelled. He rolled about choking.

The dragon said, "It won't last long. I just gave you a little dose. In a way, I suppose it's better. Yuh can dodge the flame; yuh can't dodge dis. All de knights leave quick, when I breathe out. So do all the lady dragons. Wotta life."

The dragon shook its head sadly.

Prince Delightful got shakily to his feet. The forest still smelled, but it was bearable.

He said, "Bernie, how would you like to come back to Poictesme with me and be introduced to King Faraday?"

"What? And have a million knights sticking their spears into me?"

"No, believe me. You'll be treated like a king yourself. You'll have all the bunny rabbits you can eat, and grass, too."

"How come?"

"You'll see. Trust me. I have to ride you back, though. I haven't got a horse anymore."

Prince Delightful came back on Bernie, sitting just behind his head, and viewing the world from thirty feet in the air.

At first everyone fled screaming, but Prince Delightful kept calling out, "Friends, this is a tame dragon, a good dragon. Its name is Bernie. Speak to them, Bernie."

And the dragon called out, "Hi, guys. It's just me and my friend, duh prince."

Eventually, some peasants and workmen and varlets of varying degree, braver than the rest, followed along as the dragon took his huge steps carefully, making sure it treaded on no one by accident. Its great head turned on its long neck from side to side and the prince waved majestically first to the right and then to the left.

Then, as the news spread, the populace began to line the road and by the time Bernie moved into the capital city and up the main boulevard to the castle, the cheering populace had turned it all into a triumphant procession.

The dragon said, "Hey, de human people ain't so bad when yuh get to know dem, Prince."

"They're almost civilized," said Prince Delightful.

King Faraday came out to greet them and so did Laurelene, who shouted, "Greetings, my brave Prince Delightful."

The sorcerer came out, too, and rubbed his eyes and said, "Of all things, an apatosaurus." But he often spoke gibberish and no one paid attention.

Bernie was housed in a stable as far removed from the palace as possible and King Faraday, having overseen that, returned to his throne room and said to Prince Delightful, "I admit that bringing back the monster was quite a feat, but it was not what I engaged you to do. You were supposed to kill it."

"Ah, but a tame dragon is far better than a dead one, if you'll let me explain matters to Your Majesty."

"I'm listening."

"To begin with, I assume that, as a respectable monarch, you have a neighbor who is an enemy of yours and whom you have been fighting for generations. You have laid his lands waste and he has laid your lands waste, and many people have died in agony on both sides."

"Well, of course. This is a civilized land, and we would not think of behaving in any other way. There is war between myself and the faithless, barbarous land of Lotharingia to our east."

"And at the moment, is your army attacking them, or is theirs attacking yours?"

King Faraday coughed. "At the moment, Lotharingia has contrived to attain a slight advantage over us and has advanced to within ten miles of our provincial town of Papeete."

"Would you like to destroy their forces and impose a peace of your choosing upon them?"

"Without doubt, but who would bring about such destruction?"

"Why, Bernie and I. Alone."

"The Lotharingian forces include a thousand brave knights, armed cap-a-pie. Your dragon might kill some but it will be killed itself and our people would be greatly cast down at our failure."

"There'll be no failure. Let there be a saddle designed for Bernie's neck, and a pair of reins so that I won't fall off. Ask the sorcerer to design something that I may place over my head that will purify air, and have a small force escort me to the Lotharingian army."

"A small force?"

"They may move off when Bernie and I reach the Lotharingians. Bernie and I will face the enemy alone. However, have an army waiting on the flanks, ready to move in behind the enemy forces to cut off their retreat."

King Faraday said, "It is mad, but I will do as you say. After all, you brought back the dragon, when all the others merely fled."

Saddle and reins were prepared. The sorcerer brought a device of peculiar shape that fitted over Prince Delightful's head.

The sorcerer said, "This will keep the air pure. It is a gas mask." But, as usual, no one was impressed with the words he used.

Prince Delightful and Bernard appeared before the lines of the Lotharingian army. The Lotharingians were in brave array and they bristled with spear points.

There was a tremor, however, that shook the ranks at the first sight of the dragon, with its rider high in the air and with his face hidden by some device that made him seem more fearsome than the monster he bestrode.

After all, every Lotharingian had seen pictures of dragons, but none had ever seen a gas mask, either in books or in real life.

The Lotharingian general called out bravely, however, and said, "It is only one beast upon another, my brave Lotharingians. Stand firm, acquit yourself like men. Circle the dragon, avoid its flames and hack at its tail. The pain will cause it to run."

The Lotharingians took heart and made their stand, waiting for the dragon to advance. It did not, however, but kept its distance.

Prince Delightful said, "Did you hear them? They're going to hack at your beautiful tail."

"Dat's what I hoid," rumbled the dragon, "but dey ain't gonna, because what dey said went an' got me real mad."

He opened his gigantic maw and, with a roar of thunder, there emerged a vast cloud of turbid, putrid gas. It rolled down upon the Lotharingian forces and where it struck and spread out, the armed men broke and ran, throwing away their weapons as they did so, concerned only to get away from the incredibly foul odor.

Some miles back, the army, reduced to a disorderly mob, met the waiting forces of Poictesme and few escaped either death or capture.

"You may have my beautiful and virginal daughter, Prince Delightful," said King Faraday, "and since I have no son, you will inherit my kingdom when I die and the conquered land of Lotharingia as well and your own father's kingdom, too. As for your dragon, he will be a hero to us for as long as he wishes to remain here. He shall live on the finest hay and we shall catch small animals for him when he feels the need for some."

"He would like a lady dragon or two," said Prince Delightful, diffidently.

"Even that might be arranged," said the king, "if he learns to control his passions to some extent."

Prince Delightful tripped on his train only twice during the marriage ceremony, but, as he said to Bernie in his stable afterward, "It doesn't matter. Actually, the fairy Misaprop, made it all possible. My clumsiness landed me on your neck and your noxious breath destroyed the enemy army. —And now I must go to my fair wife."

As it turned out, he was not unduly clumsy on his wedding night and he and the Princess Laurelene lived happily ever after.

PART TWO

ON FANTASY

MAGIC

ARTHUR CLARKE, IN ONE OF HIS NOTABLE oft-quoted comments, said that technology, sufficiently advanced, was indistinguishable from magic.

That's clear enough. If a medieval peasant, or even a reasonably educated medieval merchant, were presented with the sight of a super-jet streaking through the sky, or with a working television set, or with a pocket computer, he would be quite convinced that he was witnessing sorcery of the most potent sort. He might also be pretty certain that the sorcery was the devil's work. Consequently if a person from the present (his future) were to go back in time with a pocket computer, for instance, and were to demonstrate its workings, the result might well be exorcism, and perhaps even the torture chamber.

The question in my mind, though, is whether the proposition can be reversed. Is magic necessarily indistinguishable from sufficiently advanced technology? If so, you see, all the tricks of the trade of fantasy could be transferred to science fiction. After all, you don't have to describe the advanced technology in detail (if you could, you would build a working model, patent it, and become very rich, perhaps.)

For instance, as a child, I found *Ali Baba and the Forty Thieves* fascinating. Imagine coming up to a blank mountain wall, saying "Open sesame," having the wall split in two, and having the halves move apart to reveal the entrance to a cave. Now that's magic!

My wonder and bemusement at such a thing continued undiminished even after I had grown accustomed to approaching doors and having them open automatically at my approach. That wasn't magic; that was just a photocell and therefore no cause for wonder at all (even though I would agree that a medieval merchant, presented with such an automatically opening door, would surely consider it magic.)

Perhaps it is the "Open sesame" that is the real wonder of it. After all, a door that opens at the mere approach of anyone at any time shows no discretion. If there is a code word that only you know then you control the door; you have *power*.

But then, it is easy to imagine a computer which will only allow the door to open at some appropriate code word punched onto its keyboard. Indeed, the time may well come when such a computer may be designed to respond to the spoken command. In that case, it is inevitable that some jokester will have the computer open the door at the command "Open sesame!"

We might go even further and outdo the story. After all, in the tale the door opens to anyone's command of "Open sesame!" and because Ali Baba overhears it, he gains entrance to the cave and grows rich. A computer may be designed to respond only to the typical sound pattern of a particular voice and then only you may open the door, even if the whole world knows the code word.

Next, how about Snow White's stepmother, the wicked queen, who asks her mirror who is the fairest of them all and has the mirror assure her that *she* is. Well, we don't have talking mirrors, but we do have talking television screens, and the medieval merchant would see no distinction.

Some day, when it will become routine to have conversations under conditions of closed-circuit television, a fair young maid can phone her boyfriend and say, sentimentally, "Who is the fairest in the land?" and heaven help the boyfriend if his image in the mirror doesn't say, "You are the fairest in the land."

A third example that I always found impressive as a child is that of the giant who finds he must chase the hero who has gotten away with one or more of said giant's ill-gotten treasures. The giant promptly puts on his "seven-league boots" and is off on a chase. No matter how great a lead our young hero has, we may be sure he will be quickly overtaken.

Now what are seven-league boots? It is usually explained that the giant can traverse seven leagues (twenty-one miles) at every stride. The stories never explain how long it takes him to make one stride, but children always assume (at least I did) that the giant makes as many strides per minute as a man ordinarily does.

The stride of a walking man is about one yard. This is, when a foot moves from its rear position to its fore position in ordinary walking, it moves through a distance of a yard. In the same time the much huger stride of the giant moves through twenty-one miles or 36,960 yards.

A man walking in an unhurried manner travels at a speed of three miles per hour. The giant walking in an unhurried manner, travels at 36,960 times this speed, or 110,880 miles an hour. This is indeed fast; much faster than I had imagined as a child; or (I am sure) than the tale spinner who first spoke of seven-league boots imagined.

Someone equipped with seven-league boots can travel from New York to Los Angeles in 1.6 minutes, and can go around the world in 13.5 minutes.

That is astonishing even as an example of high technology. It is faster than any present-day airplane, and is even faster than the rocket ships carrying our astronauts to the Moon.

In fact, so unexpectedly fast are seven-league boots that they defeat their own purpose. Any giant moving twenty-one miles at a stride, with strides coming as frequently as in an ordinary man's ordinary walk, would be traveling with a speed some 4.4 times escape velocity. In short, he would, at his first stride, launch himself through the atmosphere, and, in a few more strides, find himself in outer space.

And yet there is nothing to keep us from developing seven-league-boot capacity. After all, that enormously speedy giant is still moving at only 1/6250 the speed of light.

———

I think I have shown then that magic can be indistinguishable from sufficiently advanced technology; but is that *always* so?

Obviously not, for it is common enough in tales of magic and sorcery to have people able to make themselves invisible, for instance; or to change a man into a frog and vice versa; or to be made capable of understanding the language of animals (and to then find that a horse can discourse as sensibly as Socrates). It is questionable whether such things are within the reasonable purview of technology, though with sufficient ingenuity, a science-fiction writer can think of a way of making such things sound technologically plausible.

However, consider that bit of magic that appeals to childhood most of all. There is no question in my mind that *the* most wonderful of all objects is Aladdin's lamp. Tell the truth, now! Haven't you ever dreamed of owning it?

Imagine having a jinn under your absolute control; one who answers "I hear and obey" to all requests, however unreasonable; one who can supply you with uncounted trays of jewels at the snap of a finger; one who can build you an elaborate and luxurious palace overnight and have it come readyfilled with beautiful and compliant damsels.

Ah! That's what I call *living*.

Now we are ready to put our finger on the vital difference between magic and however-high technology. Presented with something so strange we cannot comprehend how it's done, whether by some technological advance or some actually working magic, we have only to ask one question: "What are the limits within which the ability to do this must work?"

Magic need have no limits; technology must have.

Thus, the jinn of the lamp can build a palace overnight, or even in an instant, and it wouldn't occur to the reader to ask, "But what was the source of the energy required to perform this task?" The jinn of the lamp could travel to Jupiter to obtain the rare egg of the dyk-dyk bird and be back in twenty seconds and no one would dream of pointing out that lo! he has traveled far faster than the speed of light.

I suspect that no technology, however advanced, will ever defy the law of conservation of energy, or of momentum, or of angular momentum, or of electric charge. I suspect that no technology, however advanced, will defy the laws of thermodynamics, or Maxwell's equations, or the indeterminacy principle, or the tenets of relativity and quantum theory.

I say that I "suspect" this because I am perfectly ready to admit that we don't yet know all there is to know about the Universe, that there may turn out to be special conditions, of which we as yet know nothing, in which any or all these limits can be bent or broken.

However, even if these limits are demolished, other limits, more basic and more unbreakable, will replace them. *Some* limit there will remain, as seems absolutely unavoidable to me.

Magic, however, is unlimited; that is its essence. When a science-fiction writer presents a tale of magic that must abide by rules and respect limits (as L. Sprague de Camp does in his wonderful "The Incomplete Enchanter") then it is no longer magic; it is merely an exotic technology.

SWORD AND SORCERY

I DON'T REPRESENT MYSELF AS AN expert on the history of science fiction and its various sister fields and cousin fields, but I suspect I won't be far wrong if I say that the contemporary sword-and-sorcery tale owes its existence to the imagination of Robert Howard and to his invention of the Conan stories.

Part of the success of this type of story lies in the fascination of the bulging muscles and incredible strength and fortitude of the hero. I imagine that almost any male would at least occasionally wish he had biceps as hard as chrome steel and could wield a fifty-pound sword as though it were a bamboo cane and could use it to cleave vile caitiffs to the chine. Imagine single-handedly putting fifty assailants to flight with a sword in one hand and a fainting damsel in the other?

Oddly enough, I shudder at such things. I have lived so thoroughly effete a life, and am such a failure at suspending some kinds of disbelief, that I remain too conscious of what a hero must smell like after having performed such feats and I've never read of one of them using a deodorant even once. It seems to me that the Conans of the world must rescue maidens from fates worse than death only to subject them to other fates worse than death.

Of course, maidens might like that sort of thing, and so might damsels—but I don't really know. I've never put them to that particular test.

Heroes date back much farther than Conan, you may be sure. They are as old as literature, and the most consistently popular ones are notable for their muscles and not much else. As Anna Russell says of Siegfried, who is the hero of Richard Wagner's *Der Ring des Nibelungen,* such heroes are "very brave, very strong, very handsome, and very, *very* stupid."

You can find such heroes in almost every culture. The Sumerians had Gilgamesh, the Greeks had Heracles, the Hebrews had Samson, the Persians had Rustam, the Irish had Cuchulain, and so on. Each one of them would get into all kinds of trouble since any child could deceive and entrap them, and they then had to depend on their superhuman strength, and nothing else, to get out of the trouble.

It took the ancient Greeks to come up with something better. In the *Iliad,* the hero is Achilles, another killing machine. In the *Odyssey,* however, the hero is Odysseus, who is an efficient enough fighter (he wouldn't have been allowed in any self-respecting epic, otherwise) but, in addition, he had *brains.*

There is a tale that is not told in the *Iliad,* but is referred to in the *Odyssey* and is elaborated by poets after Homer, to the effect that after the death of Achilles, there was a question as to which of the Greek heroes deserved to take over Achilles' glorious god-manufactured armor. One of the claimants was Ajax, who was second only to Achilles in strength and was very likely the least intelligent of the heroes, and the other was Odysseus. It was a case of brawn versus brain.

In Ovid's *Metamorphoses,* the story is told particularly well. Ajax stands up to state his case to the assembled Greeks, and tells of the long, harsh battles in which he was a staunch bulwark, in which his mighty arm fended off the Trojans, and of the time he singly defended the ships at a low point in the war.

When I read this for the first time, I was impressed. Ajax convinced me. I didn't see how it was possible for Odysseus, a fighter of lesser strength, to maintain his claim to the armor. But then, the wise Odysseus arose and totally demolished Ajax's arguments. It was not simple strength, not the mere clash of sword and shield that was deciding the war, but strategy . . . policy . . . *thought*. I cheered Odysseus and so did the Greeks, and he got the armor. Poor Ajax went mad with frustration and killed himself.

There is a touching passage in the *Odyssey* that serves as a postscript. Odysseus visits the underworld, and sees relatives and friends who had passed away; including his mother and Achilles. Ajax is there, too, and Odysseus approaches the dead hero with friendly words, but Ajax moves away silently. Even after death, he cannot forgive.

In other cultures, too, there is the occasional tale of brute strength defeated. One of the great stories is that of David and Goliath, the little man defeating the giant by clever choice of weapons. Reynard the Fox defeats the threatening wolves, bears, and lions in the medieval animal tales, and so does Br'er Rabbit in the American folktales.

In this battle of brains and brawn, however, the audience is never quite at ease with the victory of brains. The uncomplicated Lancelots and Rolands are cheered to the echo, but clever victors are often met with a certain reserve and suspicion. In many post-Homeric legends, Odysseus is represented as an unprincipled schemer and physical coward. The cleverness of the fox and rabbit is usually represented as based on lies and dishonesty.

In legends, the clever character is often envisaged as someone smart enough to control aspects of the universe through his superior knowledge and wisdom. He is a magician or sorcerer. There are occasionally magicians who are on the side of right and who serve the physical hero, as Merlin serves King Arthur. Sometimes, they even *are* the hero, as Vainamoinen is, for instance, in the Finnish legends.

Very often, though, the magician is the villain, who threatens the hero with sneaky enchantments, who fights from behind the protective wall of his powers. Our poor hero, who fights in the open with simple and honest thwacks of his sword, must somehow reach and destroy the cowardly, unethical magician.

Clearly, the readers are expected to feel that it is noble and admirable for the hero to pit his own superhuman strength against the lesser physiques of his enemies, and also to feel that there is something perfidious about a magician pitting his own superhuman intelligence against the lesser wit of his enemies.

This double standard is very evident in sword-and-sorcery, in which the sword-hero (brawn) is pitted against the sorcery-villain (brain), with brawn winning every time. The convention is, furthermore, that brawn is always on the side of goodness and niceness (a proposition which, in real life, is very dubious). This is similar to the convention in westerns, in which all disputes are decided by which character can draw his gun the fastest and shoot the straightest. It is then understood that the clean and virtuous white hat is always the fastest and straightest shooter, a proposition which must surely be a variety of wishful thinking impossible to justify in any realistic fashion.

Science fiction, in its early days, often fell into this cliché of smart-is-wicked. Think of all the mad scientists who populated the stories published during the first decade of the science-fiction magazines to say nothing of the comic strips and movies ever since. Think of all the Flash Gordons who have pitted their mighty thews, and their stupidity, against the evil intelligence of the Mings—and won.

I don't say that I don't enjoy this, too. I particularly like it when it is leavened with a sense of humor, as it was in the case of the television miniseries *Wizards and Warriors*. However, the fact is that in the history of the large mammalian predators, humanity came out as sovereign by virtue of brain over brawn, and heroic fantasy would reverse the decision and give the victory to the lions and elephants. (If you disapprove of what human beings are doing to the Earth—as I do—you may wish the lions and elephants *had* won, but I'm not saying that brains are Good, merely that they are Victors.)

Present-day science fiction has, as one of the characteristics that differentiate it from other forms of fiction, a tendency toward the deification of reason. Scientists are sometimes heroes, and intelligence is very frequently the weapon that must be used, even by those who are not scientists, to solve the problems posed. In my own stories, I almost never make use of violence, and even when I do, it is never the means whereby the crisis is resolved. In my stories, it is a case of reason against reason, with the superior brain winning. (And sometimes it is not completely clear that the superior brain represents the cause of Right and Good, for I have the uneasy feeling that Right does not always triumph—or is even always clearly definable.)

The definition of "good science fiction" ought to include, then, the tendency to have problems solved by the use of brains—the human specialty—rather than by the use of stupid strength.

Not all heroic fantasy takes the reverse stand. In Tolkien's *The Lord of the Rings* intelligence is exalted. Nevertheless, I consider the typical sword-and-sorcery tale to be anti–science fiction; to be the very opposite of science fiction. It is for that reason that you are not likely to find anything of the sort published in *Isaac Asimov's Science Fiction Magazine*, unless it is particularly exceptional in its characteristics.

CONCERNING
TOLKIEN

IN MY INTRODUCTION TO THE FIRST volume of the *Isaac's Universe* series, I mentioned briefly that in inventing a multi-intelligence universe to serve as a background for these stories, I was influenced by E. E. Smith's stories of the *Galactic Patrol*.

And so I was—but in thinking about the matter since then, I realized that there was a second influence, much stronger than that first one. Why, I thought, did *Galactic Patrol* spring to mind and not *The Lord of the Rings*.

Actually, there's no mystery to it. *Galactic Patrol* was science fiction while *The Lord of the Rings* was fantasy—and when I was thinking up the background to *Isaac's Universe*, I was in a science fiction mode of thought.

So now let me break away from the bonds of sf and think about *The Lord of the Rings*.

The author of *The Lord of the Rings* was John Ronald Reuel Tolkien (1892–1973) who wrote as J. R. R. Tolkien. He was born in South Africa but lived in Great Britain as an Oxford don whose specialty was Anglo-Saxon.

In 1937, he published a children's story called *The Hobbit*. It was not, in my opinion, entirely successful. Tolkien was still feeling his way. In *The Hobbit*, he tended to write down to his readers with a kind of self-conscious coyness.

This, however, grew less marked as the story went on and Tolkien himself was caught up in it. The hero was Bilbo Baggins, the hobbit of the title, a humanoid creature about half the size of a man. The story involves the quest of a group of dwarfs to regain a treasure that once belonged to them but is now guarded by a malevolent dragon. Baggins is sent to accompany them by Gandalf (a wizard who makes his first appearance as a kind of conjurer).

Baggins goes along very much against his will, for he is scared to death. However, as the story proceeds, he grows more heroic (in a very convincing way) and by the closing scenes, he is dominant—with far more brains, more initiative, and more heroism than the other characters in the story.

In the 1950s, Tolkien decided to elaborate on *The Hobbit* and write a long, three-volume continuation designed for adults rather than for children. Bilbo makes his appearance at the start and there is much the same atmosphere as in *The Hobbit*, but he quickly passes on a new task to his nephew, Frodo, who is the hero of *The Lord of the Rings*, and with that the atmosphere changes, deepens, and becomes wholly absorbing.

The center of action is a ring, which Bilbo had come upon accidentally in the course of *The Hobbit* and which now turns out to be the key to universal power.

The story becomes a saga of the fight between good and evil. Good is represented by Frodo and his friends, and by his mentor, Gandalf, who is now portrayed as nearly all-powerful, and even, eventually, as a nearly Christlike figure. Evil is represented by the Satan figure, Sauron, who needs only the ring to establish his already fearsomely great power permanently and absolutely. It is the task of our heroes, and of Frodo, in particular, to see that the ring is destroyed and to undertake an appallingly dangerous trek for that purpose.

The forces of good win out, but the difficulties are so great and the writing is so skillful that, even after repeated readings, the suspense holds. (I have read *The Lord of the Rings* five times.)

One wonders what was in Tolkien's mind. Actually, I don't like to try to guess the thoughts and motivations in an author's mind. I know, from personal experience, that clever analysts can find a great deal more in a novel than the author ever realized he had put in. (Yes, I have been victimized in this fashion, but I also know that despite my vehement denials that I meant this or that—I cannot entirely account for the workings of my unconscious mind.)

In the same way, Tolkien is reported to have denied any application of his saga to the events of the day or any tortured symbolism of various items in the novels—but I don't believe him.

To me, it seems obvious that Tolkien, between the writing of *The Hobbit* and *The Lord of the Rings,* lived through that dramatic and heart-stopping period in which Adolf Hitler and his Germans took over the control of the European continent in the space of ten months, and Great Britain found itself facing an overwhelming enemy without allies of its own.

If that wasn't Frodo versus Sauron, what was? —And Frodo won.

Another thing. What was this ring of power that all were fighting for? It was an evil ring which took possession of its owner and bent him, all unwittingly and all involuntarily, toward evil. Even Frodo, in the end, was affected and almost failed to carry out his mission. Obviously, the ring was something one feared but perversely wanted; something that once one had one could not let go.

What does that symbolize?

The answer came to me (and an obvious answer, too, once I had it) through a remark made by my dear wife, Janet.

Sauron rules over a region called Mordor, a blasted land in which nothing grows, a land destroyed by Sauron's evil, and one which Frodo must enter to complete his task. The description of Mordor is of a horrifying place.

Well, one day, Janet and I were driving along the New Jersey Turnpike, and we passed a section given over to oil refineries. It was a blasted region in which nothing was growing and which was filled with ugly, pipelike structures, which refineries must have. Waste oil was burning at the top of tall chimneys and the smell of petroleum products filled the air.

Janet looked at the prospect with troubled eyes and said, "There's Mordor."

And, of course, it was. And that was what had to be in Tolkien's mind. The ring was industrial technology, which uprooted the green land and replaced it with ugly structures under a pall of chemical pollution.

But technology meant power, and though it destroyed the environment and would eventually destroy the Earth, no one who had developed it dared give it up or even wanted to. There is no question, for instance, that America's automobiles pollute and filthify the atmosphere, and kill uncounted people with respiratory ailments. Yet is it conceivable that Americans would give up their automobiles, or even curtail their use somewhat? No, the ring of technology holds them in its grip and they won't give it up even if they are gasping for breath and dying.

(Mind you, I don't entirely agree with Tolkien's view of technology. I am not an Oxford don used to the calm pleasures of an upper-class Englishman in a preindustrial day. I know very well that the mass of humanity—including me and mine—derives what comfort they now have from the advance of technology and I do not want to abandon it so that upper-class Englishmen can substitute servants for machines. I don't want to be a servant. While I recognize the dangers of technology, I want those dangers corrected while keeping the benefits.)

Now comes the key question: What has all this to do with *Isaac's Universe?*

The Lord of the Rings is set on a mythological Earth, in which the very geography is unrecognizable. Human beings exist and there is a strong suggestion that they are in the process of taking over and that pretty soon "Middle-Earth" (Tolkien's world) will become the Earth we live on.

In addition to human beings, however, there are a wide variety of other creatures. There are the elves, who are more beautiful and intelligent than human beings, and who are essentially immortal. They are creatures of the pleasant forests and may, for Tolkien, have represented the British preindustrial upper classes.

There were also dwarfs, strong and long-lived; ents who are virtual personifications of the forest; wizards like Gandalf, and, of course, hobbits, who clearly represent the tame farmers of preindustrial times.

On the side of evil are the orcs, who were called goblins in *The Hobbit* and who, to me anyway, are representative of the new industrial workers as seen by the disapproving upper-class eyes of Tolkien. In *The Hobbit* he has trolls who speak pure London cockney, but he abandoned that quickly as too broad a representation.

There are also individual creatures that seem to exist all by themselves. On the side of good is Tom Bombadil, who represents nature; on the side of evil is the monstrous spider, Shelob, who perhaps represents the overpowering multinational conglomerates that now dominate Earth's economy.

There are super-wolves on the side of evil, supereagles and a super-bear on the side of good.

Most of all there is Gollum, who is, apparently, a hobbit perverted by the long possession of the ring, and who is the most ambiguous creature in the story. Within him is the constant battle between good and evil; and although the weakest and most helpless character in the saga, he manages, in some ways, to achieve the most. It is he, in fact, who, without meaning to, brings the tale to its satisfactory conclusion. I have always sympathized with Gollum and considered him more sinned against than sinning.

This rich mix of different types of intelligent creatures lends unimaginable strength and variety to *The Lord of the Rings* and it had to be in my mind when I thought up a universe with different types of intelligent creatures in it.

IN DAYS
OF OLD

THERE ARE SOME WORDS THAT REEK of romanticism, and "knight" is one of them. Yet its lineage is rather low. It is from the Anglo-Saxon *cniht,* which meant "boy" or "attendant." He was someone who attended his master and waited upon his needs. The German homologue, *Knecht,* still means "servant" today.

Of course, if it is the king we are talking about, his attendants were often fighting men, and in medieval times, that meant someone who could afford a horse and armor, and that, in turn, meant an aristocrat.

In other languages, it is the horse that was stressed rather than the service. In ancient times, to ride a horse was the surest sign of aristocracy (a warhorse, of course, and not a plow horse), just as driving a Cadillac or Mercedes (not a Chevrolet or Volkswagen) does the trick today.

In literary Latin, the word for "horse" is *equus,* but in soldier lingo, a horse was *caballus* (equivalent in English to "nag" or "hack"). It was the latter that came to be used for "warhorse." In Spanish, *caballus* became *caballo,* in Italian it became *cavallo,* and in French it became *cheval.*

Consequently, a horseman was *caballarius* in Latin, *caballero* in Spanish, *cavaliere* in Italian, and *chevalier* in French. All were equivalent to the English "knight." If we want to speak of the whole body of knights, you might talk of the "knighthood" of England, but it is more common to turn to French (for Norman-French, at least, was the language of the English aristocracy from the twelfth to the fifteenth century) and speak of "chivalry." To behave like a knight—that is, with courtly manners, instead of with the boorish behavior of malapert peasant knaves and varlets—is to be "chivalrous."

Actually, however, the romantic glow that makes knights seem so wonderful is totally a matter of fiction. In actual fact, knights, presuming on their horses and armor, were arrogant and insufferable in their behavior, especially to people unarmed and on foot. In English, we have another word for "knight"—"cavalier" (usually used for the arrogant fools who fought for King Charles I)—and we all know what "cavalier treatment" means.

Incidentally, I made use of the word "knave" a few lines back. This means "boy" or "attendant", and the German homologue, *Knabe,* means "boy" even today. As you see, "knave" and "knight," which are now treated as opposites, meant precisely the same to begin with. (The German word for "knight," by the way, is *Ritter,* meaning "rider.")

Ever since 2000 B.C., aristocrats did not fight on foot in the way the peasant scum were forced to. The Homeric heroes fought in chariots whenever they could, and the Greek and Roman aristocrats were in the "cavalry" (the Latin equivalent of the French/English "chivalry").

Nevertheless, until the end of ancient times, the cavalry never served anything but a supporting role. They were mainly important because of their speed of progress. They could spy out the enemy, and they could pursue an already broken and fleeing foe. The actual fighting, however, was done by the steady and disciplined "infantry," the Greek line of hoplites, the Macedonian phalanx, the Roman legion. (The very word "infantry" is akin to "infant" and is another word meaning "boy." The term is a measure of the contempt held for the foot soldier by the aristocrats.)

The role of the cavalry changed with the invention of the metal stirrup by the nomads of central Asia some time in the early centuries of the Christian era. What a difference it made. Without a proper stirrup, the cavalryman was insecurely balanced on his horse, and if he used a spear too incautiously he could be easily pulled or pushed off his mount. Under those conditions, horsemen were better off using arrows, as the Parthian cavalry did. With a good stirrup, on the other hand, the cavalaryman could wedge his feet securely and place the full weight of himself and his horse behind the spear. No footman of the period could stand against that.

When the Goths were fleeing from the Huns in the fourth century, they did manage to borrow the Hunnish stirrup, and in 378, the Gothic horsemen demolished the Roman legions at the Battle of Adrianople. The cavalry was then supreme for a thousand years, and the era of knighthood began.

Still, however much knights were idealized and heroicized in fiction, in actual life they were cruel, despotic, and ferocious in their treatment of the lower classes, and when they were finally and disgracefully defeated, we all cheered.

The time came when the lower classes learned to fight the horsemen by keeping them at a distance and skewering them. In this the lower classes were greatly aided by that inevitable accompaniment of arrogant aristocracy—invincible stupidity. The Flemish burghers learned how to use the long pike in a steady line (the rebirth of the Macedonian phalanx) and slaughtered the French horsemen at the Battle of Courtrai in 1302. The English longbowmen massacred French horsemen from a distance at the Battles of Crécy (1346), Poitiers (1356), Agincourt (1415), and Villeneuve (1420). The Swiss pikemen demolished the Burgundian horsemen in 1477, and by then gunpowder had established itself and knighthood was all over.

But we still remember it in a golden glow of romance and, most of all, in the Arthurian legend—the tales of King Arthur of Britain and his Knights of the Round Table. In fact, anytime we speak of "knights" we think of those tales and, most of all, of Sir Lancelot.

The Arthurian legend began with Geoffrey of Monmouth, who, in about 1136, wrote his *History of British Kings,* and in the process talked of Uther Pendragon, his son Arthur, and their helpful wizard, Merlin. It is not history, but myth and legend, yet it fascinated its readers, who then, as today, would rather have history appeal to their superstitions and patriotism than to any abstract and bloodless passion for truth. If you want an excellent modern retelling of Geoffrey's tales, read *The High Kings* by Joy Chant (1983).

About 1170, a French poet, Chrétien de Troyes, took up the tale and added straightforward romance. It was he who first invented the adulterous passion of Lancelot and Guinevere, and the mystical tale of the search for the Holy Grail. Since Chrétien made no pretense to even the shadow of historical truth, his tales were even more popular than Geoffrey's.

Sir Thomas Malory put together the scattered fragments of the Arthurian legend into *Morte d'Arthur* ("The Death of Arthur"), and it is his version, published in 1485, that we know best today.

The legend has never died, and in each century it has been retold. In modern times there are Alfred, Lord Tennyson's *Idylls of the King* (1859), Mark Twain's *A Connecticut Yankee at King Arthur's Court* (1889), and T. H. White's *Once and Future King* (1958). From the last of these, the musical *Camelot* was taken. Most recently, there is Marion Zimmer Bradley's *The Mists of Avalon* (1982).

The Arthurian legend is strictly fantasy. It is loaded with wizards, enchantresses, spells, and magicking. Those who attempted to remove the fantasy and present the legend in a realistic manner were least successful. I found Tennyson to be dishwaterishly dull, for instance. Twain introduces the time-travel motif, which makes for anachronistic amusement, but by turning Merlin into a flim-flam faker, he greatly detracts from the interest of the tale.

White, on the other hand, especially in *The Sword in the Stone* (1939), which is the first volume of his tetralogy, even adds to the fantasy, and his version rises superior to Malory for that reason (in my opinion). The same can be said of Bradley's painstaking tour de force.

It is not surprising, then, that modern fantasy writers turn every now and then to knightly romanticism and, in particular, to aspects of the Arthurian legend and try their teeth on it.

GIANTS IN THE EARTH

GIANTS ARE SUCH A COMMON ELEMENT in fantasies, myths, and legends of all societies that one must wonder where the notion comes from. Even the Bible adds its voice to the subject: "There were giants in the earth in those days" (Genesis 6:4).

To be sure, there are giants in the earth *these* days. The blue whale of Antarctic waters is not only the largest animal alive today but is probably the largest animal that ever lived. The sequoias and redwoods of the Pacific Coast are not only the largest and tallest plants alive today but probably the largest plants that ever lived.

People lived parochial lives in ancient times, rarely traveling more than a few miles from home, and tales of large animals in foreign climes must have lost nothing in the telling. As the tales passed from mouth to mouth, they undoubtedly grew ever more dramatic. Thus, whales became biblical "leviathans" and hippopotamuses became biblical "behemoths," and in the tales of the medieval rabbis, both leviathans and behemoths became monsters of truly mountainous size.

But giants need not merely be the magnifications of distant

truths. They can be the outcome of reason. In mythmaking days, it was natural to suppose that the forces of nature were expressions of life. The wind was the breath of gods; storms were the result of their anger; the lightning was their hurled artillery. Volcanoes arose from the overflowing forges of underground gods, and earthquakes from their uneasy shifting when asleep, or in chains. Naturally, for living things (presumably humanoid in shape) to produce these effects, gods must be colossal in strength and size. It makes sense, doesn't it?

Then, too, in ancient times, it sometimes happened that a settled civilization decayed, stumbled, and was overrun by a more primitive, but more vigorous, band of warriors. We can picture the warriors wondering at the works of the civilization they have conquered—the massive walls surrounding the cities, the large temples or other structures, and so on.

Being innocent of the advanced technology developed by the civilization they have conquered, they cannot imagine how those structures were made. They themselves could not have done it, and it would therefore be ridiculous to suppose that the inferior people they had conquered could have done it. The logical assumption was that a race of giants did it.

The Dorian barbarians who overthrew the Mycenaean kingdoms of Greece noted the thick, large-stoned walls of Mycenae and assumed they were built by those giants called Cyclopes. We still speak of large walls built of unpolished stones held in place by their own weight rather than by mortar as "cyclopean."

And it's not only naive ancients who believed this. Some people today, surveying the pyramids of Egypt and convinced that the ancient Egyptians could not have built them, fantasize their own version of giants and demigods as having built them. They naively suggest that astronauts from other worlds did the job. (Why astronauts, with technologies capable of interstellar flight, should have constructed huge piles of stone rather than have built something of steel and concrete beats me.)

We have the advantage today of knowing that there were indeed giants in the past—in the long, long past. For a period of a hundred million years, the land thundered under the legs of giant reptiles. The brachiosaur was the bulkiest and most massive land animal that ever lived, the tyrannosaur the most dreadful carnivore. There were pteranodons, which were flying reptiles that, in some cases, were as large as a large airplane.

Could some "racial memory" have implanted in the human mind giants and monsters derived from these reptiles, all of whom died out some sixty million years before the first primitive hominids made their appearance? As an example, could the dragons of so many myths be the pteranodons in reality? Not likely. It is much more reasonable to suppose that dragons were originally an expression of the giant pythons and anacondas that do exist. They were trimmed out with wings merely because that was commonly done as an expression of speed (think of winged horses such as Pegasus), and their fire-breathing is an expression of the poison venom of some snakes.

Of course, if an extinct creature is only recently extinct, it might serve. The elephant bird, or aepyornis, of Madagascar still survived in medieval times. It weighed half a ton and was the largest bird that ever existed. It must surely have been the inspiration for the flying bird-monster, the "roc," that we find in the Sinbad tales of *The Arabian Nights*.

Of course, even creatures never encountered in life by any human beings leave their bones behind, bones that are fossilized to a greater or lesser extent. It was only in the nineteenth century that these fossil remnants were correctly interpreted, but that doesn't mean they weren't found, and misinterpreted, in earlier centuries.

In prehistoric times, for instance, there were pygmy elephants and hippopotamuses on the Mediterranean islands. Even a pygmy elephant has a large skull, and some of these were dug up in historic times on the island of Sicily. It was natural to assume them to be remnants of humanoid giants. The nasal cavity in the skull looked as though it might represent a large centrally located single eye. That could be the origin of the giant one-eyed Cyclops (Greek for "circular eye") in the *Odyssey*.

Did humanoid giants ever exist? The closest example, as far as we know, is a giant primate that lived until a few million years ago.

Human beings are themselves giant primates, for we are among the largest of the entire group. The only primate that is clearly larger and more massive than we are is the male gorilla, but there was once a super-gorilla we call *Gigantopithecus* (Greek for "giant ape"). He could stand up to nine feet tall and must have weighed something like eight hundred pounds.

The diet of *Gigantopithecus* was apparently very much like that of human beings, and it had teeth that were very human in shape but were, of course, much larger. In fact, when modern paleontologists first came across such teeth, it seemed possible that they might be those of outsize human beings. It took a while before other bones were discovered that made the apishness of *Gigantopithecus* abundantly clear.

It might well be that such teeth, showing up here and there, seemed evidence of the one time existence of fearsome humanoid giants.

There remains one other point to make. We have all—every one of us—at one time lived in a world of giants. When we were infants and small children, we were surrounded by giants. These were, for the most part, benevolent giants, but not in every case. And even when benevolent, the giants often denied us what we wanted and it was clear that we could not fight their power. So it was a frightening and frustrating world, and we may all be permanently scarred with the fear of the large in consequence.

WHEN FANTASY BECAME FANTASY

IN SOME WAYS, ALL FICTION WRITING is fantasy. If a tale is truly fiction, it never happened; and if it never happened, it is fantasy; it is a creation of the mind, the imagination. For that matter, if we want to be very strict about it, much supposed "nonfiction" is fantasy, too.

The fact is, though, we *don't* want to be very strict about it. If we define fantasy in such a way as to include almost everything, then the word loses its force and it comes to mean no more than "writing."

Let us look for a different definition. Fantasy should mean not only something that is not so and therefore exists only as an idea, but also something that *could not possibly be so* and therefore can exist *in no other way* than as an idea.

Thus, Charles Dickens's *Nicholas Nickleby* is not a fantasy. Though its characters never existed and its events never took place, those characters and events could have existed without upsetting the accepted order of the universe.

On the other hand, Dickens's "A Christmas Carol" is clearly a fantasy, for it deals with ghosts and with abstractions such as

"Christmas Past," which have been made concrete. The accepted order of the universe does not include ghosts and concretized abstractions.

In fact, we can be stricter still and insist that fantasy must deal not only with matters that we conceive as not capable of existence in our universe, but which we insist are incapable of existence even in a universe modified by reasonable scientific advance. If reasonable scientific advance *could* make them possible, then we would have science fiction. (To be sure, an ingenious person can manipulate the possibilities of scientific advance in such a way that what we would casually think of as fantasy can be made into a kind of science fiction. Usually, however, the manipulation is not bothered with, so that fantasy and science fiction remain distinct.)

And now that we have an idea as to what we mean by fantasy as a restricted branch of literature, we have a right to ask how old it is. It might seem a fair guess that fantasy is forever; that it is as old as language; as old as the human imagination.

It would seem that over the Stone Age campfires, our uncivilized ancestors froze each other's blood with tales of monsters, and ghosts, and demons of all sorts.

We'll never know that for sure, of course, so if we prefer to cling to greater certainties, we have to turn to the oldest surviving scraps of literature, and these, we find, are quite likely to deal with fantasy.

The Epic of Gilgamesh, written by nameless Sumerians about 2700 B.C., is, I believe, the oldest surviving work of fiction, and it contains elements of fantasy—gods, monsters, plants that confer immortality, and so on. The *Iliad* and *Odyssey* are to some extent fantasies, especially the latter. The tales of Polyphemus the Cyclops and of Circe the Witch remain, to this day, among the most popular fantasies in existence.

Folk tales are almost invariably fantasies; *The Arabian Nights* are fantasies, for instance, as are *Snow White* and *Cinderella*. Every age has its fantasies and even the twentieth century has developed some that rival those of the past in skill and popularity. Consider *Mary Poppins, The Hobbit,* and *Watership Down.*

And yet—when is a fantasy not a fantasy?

The answer, surely, is this: When its events are not accepted as running contrary to the accepted order of the universe. Even more so, when its events, however fantastic they may seem, are accepted as literal truth.

Thus, the Bible is filled with wonder tales—the speaking serpent in the Garden of Eden; the speaking ass that Balaam bestrode; the parting of the Red Sea; the deeds of Elijah and Elisha; the activities of Jesus as a healer. If these were encountered by some well-educated Chinese scientist who had never heard of the Bible before, he would have no hesitation in labeling the book a fantasy collection. Naturally, pious Jews and Christians would reject such a view with horror and would consider it blasphemous.

In the same way, unsophisticated people of the past who believed in the Olympian gods and goddesses and who had no doubt that strange monsters existed in the misty regions beyond the small patch of ground they knew well, would accept Homer's tales as accurate history in all its details.

And, in later times, those who believed in ghosts, or afreets, or ghouls, or fairies, or elves would accept tales involving them as at least true in concept, if not necessarily in detail, and they would not be thought of as fantasies at all.

How far into the present does this notion of fantasies that are not fantasies extend? Obviously, right into the present and, probably, into the future as far as the mind can see. Every religion seems like a fantasy to outsiders, but as holy truth to those of the faith. There are always people who are unsophisticated, because of youth or lack of modern secular and scientific education, who believe in Santa Claus, in zombies and voodoo, in the tooth fairy and the Easter bunny, and so on.

There are even adults who, to all appearances, are intelligent, educated, and sophisticated, who are nevertheless believers in astrology, spiritualism, creation science, or other irrationalities that seem like nonsensical fantasy to those of us who are untainted by such things.

In that case, when, if ever, did we start thinking of fantasy as *fantasy*?

No doubt there were always some sceptics, some people we would view today as hard-headed realists, in even the most superstitious and faith-ridden times. These people scorned anything not based on observational and rational evidence, and were firm in the belief that what most people accepted without question was, in actuality, mere fantasy.

This is, however, not enough. The occasional skeptic can barely make a mark on society. Did there come a time, however, when such rationalism became an accepted part of a secular society and when people in reasonably large numbers were educated into the belief that the universe could be understood only by reason, so that anything beyond that was fantasy?

Such a state of affairs began to arrive in the western world after the end of the period of the religious wars and the coming of the Age of Reason. The latter half of the seventeenth century, the time of the Royal Society and of Isaac Newton, marks the dividing line.

Even then, however, rationality was confined to a rather thin layer of the educated. It was not till the nineteenth century that, in the western world, there gradually arose the notion of mass education under the control of a secular state. For the first time, there were extensive regions in which large percentages of the population were educated in school systems that were not run by some religious group or other. And then, for the first time, there arose large numbers of individuals who could tell what fantasy was and who enjoyed it all the more because they recognized it as pure exercises of untrammeled imagination.

THE RELUCTANT CRITIC

WRITERS RARELY AGREE ON ANYTHING about their craft, but they do tend to join forces against the critic. I am far too gentle a soul myself to say nasty things about people, but here is what I managed to say in a book of mine called *Familiar Poems Annotated* while talking about Robert Frost:

"His poetry seems to please the critics, and because it is plain-spoken, rhymes and scans, it pleases human beings as well."

Here's what Lord Byron says: "As soon / Seek roses in December, ice in June; / Hope constancy in wind, or corn in chaff; / Believe a woman or an epitaph, / Or any other thing that's false, before / You trust in critics."

Coleridge's opinion is this: "Reviewers are usually people who would have been poets, historians, biographers, etc., if they could; they have tried their talents at one or at the other, and have failed; therefore they turn critics."

And Lawrence Sterne's: "Of all the cants which are canted in this canting world, though the cant of hypocrites may be the worst, the cant of criticism is the most tormenting!"

Enough! You get my point!

And yet—every once in a while—I find myself trapped—forced to the wall—driven into the ground—and very much against my will—

I am forced to be a critic!

Science Digest asked me to see the movie *Close Encounters of the Third Kind* and write an article for them on the science it contained. I saw the picture and was appalled. I remained appalled even after a doctor's examination had assured me that no internal organs had been shaken loose by its ridiculous sound-waves. (If you can't be good, be loud, some say, and *Close Encounters* was very loud.)

To begin with there was no accurate science in it, not a trace; and I said so in the article I wrote and which *Science Digest* published. There was also no logic in it, not a trace; and I said that, too.

Mind you, I'm not one of these purists who see nothing good in anything Hollywood does. Hollywood must deal with large audiences, most of whom are utterly unfamiliar with good science fiction. It has to bend to them, meet them at least halfway. Fully appreciating that, I could enjoy *Planet of the Apes* and *Star Wars*.

Even when my good friends, Ben Bova and Harlan Ellison, denounced the latter unstintingly, I remained firm. *Star Wars* was entertainment for the masses and did not try to be anything more. Leave your sophistication at the door, get into the spirit, and you can have a fun ride.

Close Encounters, however, took itself seriously or put on a show of doing so. It was *pretentious,* and that was fatal. What's more, it made its play for UFOlators and mystics, and—in its chase for the buck—did not scruple to violate every canon of good sense and internal consistency.

I said all this in my article and then the letters came.

Some of them complained that I had ignored the virtues of the picture. "What about the special effects?" they asked. (They were referring to the flying chandelier at the end.)

Well, what about them? Seeing a rotten picture for the special effects is like eating a tough steak for the smothered onions, or reading a bad book for the dirty parts. Optical wizardry is something a movie can do that a book can't but it is no substitute for a story, for logic, for meaning. It is ornamentation, not substance. In fact, whenever a science fiction picture is praised overeffusively for its special effects, I *know* it's a bad picture. Is that all they can find to talk about?

Some of those who wrote me were hurt and appalled that anyone as obviously good-natured as I could possibly say such nasty things. I did rather bite my lips at that; it's no fun to force one's self into the twisted semblance of a critic. Yet there comes a time when one has to put oneself firmly on the side of Good.

Some asked me angrily who I thought I was and what made *me* a judge of science fiction anyway. They had seen every science fiction movie made in the last five years and they knew a lot more about science fiction than I did. —Well, maybe they did; I didn't argue the point.

And one and all, they came down to the same plaintive cry, "Why do you criticize its lack of science, Dr. Asimov? It's *just* science fiction."

God, how that stings! I've spent a lifetime loving science fiction, and now I find that you must expect nothing of something that's *just* science fiction.

It's *just* science fiction so it's allowed to be silly, and childish, and stupid. It's *just* science fiction, so it doesn't have to make sense. It's *just* science fiction, so you must ask nothing more of it than loud noise and flashing lights.

That's the harm of *Close Encounters:* that it convinces tens of millions that that's what *just* science fiction is.

My favorite letter, though, came from someone whose name was familiar to me. He had written me on a number of earlier occasions and I quickly learned never to answer. He has ideas on every possible scientific subject; and in every single case he is wrong, calamitously wrong, mastodonically wrong. He is an unappreciated national treasure, for he is so unanimously wrong that by taking the direct opposite of his views you will be more often right than if you listened to the wisest sage.

His Erroneousness took issue with my comment that the aliens in *Close Encounters* acted with utter illogic (and I had cited a number of instances). They're *aliens,* he said, explaining it to me carefully so that I would understand. They're *supposed* to be illogical.

Well, then, I suppose all you need are illogical writers, writers who never heard of logic. Illogic would come so naturally to them that they would have no trouble portraying aliens.

It was a well-rounded incomprehension totally worthy of my correspondent.

John Campbell once issued the challenge: "Show me an alien thinking as well as a man, but not *like* a man."

Easy? I've tried many a hard thing in my science fiction career, but I've never had the nerve to tackle that one (except maybe a little in the second part of *The Gods Themselves*). Stanley Weinbaum managed a bit of it in the case of Tweerl in *A Martian Odyssey*. Olaf Stapledon managed a bit of it in the case of John in *Odd John*.

Do you suppose that those fellows who put together the screenplay of *Close Encounters* could do it by just pushing in some of their own native illogic?

Let me give you an example of what I mean in the other direction.

Suppose you wanted to portray an amiable nitwit, a pleasant simp with about as much brains as you can pack into a thimble. And suppose you want him to be the first-person narrator. Do you suppose you can find yourself an amiable nitwit or a pleasant simp and have him write the book? After all, he *is* one; whatever he writes is what an amiable nitwit or a pleasant simp would say.

Let me point, then, to P. G. Wodehouse's books about Bertie Wooster and Jeeves. Bertie Wooster tells the story and with every line reveals himself to be an amiable nitwit, a pleasant simp. But those books are perfectly written by someone who is nothing of the sort. It takes damned clever writing to have someone betray himself as a silly ass in every line and yet do it so smoothly you never ask yourself, "How is it that that silly ass is telling the story so well?"

Or to come closer to home, consider Daniel Keyes's *Flowers for Algernon* in which the narrator begins a moron, becomes brighter and brighter, then duller and duller, and ends as a moron. The moron-parts were clearly the hardest to write, for Keyes had to make Charlie *sound* like a moron without making the story sound moronic. If it were easy, the best way to do it would be to have a moron write it.

So *Close Encounters* has its uses, too. It is a marvelous demonstration of what happens when the workings of extraterrestrial intelligence are handled without a trace of skill. It makes one feel added wonder and awe at stories in which extraterrestrial intelligence and other subtleties are handled with painstaking skill—as in those we try to find for this magazine.

THE UNICORN

A RECENT ANTHOLOGY I HELPED EDIT is entitled *Mythical Beasties* and contains thirteen fantasies, each featuring a different well-known but nonexistent animal. Of course, that's fantasy, not science fiction, but I got to thinking—

People of all ages and places have, at one time or another, invented nonexistent animals and added copious detail. The process is very likely the same as that which science fiction writers use to invent extraterrestrial creatures. Our ET organisms are as nonexistent and, if we're lucky, as plausible, as those that are invented for myths and legends. Perhaps the same process is involved, and if we consider the legendary creatures we may get some insight into a way in which we build up zoological and botanical denizens of a world circling Alpha Centauri A.

Picking a mythological beast at random, let's consider the unicorn. How did the unicorn come to be imagined?

To many a person it *wasn't* imagined. It was real. The evidence? The very best. The unicorn is mentioned in the Bible, and the Bible is God's word, is it not?

Here's a biblical description of God: "God hath brought them [the Israelites] out of Egypt; he hath as it were the strength of an unicorn." (Numbers 23:22). Another description—this time of the tribe of Joseph: "His glory is like the firstling of his bullock, and his horns are like the horns of unicorns:" (Deuteronomy 33:17).

God asks Job the following question: "Canst thou bind the unicorn with his band in the furrow?" (Job 39:10). The psalmist begs God, "Save me from the lion's mouth: for thou has heard me from the horns of the unicorns." (Psalms 22:21). He also says, "But my horn shalt thou exalt like the horn of an unicorn." (Psalms 92:10). And Isaiah says, "And the unicorns shall come down with [them] . . ." (Isaiah 34:7).

Of course the Bible from which I have been quoting isn't the inspired word, exactly. It is the Authorized Version (the King James) and it is only a translation. The translators may, after all, have made a mistake. The Hebrew word translated as "unicorn" is, in each case, re'em. What does that *really* mean?

If we turn to the New English Bible, the most accurate translation yet made, we find that the Numbers quotation reads as follows: "What its curving horns are to the wild ox, God is to them, who brought them out of Egypt." In every other reference I've cited, re'em is translated as "wild ox."

The wild ox is the "aurochs" (from a German word meaning "primeval ox"). Its scientific name is *Bos primigenius,* which is Latin for "ox, firstborn." It is probably the ancestor of domestic cattle. It was a large and fierce bovine, standing six feet at the shoulder, with large horns spreading far outward. The horns and strength of the wild ox were worth using metaphorically, but the animal is no more. The last living aurochs is supposed to have died in Poland in 1627.

But how did we ever go from "wild ox" to "unicorn"?

Well, the Assyrians carved wild oxen in bas-relief to serve, I presume, as symbols of strength and vigor. The Assyrians, however, were not masters of perspective. They carved a side view and simplified matters by letting the horn on the side of the viewer overlap exactly the far horn.

What one saw was a single horn, so the Greeks called it, slangily, *monokeros* ("one-horn" in Greek) and that became the word for re'em in the Septuagint, the Greek translation of the Bible. In the Latin translation of the Bible it became "unicorn" ("one-horn" in Latin) and unicorn it stayed in the King James.

178

Of course, the biblical references speak only of horns and strength. Where do the rest of our notions of the unicorn come from? For that we have to turn to non-biblical sources.

About 400 B.C., there was a Greek physician and scholar, named Ctesias, who lived for some years in Persia and who wrote a history of the Asian kingdoms: Assyria, Babylonia, Persia, and India.

In his books (which have not survived and which we know of only from scattered commentaries by other Greek writers) he referred to one Indian animal which he described as a kind of wild ass, white in color, and with an eighteen-inch-long, straight horn in its forehead. That is essentially the picture of the unicorn we have to this day—a graceful horselike creature with one long horn in its forehead.

We can guess that no such creature exists. If it was horselike then it must belong to the group of animals that include the horses, asses, and zebras, and not one of this group, not one, either living or extinct, has ever had horns, let alone a single horn. Consequently, any report that the unicorn is horselike can't be so.

Where did Ctesias get his description from, then? He was probably an honest man who did his best to tell the truth, but people do tend to be gullible, and he was undoubtedly repeating hearsay that had become distorted even before it had reached his ears.

As it happens, there *is* a one-horned animal in India—the Indian rhinoceros. Of course, the horn is not a true horn but a concretion of hair. It is not on the forehead, but on the snout. It is not long and straight but rather short and curved. And although the rhinoceros is more closely related to the horse than it is to the wild ox, it is not horselike in appearance.

Could there be a confusion with another animal? Very likely. There is an antelope called the oryx, rather rare now, but common in ancient times, when it was found widely in Arabia and Babylonia. It has a long horselike face, so that it might be considered to be a kind of wild ass (even though it isn't). And on its head, it has two long, straight horns, so that it is sometimes called the scimitar-horned oryx. Seen from the side, the two horns overlap and you seem to see a one-horned horselike creature.

Ctesias might thus have combined the appearance of the oryx, which he must have seen, and which he must have known had two horns, however it might have seemed like one from the side, with the tale of the strange Indian animal that travelers agreed had only a single horn.

It was the horn that made the unicorn so valuable to people who believed in its existence. All kinds of wild legends grew up about the horn. It was supposed to be an aphrodisiac if it was ground up and added to drinks. It was also supposed to be a supreme antidote to poison, so that the powder some might think would increase one's manly vigor, others might think would purify and make harmless the wildest poisons. Either way, the horn was something greatly to be desired.

Naturally, people, such as sailors, who were known to have traveled to far countries and to have seen strange sights were likely to be believed if they came back with horns they said had been obtained from unicorns. They could sell those horns at enormous prices, and they often did.

The horns that were thus sold to gullible landlubbers were indeed long and straight, and were also twisted into a tight left-handed spiral. It is for this reason that most drawings of unicorns show the horn to be twisted in such a spiral.

Where did sailors get such horns?

Well, there is a small whale, about fifteen feet long, called the "narwhal," a name which may come from a Scandinavian expression meaning "corpse-whale" because of its dead-white color. Its scientific name is *Monodon monoceros,* which is Greek for "one-tooth, one-horn."

Despite the Greek name, the narwhal has two teeth. In the male narwhal, however, the left tooth develops into a straight tusk, sticking forward out of the mouth, a tusk which may grow to be as much as nine feet long, half the length of the body or more. The tusk is grooved in a left-hand spiral and looks exactly like the horn we see in pictures of the unicorn.

In fact, the unicorn horn *is* the narwhal tusk, for that is what sailors tended to bring home and palm off on the unsophisticated as the genuine, miracle-working horn of the unicorn.

And now we see how a mythological animal gets its form and shape. It is usually built up out of bits and reminiscences from real animals. Contributing to the unicorn in one way or another are the wild ox, the rhinoceros, the oryx, and the narwhal.

And this is how science fiction writers tend to get their extraterrestrial creatures, too. It is very difficult to be totally original.

Once, though, there was a very early story I wrote (in 1940 actually) called "Half-Breeds on Venus" which made the cover of the magazine in which it appeared. The artist drew a creature that looked very dinosaurian, except that it had a single fang right in the front of its upper jaw. No such single fang is to be found in any bilateral animal, living or extinct, and it was beautifully original. I thought it was the only good thing about the story. (To be sure, Ollie the Dragon in *Kukla, Fran, and Ollie* had just such a fang, but he came along years later.)

UNKNOWN

DURING THE LAST FEW DAYS, I HAVE been leafing through *The Fantasy Almanac* by Jeff Rovin (Dutton, 1979) with a certain amount of pleasure. Rovin is very good on the Greek myths, folktales, and traditional monsters, though I'm a little ho-hum on the modern ephemera of superheroes and movie monsters.

There was, however, one entry which struck me as superfluous and that was "Asimov, Isaac." What Rovin said of me was accurate enough but there was nothing to give any hint that I had any connection with fantasy. The few works of mine which he cited were strictly science fiction. One of the spurs to my working my way through the book, then, was to see if I could find any justification for the inclusion.

I finally found it, for there, in the S's, was "Starr, Lucky," under which he listed my six Lucky Starr novels, originally published under the pseudonym of Paul French. At first, I thought this another gratuitous inclusion since my Lucky Starr books were strictly science fiction (nor does he imply anything else.) I then realized that he was thinking of Lucky Starr as a superhero, in the long line ranging

183

from Gilgamesh to the Incredible Hulk. Well, *I* don't think Lucky is anything more than a plain ordinary hero, but at least I have my explanation, which was all I wanted.

Much worse than the inclusion of your unhumble servant, however, was an exclusion. Rovin includes an entry on *Weird Tales,* as he should, but he does not include *Unknown,* the best fantasy magazine that ever existed or, in my opinion, is ever likely to exist.

The way it started, according to the story I heard at the time, was this. Eric Frank Russell submitted a story called "Forbidden Acres" to John W. Campbell, editor of *Astounding Science Fiction.* It was a very powerful story of an Earth that is secretly controlled by extraterrestrials with an advanced technology. Certain Earthmen learn that "we are property" and try to fight it. Campbell wanted the story intensely but he felt that it was not legitimate sf and did not belong in the pages of *Astounding.* Rather than reject it, however, he determined to start a new magazine, one devoted to "adult fantasy." This magazine he named *Unknown* and its first issue was dated March, 1939. Its lead novel was the Eric Frank Russell tale, retitled "Sinister Barrier."

How well I remember the day that first issue arrived in my father's candy store. (Good heavens, it was almost half a century ago—and it seems like yesterday.) I devoured the issue. "Sinister Barrier" was absolutely absorbing and the short stories that filled out the issue were like nothing I had ever seen before. One of them was Horace Gold's "Trouble With Water," a very funny story about an offended water spirit.

The issues kept coming. The second issue featured L. Ron Hubbard's "The Ultimate Adventure," an Arabian Nights story of a kind Scheherazade might have told if she had had a better imagination. It also had the first part of L. Sprague de Camp's "Divide and Rule" a story of modern knights that put *Morte d'Arthur* way in the shade. Later issues contained de Camp's "Lest Darkness Fall," "The Mathematics of Magic," "The Roaring Trumpet," and "The Wheels of If"; Horace Gold's "None But Lucifer"; John MacCormac's "Enchanted Weekend"; Hubbard's "Slaves of Sleep," "Fear," and "Typewriter in the Sky"; Jack Williamson's "Darker Than You Think"; Fritz Leiber's "Conjure Wife"; Theodore Sturgeon's "It," "Shottle Bop," and "Yesterday was Monday" and so on, and so on.

The magazine continued for twenty-six glorious monthly issues but by the August 1941 issue the war in Europe was coming ever closer to the United States and the price of paper was going up. *Unknown's* circulation did not match that of *Astounding* and what paper could be obtained had to be reserved for the latter. *Unknown* therefore went bimonthly but moved to a larger size in an attempt to make up for it. It changed its name to *Unknown Worlds*, too. With the June 1943 issue it was back to a smaller size, and the October 1943 issue was its last. After thirty-nine issues, it died a war casualty.

Nor could it ever be revived. After the war, in 1948, Campbell edited a one-shot issue called *From Unknown Worlds*, containing a selection of reprints from the magazine, but it apparently didn't do well enough to warrant a revival, especially since Street & Smith, which had published the magazine, was about to put an end to all its pulp magazines, with the single exception of *Astounding*.

In 1939, the year of *Unknown's* birth, I was desperately trying to sell stories of my own and, indeed, I had sold two stories before ever *Unknown* appeared, and two more in the month of its appearance. Naturally, considering my extravagant admiration for the magazine, I was bound to try to place a story in its pages.

Believe me, I hesitated. The writing that appeared in the magazine seemed to me to be so skilled that I despaired of equaling it. Nevertheless, shamefaced bashfulness is no part of my nature, and I tried. In July, 1939, I made my first attempt to penetrate the magazine's sinister barrier with my seventeenth story, "Life Before Birth." The next month, I tried my twenty-second story, "The Oak." In January, 1941, I sent in my twenty-seventh story, "Little Man on the Subway," in February, 1941, my twenty-ninth story, "Masks," and in June, 1941, my thirty-fourth, "Legal Rites."

All five stories were rejected at once and deservedly, since all five stories were simply terrible. (And this despite the fact that, in the months in which these stinkers had been turned out, I also wrote such well-regarded stories as "Reason," "Liar," and even "Nightfall.")

Two of those five stories, "Little Man on the Subway" and "Legal Rites" eventually appeared elsewhere, but I attribute this to the fact that Fred Pohl collaborated with me on them—the only times he and I ever collaborated. The other stories never appeared anywhere and the manuscripts (thank goodness) are now lost.

On December 7, 1941, Pearl Harbor was bombed and in April 1942, I departed for Philadelphia to work at the U.S. Navy Yard there. What's more, in July 1942, I got married. Between my new job and my new wife, I did no writing for eleven months. (There were sizable gaps also when I finally found myself in the army, and when I was deeply engaged in my Ph.D. research, but in the last forty years, I am glad to say, I have never been completely away from my typewriter for more than a few days at a time.)

In January 1943, I finally felt the urge to write again, and, once again, I decided to attempt an *Unknown* story. Why not try again? It took me a while, for a six-day-a-week job and a seven-day-a-week wife cut into my time somewhat, but in April 1943, I sent off my forty-third story, "Author! Author!" And it was at once *accepted.* At last, at last, I was an *Unknown* author.

It takes roughly six to nine months to get a story into print after acceptance, so I didn't expect to *see* myself an *Unknown* author until early 1944, but it was never to be. I told you earlier that the October 1943 issue of the magazine was its last, and I got the news of the forthcoming shutdown on August 2, 1943. My story would not appear.

It was a terrible shock, and it might well have turned me off writing for an indefinite period to come, had I not, in the euphoria of the "Author! Author!" sale, promptly written my forty-fourth story, a science fiction story, "Death Sentence" and sold it. It appeared in the November 1943 *Astounding.* That was the first month in which *Astounding* appeared in "digest-size," which is now the common size for science fiction magazines. That second sale kept me going.

There is an odd epilogue to the saga of my never getting to be an *Unknown* author.

In 1963, twenty years after the demise of *Unknown,* the writer Don Bensen was putting out a paperback collection of five stories from that magazine. He asked me to write the introduction and, of course, I did—and I was pleased at the chance of doing it, too.

In the course of the introduction, I told the sad tale of how I had tried to be an *Unknown* author, and had failed, and had continued to fail even though I finally sold a story to the magazine.

Bensen accepted the introduction, and sent me an excited letter. He had not known that I had had a story accepted by *Unknown.* Had he but known, he would have tried to include it in the collection. Since he now knew, he was going to arrange a second collection of stories that would include "Author! Author!" I was certainly willing, but I pointed out that the story was twenty years old and contained topical references that now dated it badly. Also, I said, *Astounding* controlled the reprint rights. Bensen dismissed the outdatedness with a shrug and negotiated a release from *Astounding*.

In 1964, then, the paperback anthology, *The Unknown Five* (Pyramid), appeared, with "Author! Author!" as the lead story.

I was an *Unknown* author at last, and the interval of twenty-two years between acceptance and publication is the longest such interval I ever suffered or am ever likely to suffer.

EXTRA-ORDINARY VOYAGES

ONE OF THE PET PARLOR GAMES PLAYED by those interested in science fiction—writers, editors, fans, readers—is to define science fiction. What the devil is it? How do you differentiate it from fantasy? From general fiction?

There are probably as many definitions as there are definers; and the definitions range from those of the extreme exclusionists, who want their science fiction pure and hard, to those of the extreme inclusionists who want their science fiction to embrace everything in sight.

Here is an extreme exclusionist definition of my own: "Science fiction deals with scientists working at science in the future."

Here is an extreme inclusionist definition of John Campbell's: "Science-fiction stories are whatever science-fiction editors buy."

A moderate definition (again mine) is: "Science fiction is that branch of literature that deals with human responses to changes in the level of science and technology." This leaves it open as to whether the changes are advances or retrogressions, and whether, with the accent on "human response," one need do more than refer glancingly and without detail to those changes.

To some writers, in fact, the necessity for discussing science seems so minimal that they object to the use of the word in the name of the genre. They prefer to call whatever it is they write "speculative fiction," thus keeping the abbreviation "sf."[1]

Occasionally, I feel the need to think it all out afresh and so why not approach the definition historically. For instance—

What is the first product of western literature, which we have intact, and which could be considered by inclusionists to be science fiction?

How about Homer's *Odyssey?* It doesn't deal with science in a world which had not yet invented it; but it does deal with the equivalent of extraterrestrial monsters, like Polyphemus, and with people disposing of the equivalent of an advanced science, like Circe.

Yet most people would think of the *Odyssey* as a "travel tale."

But that's all right. The two views are not necessarily mutually exclusive. The "travel tale," after all, was the original fantasy, the natural fantasy. Why not? Until contemporary times, travel was the arduous luxury of the very few, who alone could see what the vast hordes of humanity could not.

Most people, till lately, lived and died in the same town, the same valley, the same patch of earth, in which they were born. To them, whatever lay beyond the horizon was fantasy. It could be anything—and anything told of that distant wonderland fifty miles away could be believed. Pliny was not too sophisticated to believe the fantasies he was told of distant lands, and a thousand years of readers believed Pliny. Sir John Mandeville had no trouble passing off his fictional travel tales as the real thing.

And for twenty-five centuries after Homer, when anyone wanted to write a fantasy, he wrote a travel tale.

Imagine someone who goes to sea, lands upon an unknown island, and finds wonders. Isn't that Sinbad the Sailor and his tales of the Rukh and of the Old Man of the Sea? Isn't that Lemuel Gulliver and his encounters with Lilliputians and Brobdingnagians? As a matter of fact, isn't that King Kong?

The Lord of the Rings, together with what promises to be a vast horde of slavish imitations, are travel tales, too.

Yet are not these travel tales fantasies, rather than science fiction? Where does "real" science fiction come in?

Consider the first professional science fiction writer; the first writer who made his living out of undoubted science fiction—Jules

Verne. He didn't think of himself as writing science fiction, for the term had not yet been invented.

For a dozen years he wrote for the French stage with indifferent success. But he was a frustrated traveler and explorer and in 1863, he suddenly hit pay dirt with his book *Five Weeks in a Balloon.* He thought of the book as a travel tale, but an unusual one since it made use of a device made possible by scientific advance.

Verne followed up his success by using other scientific devices, of the present and possible future, to carry his heroes farther and farther afield in other *voyages extraordinaires*—to the polar regions, to the sea bottom, to the Earth's center, to the Moon.

The Moon had been a staple of the tellers of travel tales ever since Lucian of Samosata in the 1st century A.D. It was thought of as just another distant land, but what made it different in Verne's case was that he made the effort to get his heroes there by scientific principles that had not yet been applied in real life (though his method was unworkable as described).

After him, other writers took men on longer voyages to Mars and to other planets; and finally, in 1928, E. E. Smith, in his *The Skylark of Space,* broke all bonds with his "inertialess drive" and carried humanity out to the distant stars.

So science fiction began as an outgrowth of the travel tale, differing chiefly in that the conveyances used do not yet exist but might exist if the level of science and technology is extrapolated to greater heights in the future.

But surely not all science fiction can be viewed as travel tales. What of stories that remain right here on Earth but deal with robots, or with nuclear or ecological disaster, or with new interpretations of the distant past for that matter?

None of that, however, is "right here" on Earth. Following Verne's lead, whatever happens on Earth is made possible by continuing changes (usually advances) in the level of science and technology so that the story must take place "right there" on future Earth.

What, then, do you think of this definition: "Science fiction stories are extraordinary voyages into any of the infinite supply of conceivable futures"?

1. I don't favor the term "speculative fiction" except insofar as it might abolish that abominable abbreviation "sci-fi." But then it might substitute "spec-fic" which is even worse.

FAIRY
TALES

WHAT ARE "FAIRY TALES"?

The easiest definition is, of course, that they are tales about fairies where a fairy is a kind of imaginary being possessing many supernatural powers.

We most commonly picture fairies, in these Disneyish degenerate times of ours, as being cute little beings with butterfly wings, whose chief amusement is nestling in flowers. That, however, is a foolish narrowing of the notion. Properly fairies are *any* imaginary beings possessing many supernatural powers. Some are large and grotesque.

Therefore, stories dealing with witches, wizards, giants, ogres, jinn, afrits, baba-yagas, and many of the other creatures of legend may fairly be considered to be "fairy tales." Since the powers of such "fairies" include the granting of wishes, the casting of spells, the conversion of men into other creatures or vice-versa, fairy tales are obviously a kind of fantasy, and some might even consider them one of the strands that went into the making of modern science fiction.

Because many fairy tales have unknown authors and were transmitted in oral form for many generations before they were written down by students of such things, and because, as a result, they lack polished literary form, they have been called "folktales." But then some of our most beloved fairy tales have been written by known authors in comparatively modern times (for instance, *Cinderella* and *The Ugly Duckling*), so I think we had better stick to "fairy tales."

Fairy tales have always been considered suitable reading for youngsters. Adults who have forgotten them, or who have never read them in the first place, seem to think of them as charming little stories full of sweetness and light. After all, don't they all end, "And they all lived happily ever after"? So we all say, "Oh, my, wouldn't it be great if our lives were just like a fairy tale."

And we sing songs that include lines like, "Fairy tales can come true/It can happen to you . . ."

That's all nonsense, of course, for, you see, not all "fairies" are benevolent. Some are mischievous, some are spiteful, and some are downright wicked, so that some of the fairy tales are rough going.

This all hit home once, about a quarter of a century ago, when I was even younger than I am now. At that time, I had two young children and I was wondering what I ought to do with them, so I attended some sort of parents/teachers meeting at the local school. At that meeting, a woman rose and said, "Is there some way we can keep children from reading the awful science fiction things they put out these days? They're so frightening. Why can't they read the delightful fairy tales that *we* read when we were young?"

Of course, I wasn't as well known in those days as I am now, so I'm sure she didn't mean it as a personal blow at me, but I reacted very promptly just the same, as you can well imagine.

I got up as though someone had shoved a long pin up through the seat of my chair and began to recite some of the plots of those delightful fairy tales.

How about *Snow White*. She's a nice little girl, whose mother had died and whose father has married a beautiful woman as a second wife. The new stepmother doesn't like Snow White, and the more good and beautiful the girl comes to be, the more her stepmother doesn't like her. So stepmother orders an underling to take Snow White into the woods and *kill* her and, just as a little added attraction, she orders him to cut out her heart (after she is dead, I hope, though the stepmother doesn't specify) and bring it back to her as evidence.

Talk about child abuse!

The wicked stepmother theme is a common one in fairy tales. Cinderella had one also, and two wicked stepsisters to boot, and she was mistreated by them all constantly—ill-fed, ill-dressed, ill-housed—and forced to watch those who abused her swimming in cream while she slaved away for them.

Sure both stories end happily but how many children are scarred forever by these horribly sadistic passages. How many women, innocent and good, who marry a man with children and are prepared to love and care for those children, are met with undying suspicion and hostility by those children because of the delightful fairy tales they've read.

There are wicked uncles, too. *The Babes in the Wood* is a short, all-time favorite. They are driven into the woods by their wicked uncle and starve to death there. Of course, the robins cover them with leaves, if you want to consider *that* a happy ending.

Wicked uncles were so popularized by fairy tales that they are to be found in formal literature. They make excellent villains in Stevenson's *Kidnapped,* and in Dickens's *Nicholas Nickleby.* If you have read fairy tales and are young, I wonder if you don't view some perfectly pleasant uncle of yours with careful wariness.

Or how about *Little Red Riding Hood,* in which an innocent little girl *and* her grandmother are swallowed by a wolf. Permanently, too, because if you've ever watched a wolf eat a little girl, you know that she gets torn apart. So don't believe that bit about the hunters coming and cutting open the wolf, in order to allow the kid *and* her grandmother to jump out alive. That was made up afterward by people who had watched kids going into convulsions after reading that delightful fairy tale in its original form.

My favorite, though, is *Hansel and Gretel.* Here are two perfectly charming little children who have the misfortune to have a father who is a poor woodcutter. There happens to be a famine and they run out of food. What happens? The children's mother (*not* their stepmother, but their very own mother) suggests they be taken deep into the woods and left there. In that way, there will be two less mouths to feed. Fortunately, they found their way back, to the disappointment and chagrin of their mother. Consequently, when famine struck again, the mother was right on the ball with her insistence that a second attempt be made to get rid of those little pests. This time the device is successful.

Can you imagine how much confidence this instills in any child reading the story? Thereafter, he keeps a sharp eye on the refrigerator and the pantry to see if the food is running short, for he knows who's going to be taken out to the garbage dump and left there in case the family runs short.

But that's not the worst. In the forest, Hansel and Gretel come across a gingerbread house owned by a witch, who promptly imprisons Hansel and starts fattening him up for a feast, with him as main course. Cannibalism—just in case the kid reader didn't get enough kicks out of abandonment and starvation. Of course, it ends happily because the kids get away from the witch (killing her by burning her in an oven, of course) and come home to their loving father. Their mother (hurray, hurray) has died.

Can you imagine mothers wanting their children to read stuff like this, instead of good, wholesome science fiction? Why if we printed stories à la Grimm (grim, indeed) in our magazine, we'd be harried out of town by hordes of indignant citizenry.

Think of that when next you feel moved to complain about the "violence" in some of our stories. Why, they're mother's milk compared to the stuff you expect your eight-year-olds to read.

Of course, fairy tales reflect the times in which they were told. Those were hard times. Poor woodcutters were *really* poor and there was no welfare roll they could get onto. Famines were *really* famines. What's more, mothers frequently died in childbirth, and fathers had to marry again to have someone take care of the youngster. Naturally, the new wife promptly had children of her own (or had them already by an earlier husband) and any woman would favor her own children over some stranger. And fathers did die young and leave their property to an infant child and appoint a brother the guardian of both child and property. Naturally, the brother, knowing that once the child grows up and takes over the property in his own right, he himself is out on his ear, is tempted to prevent that dire possibility from coming to pass.

Nowadays with children less likely to be orphaned before they have reached the age of self-care, those plots are passé and seem needlessly sadistic. They were realistic in their own times, however.

Nevertheless, if some of the problems of the past have been ameliorated, others have cropped up. Parents are less likely to die while their children are infants; but are more likely to get divorced.

If wicked uncles are passé, wicked landlords are not. If wolves don't roam the suburbs much anymore, drug pushers do.

Some define science fiction as "today's fairy tales." If so, you have to expect them to deal with the realistic dangers of today, but we at *Isaac Asimov's Science Fiction Magazine* will try to keep them from falling into the depths of depravity of yesterday's fairy tales.

DEAR JUDY-LYNN

(*Judy-Lynn del Rey was, with her husband Lester del Rey, the guiding genius of Del Rey Books, the outstanding personality in the science fiction publishing world, and a dear friend of mine of seventeen years standing. She will never read this letter, but I must now write it. She was also the person most responsible for the rise of modern fantasy in the book publishing field.*)

Dear Judy-Lynn:

You were born some forty years ago with a genetic deficiency that meant you would be unusually short all your life. Fortunately, you were born to loving and supportive parents, who were determined to treat you as though you were a perfectly normal child in every way.

The result was that you never asked for sympathy or expected to be treated in any favored way. You met the world on its own terms, completed college brilliantly, made your mark afterward as well, and won the admiration of all who knew you.

In this you were helped, of course, by the fact that your intelligence was far above average. Of all the women I have ever met you were the keenest, the quickest, the most brilliant. All it needed was a little time and that characteristic of yours drowned out everything else in anyone's estimation.

You were also a happy person, an uncomplaining one, and a

loving and giving one. I never heard you whine or grouse. And you had a sense of humor—but I'll get to that.

I met you at a science-fiction convention in April 1968. I was delighted with you and, for the next few years, we were inseparable at conventions. It was a pleasure to be able to extend myself in bantering conversation, knowing that you could take care of yourself perfectly well. In fact, only once did I really manage to get past your guard.

As you well know—as everyone knows—I myself have a peculiar deficiency. It consists of a total lack of common sense; a dreadful propensity to believe people. In fact, I am what is commonly known as a "jerk," or, in the nonsexual sense, a "prick," and I have been frequently told so by any number of dear friends who felt I ought to learn to be worldly-wise.

In any case, I was sitting next to you at a convention dinner and you said to me, sardonically, "You're all heart, Asimov." To this, I replied, just as your napkin happened to slip from your lap to the floor, "No, I'm not. I'm part prick."

You bent to retrieve the napkin and as you straightened up again, I said, innocently, "Were you checking to see if I was correct?"

You turned a very pretty magenta and said, "Damn it, Asimov, you've made me blush," which was something, apparently, you hadn't done since you were fourteen.

It may have been that which caused you to embark on a campaign designed to prove I was indeed what I had called myself. At that time you were working at *Galaxy* and you used its facilities to plague me.

You sent me the proofs of a cover of an issue in which I was to have a story, and you made sure that my name was horrendously misspelled. Naturally, I was on the phone in half a second in a fever of concern, and you promised to correct the situation.

On another occasion, you sent me a review of a television special I had written, a review that had been printed up in such a way as to appear to be a newspaper clipping. The review was incredibly insulting in a dozen different ways, for it was written by Lester del Rey, who aided and abetted you in your design to teach me a lesson and who (devil that he is) knew all my buttons. I was again on the phone demanding to know the name of the newspaper so that I could write them a nasty letter. It took a little while to calm me down.

Each time you pulled one of these tricks, someone in your vicinity would warn you that I would never fall for it. You would bet a dinner that I would and later on you would go out for a meal at the doubter's expense. I don't know how you managed to get anyone to bet on my worldly wisdom twice. In any case, you had lots of free meals.

Once I got a letter telling me that you had been fired. It was signed by Fritzi Vogelgesang, who introduced herself as your successor. I was dreadfully upset but Fritzi was so pleasant and so innocently flirtatious that a correspondence was quickly set up and in no time at all I was being suave all over the place. And then, when Fritzi had me jumping through hoops, she disappeared forever, for she had been you all the time. "So, Asimov," you wrote, "how quickly you forgot all about me."

But your most elaborate trick came on April 1, 1970, when I got a call from the secretary of Larry Ashmead, my editor at Doubleday. The news I got was that Larry had eloped with you and that the two of you were married. I was certain that that couldn't be, but when I called you, you weren't at work. I couldn't locate anyone who could give me information. I was on the phone all day, calling different people without satisfaction (you had everyone properly primed), and the fact that it was April 1 made no impression on me.

You felt it to be your masterpiece, I think. On April 15, 1985, I took you out, along with Lester, and Larry, in order to celebrate the fifteenth anniversary of that "wedding." We had a wonderful time rehashing all those old tricks.

Lester's wife had died in January 1970, and you, who were a dear friend of both, made sure that Lester bore up under the strain. The two of you grew closer with time and (with my enthusiastic encouragement) were married in March of 1971. I was at the wedding grinning all over the place, quite triumphantly convinced it was all my doing.

Long afterward, you said that when the ceremony reached its climax, you had the impulse to turn to me and say, "Fooled you again, Asimov. This whole thing is just a setup."

You said you wanted to watch me turn green and faint. I said, "But Judy-Lynn, I might have had a heart attack."

You said, "I was willing to chance that. The only trouble was that my mother might have had a heart attack, too, and I didn't want to chance that."

I suppose you always regretted your inability to pull off that perfect practical joke on your favorite patsy.

That marriage was the best thing that ever happened to you, Judy-Lynn, and it was also the best thing that ever happened to Lester. The two of you were perfectly matched. Lester had his encyclopedic knowledge of science fiction and fantasy and his unparalleled editorial ability; you had your drive, your genius for spotting worthwhile material, and your sure touch at promotion.

You were working with Ballantine Books at the time, which had been bought by Random House. You were promoted steadily by people who understood your worth, you were given your own imprint, Del Rey Books, and you became a vice president. And you were worth every penny to Random House. There was scarcely a moment when the *New York Times* didn't have at least one Del Rey Book on the hardcover best-seller list and another on the softcover best-seller list.

It is impossible these days for any one editor to dominate the field in the way that John Campbell did in the 1940s; however, you came the closest to doing so, and it may be that no one will ever come so close again.

On the personal side, you bought reprint rights to my new generation of science fiction novels, beginning with *Foundation's Edge,* and when Ballantine Books took over Fawcett, you put out new editions of all my Fawcett paperbacks. It was such a pleasure to find myself side by side with you again, looking at possible covers, writing up new introductions, going over old books to correct old typographical errors.

All this time, too, we had been socializing. On my fiftieth birthday, you had arranged a surprise party for me with the help of Austin Olney, my editor at Houghton Mifflin. Ever since, it became traditional that on my birthday Janet and I would host a dinner out with you and Lester. Even on January 2, 1984, when I was two days out of the hospital after my triple bypass, I managed to make it to the nearest restaurant to celebrate my sixty-fourth, and you were there.

You were also at the publication party for my latest novel *Robots and Empire* on September 18, 1985. Then, on October 4, the four of us had dinner and we talked about the series of paperbacks you were publishing that would contain all the old Barnaby comic strips by Crockett Johnson.

But that was the last. On October 16, you suffered a sudden brain hemorrhage and passed into a coma. On February 20, you passed from us forever. It is a dreadful loss to Lester, and to me, and to everyone who knew you.

Most of all it is a dreadful loss to science fiction, none greater since the death of Campbell. Campbell had, it seemed, passed his peak at the time of his death, but you were still on your way up. So for many, many reasons, the parting is a very painful one, dear Judy-Lynn.

FANTASY

SOME READERS HAVE BEEN OBJECTING to a few stories we have published in *Isaac Asimov's Science Fiction Magazine* as being "fantasy." We printed one or two of these letters and promptly (and predictably) got a rash of letters objecting to the objection and urging us to include fantasy, if we wished.

This is part of the difference between what I might term the "exclusivists" and "inclusivists" among ourselves. Exclusivists are those people who have firm definitions of what science fiction is and who resent the inclusion of any story that doesn't meet that definition. They would, in other words, exclude the marginal stories. Once you know that, you automatically know what an inclusivist is, don't you? Inclusivists either lack a firm definition, or have one but aren't wedded to it. Either way, they would include all sorts of things.

I, myself, am an exclusivist, in my capacity as a writer and, to a certain extent, as a reader. The science fiction I write is generally "hard," deals with science and scientists, and eschews undue violence, unnecessary vulgarity, and unpleasant themes. There is no philosophic reason for that; it merely happens to fit my way of thought. And, as a reader, I tend to enjoy the kind of science fiction I write, and to give but brief attention to other kinds.

As editorial directors, however, Shawna McCarthy (1983-1985) and I are inclusivists, and we must be. We can't rely on all readers having our tastes exactly, and if we insisted on catering only to those who did, we would narrow the basis of support of the magazine to less than might suffice to support it. Rather than pleasing x people 100 percent of the time, it would be safer to please $10x$ people 90 percent of the time.

Therefore, if we were to come across a good and thought-provoking story that might be considered a fantasy by the exclusivists, we would be strongly tempted to publish it—especially if we were short on good thought-provoking "straight" science fiction.

(At this point, I might point out—and not for the first time—that we are at the mercy of authors and of circumstance in designing the makeup of the magazine. Readers sometimes seem to have the notion that we are, for some mysterious reason of our own, deliberately filling the magazine with novelettes and skimping on the short stories, or having too many downbeat stories in one particular issue, or too many first-person stories. The trouble is that if we have a several-months stretch in which very few lighthearted—or third-person—or very brief—stories reach us that are good, we can't avoid running short on them. We can't print bad stories just because we need one that's funny, or short, or whatever. This also goes for readers who berate us at times for not including stories by so-and-so in the magazine. We would love to include such stories, but the author in question has to send them to us first. *Please* keep that in mind.)

But back to fantasy. Fantasy is from the Greek *phantasia,* which refers to the faculty of imagination. The word is sometimes spelled "phantasy" in homage to Greek, but I find that foolish. (In fact, I find the Greek "ph" foolish altogether and think it would be delightful if we spoke of fotografs and filosofy, as the Italians do.) A contracted form of fantasy, with a similar meaning, is "fancy."

In a very broad sense, all fiction (and a great deal of nonfiction) is fantasy, in that it is drawn from the imagination. In our group, however, we give the word a special meaning. It is not the plot of a story that makes it a fantasy, however imaginative that plot might be. It is the background against which the plot is played out that counts.

The plot of *Nicholas Nickleby,* for instance, is entirely imaginative. The characters and events existed entirely in Charles Dickens's imagination but the background is the England of the 1830s exactly as it was (allowing for a bit of amiable, and in some cases, unamiable satire). This is realistic fiction. (We can even use the term where the background is made artificially pretty. Surely, the cowboys of real life must have been pretty dirty and smelly, but you'd never think it to look at Gene Autry or Randolph Scott.)

If, on the other hand, the background does not describe any actual background as it is (or once was) then we have "imaginative fiction." Science fiction and fantasy are each an example of imaginative fiction.

If the nonexistent background is one that might conceivably exist someday, given appropriate changes in the level of science and technology, or given certain assumptions that do not conflict with science and technology as we know it today, then we have science fiction.

If the nonexistent background cannot ever exist no matter what *reasonable* changes or assumptions we postulate, then it is fantasy.

To give specific examples, the Foundation series is science fiction, and *The Lord of the Rings* is fantasy. To be more general about it, spaceships and robots are science fiction, while elves and magic are fantasy.

But there are all kinds of fantasy. There is "heroic fantasy," in which the characters are larger than life. In this case, the outsize nature of the characters may be so enormous as to verge on the grotesque, as in the case of Superman or the other superheroes; or may be so human in many ways that we find ourselves accepting them as real, as in the case of the elves and hobbits of Tolkien's masterpiece. The so-called "sword-and-sorcery" tale, of which Robert E. Howard's Conan saga is the progenitor, is a subdivision of this.

There is "legendary fantasy," which deliberately mimics the myth-making activities of an earlier age. We can have modern retellings of the Trojan War, or the voyage of the Argonauts, or the saga of the Ring of the Nibelungen, or of King Arthur and his Knights of the Round Table. A marvelous recent example of this last is Marion Zimmer Bradley's *The Mists of Avalon.*

There is "children's fantasy," of which the well-known "fairy tales" are the best example, though these were definitely adult folk tales to begin with. Modern examples can stretch from the inspired madness of Lewis Carroll's *Alice in Wonderland* to the realism of Hugh Lofting's *Dr. Dolittle* tales (so realistic we almost forget that animals which talk and think in human fashion are actually fantasy).

There is "horror fantasy," in which tales of ghosts and malign beings such as devils and ghouls and monsters are used to thrill and frighten us. The motion pictures are rich in this type, from the satisfying greatness of *King Kong* and *Frankenstein* to the good-natured foolishness of Godzilla.

And there is "satirical fantasy," such as the marvellous tales of John Collier (did you ever read "The Devil, George, and Rosie"?)—and this, frankly, is my favorite type of fantasy.

There may be other types, and numerous subdivisions of each; in fact, you may have a different system of classification altogether. However, the salient fact is that fantasy is a very broad and heterogeneous field of literature, and that each variety can vary in quality from the very good to the very bad. In every case, the very good will tempt us. After all, fantasy, like science fiction, is imaginative literature and there are times when this courtship can excuse our being inclusivistic.

In fact, it doesn't take much to switch from fantasy to science fiction, and it can be done easily enough if you are a skilled practitioner. I, myself, rarely write fantasy; but when I do, once in a while, I tend to write what I can only think of as Collier-influenced material.

I began writing my George-and-Azazel stories as unabashed fantasies, and my reason for wanting to do them was because the satirical element made possible elaborate overwriting and straight-faced slapstick. My science fiction is chemically free of such things, and I'm human enough to want to indulge now and then.

I sold two specimens to a competing magazine and the beauteous Shawna objected.

"But they're fantasies," I said, "and we almost never do fantasies."

Shawna said, "Well, then, make them science fiction."

And I did. Azazel is no longer the demon he was at the start; he is now an extraterrestrial creature. Earlier I had assumed he was brought to Earth and into George's control by means of some magical spell—but I had never described it. I still don't, but you are free to suppose that he is pulled through a space warp.

What he does is no longer outright magic. I manage to describe it in terms of rationalistic (if imaginary) science. The result is science fiction, even if not of a very "hard" nature.

Now some of you may find George-and-Azazel stories too nearly "fantasy" for your tastes, but I will continue to write them and hope that Shawna will buy one or two of them now and then, because I love them. And someday, when I have written enough of them, I will collect them into a book.

PART THREE
BEYOND FANTASY

READING
AND
WRITING

A (AREFUL SURVEY (OMPLETED EARLY in 1990 has shown that American school children have not improved their ability to read or write over the past 18 years. We're not talking math and science, or history and geography. We're talking reading and writing. A distressingly large proportion of children simply cannot read or write at a level considered appropriate for their age.

What this means is that we have built up, and are continuing to build up, a large reservoir of Americans who are only fit for unskilled labor in a technological society that has almost no use for unskilled labor. This, in turn, means a reservoir of unemployables or those who will be forced to work at rock-bottom wages in the most menial forms of labor. And this in turn means we will have a large demand for drugs as the only means of making the unbearable seem bearable. The drug culture—and we all know what that means—will tighten ever more forcefully on our nation.

But why can't we teach our children to read and write? The report lists three reasons:

ISAAC ASIMOV

1. Too much television;

2. Too little reading matter; books, magazines, newspapers in the home;

3. Too little homework.

All this sounds reasonable, but what do we do about it? The report suggests that parents grow more involved in their children's work and progress.

Here I feel a little cynical. I'm afraid that the parents of children who are backward in reading and writing are themselves likely to be similarly backward and could not, even if they wished, be of much help.

I think the problem is more fundamental. American society knows very well what it desires and admires. It desires to be amused. Fame and fortune are showered on show business personalities, on sports stars, on rock singers, and so on. Americans also desire to make money, a great deal of money, preferably without working too hard for it. So we admire wheeler dealers who manipulate junk bonds and dubious investments in order to make vast sums of money. Many of the rest of us keep hoping to win a few million in the lottery.

All this is perfectly understandable, and I do not intend or even wish to fight the universe on such matters. Of course people want amusement and easy money.

But in a technological society such as ours—and we boast that the United States is the most technologically advanced society in the world—why is learning and scholarship held in such contempt?

We see movies in which college students who are actually interested in their studies are called "nerds" and are pictured—male and female—as dumpy, plain, weak, unattractive. Opposed to them are the glorious "jocks" and "pinup girls," who are all pictured as Hollywood starlets and whose pleasure lies in endlessly humiliating the nerds—to the laughter of the audience.

I believe this reflects reality, and that at many schools students who try to pursue their studies are derided and scapegoated by the others. (I seem to recall such incidents in my own childhood years.)

Why is this? I have heard some explain it by saying America arose as a pioneer society where strong arms and sturdy frames

214

were needed to tame a wilderness, with no use for stoop-shouldered professors. But we are no longer a pioneer society and we are no longer taming a wilderness—we are despoiling an environment, and now we need professors.

I have also heard it said that our dismissal of scholarship and learning is purely a matter of money. Becoming a learned man is no way to get rich and that is the measure of its worthwhileness. Yet surely that is a rather sleazy way of setting a value on human activity. How much more ought we to respect a $60 billion drug lord than a $60,000 professor?

The fact is that America (and the whole world for that matter) desperately needs its scientists. We need only rapidly go through the litany of disasters that faces us—the pollution and poisoning of the environment, the destruction of the rain forests and wetlands, the disappearing ozone layer, the threatening greenhouse effect. These are problems that for possible solutions require technological advance and understanding.

It can be argued that the problems, even something as fundamental as the ever-increasing world population, have been caused by technological advance. There is truth to this. But these problems have resulted from the short-sighted *use* of technology by people who grabbed for the immediate short-term benefits of new discoveries and new techniques without sufficient consideration of long-term effects.

What we need, you see, are not merely scientists, engineers, and technologists, but political and industrial leaders willing to try to understand the world of science and technology in depth and to avoid basing their judgments on the "bottomline"—of instant profit or loss.

Consider the disputes that fill the minds of human beings today. The endless conflict of Catholics and Protestants in Northern Ireland, of Azerbijanis and Armenians in the Soviet Union, of Palestinians and Israelis in the Middle East, of Bulgars and Turks in Bulgaria. These and dozens of other such disputes are devils dancing at the lips of a volcano about to erupt. Money, effort, and emotion are expanded endlessly on these apparently insoluble problems right when the Earth is sliding down the chute to destruction for all the disputants alike.

And America's responsibility in all this? As the most advanced, the strongest, the richest nation in the world, we owe the world leadership. We can't solve the problems by ourselves, but we can show the way, we can rally our allies, alert even our enemies.

But we are also the freest nation in the world, so we have no dictator to pull us along. We have an elected president, an elected legislature, elected officials at every governmental level. We must depend on them to understand the state of the world and the nature of the measures that must be taken.

Because we are a democracy, it is the people themselves who must choose adequate leaders. Smiles are not enough, nor is flag-waving oratory. We must have understanding, or if you want to put it in another way, scholarship and learning.

And for that we must turn to an electorate, many of whom cannot even read or write. Does this not make a mockery of democracy? Frankly, as the 1990s opens, the state of American education freezes my blood with fear for all humanity.

THE RIGHT ANSWER

THE NUMBER OF GENERAL CONCLUSIONS one can come to about the Universe, or about any significant part of it, is usually limited, and the various sages of the world, past and present, have (with their eyes closed and their intuitions working) come up with every one of them.

It follows, then, that whatever conclusion scientists arrive at concerning anything, it remains always possible to quote some item in Eastern speculation or Celtic mythology or African folklore or Greek philosophy, that sounds the same.

The implication, on making the comparison, is that scientists are foolishly wasting a lot of money and effort in finding out what those clever Eastern (Celtic, African, Greek) sages knew all along.

For instance:

There are exactly three things that might be happening to the Universe in the long run.

I. The Universe may be unchanging on the whole and therefore have neither a beginning or an end.

217

2. The Universe may be changing progressively, that is in one direction only, and therefore have a distinct beginning and a different end.

3. The Universe may be changing cyclically, back and forth, and therefore ends at the beginning and starts over.

All the sages who have speculated on the Universe intuitively must come up with one of these three alternatives and, all things being equal, there is a one-in-three chance of their having duplicated whatever conclusions science eventually comes to on the subject.

At the present moment, scientists are inclined to accept the second alternative. The Universe seems to have begun in a big bang and to be changing progressively so as to end in infinite expansion and maximum entropy (with or without black holes).

If you pick out the proper verses of the Bible, then, and interpret them with sufficient ingenuity, you can maintain that the Bible says the same thing. All you need to do is to decide, for instance, that "Let there be light" is the theological translation of "big bang" and that six days is not very different from fifteen billion years and you can freely state that the latest astronomical theories support Genesis.

What characterizes the value of science, however, is *not* the particular conclusions it comes to. Those are sharply limited in number and guesswork will get you the "right" answer with better odds than you'll find at the racetrack.

What characterizes the value of science is its *methodology,* the system it uses to arrive at those conclusions.

A hundred sages, though speaking ever so wisely, can never offer anything more persuasive than an imperative "Believe!" Since human beings can be found to believe each of the hundred, there are endless quarrels over points of doctrine, and people have hated vigorously in the name of life and have murdered enthusiastically in the name of peace.

Scientists, on the other hand, begin with observations and measurements and deduce or induce their conclusion from that. They do so in the open and nothing is accepted unless the observation and measurement can be repeated independently. Even then the acceptance is only tentative, pending further, better, and more extensive observations and measurements. The result is that despite controversy in the preliminary findings, a consensus is arrived at eventually.

Consequently, what counts about science is *not* that it has currently (and tentatively) decided that there was a big bang; what counts is the long chain of investigation that led to the observation of the isotropic radio wave background that supports that conclusion.

What counts is *not* that science has currently (and tentatively) decided that the Universe is changing progressively by way of an apparently endless expansion; what counts is the long chain of investigation that led to the observation of red-shifts in galactic spectra that supports that conclusion.

Don't tell me, then, that those clever Eastern (Celtic, African, Greek, or even Biblical) sages have spoken of something that sounds like the big bang or like endless expansion. That's idle speculation.

Show me where those sages worked out the isotropic radio wave background, or the red-shifts in galactic spectra, which alone support those conclusions on anything more than a mere assertion.

You can't. Science stands alone!

IGNORANCE
IN AMERICA

FOR A LONG TIME NOW, SCIENTISTS have been concerned about the low level of scientific and mathematical instruction in American schools. Recent reports in 1988 and 1989 are unanimous in indicating not only that American students are scientifically and mathematically illiterate, but that they are more so than students in any other industrial society studied.

This is depressing in the extreme. The United States is the scientific leader of the world. Partly this may be due to the steady influx of scientists who were educated in other parts of the world. During the 1930s, Nazi oppression drove numerous scientists to Great Britain and the United States, and they were a key factor in the development of the nuclear bomb—a development widely touted in the United States as based on "Yankee know-how." Except that virtually all the Yankees had foreign accents.

And where do we stand today? Must we depend on the continued maintenance of our scientific lead on foreign imports?

Increasingly, our leaders must deal with dangers that threaten the entire world, where an understanding of those dangers and the possible solutions depend on a good grasp of science. The ozone layer, the greenhouse effect, acid rain, questions of diet and of heredity—all require scientific literacy. Can Americans choose the proper leaders and support the proper programs if they are scientifically illiterate?

The whole premise of democracy is that it is safe to leave important questions to the court of public opinion—but is it safe to leave them to the court of public ignorance?

Let us take an example. In July 1988, Jon Miller of the Public Opinion Laboratory at Northern Illinois University conducted a telephone poll of 2,041 adults and asked each about 75 questions on basic science. The results of the questionnaire showed that almost 95 percent of those questioned were ignorant of basic and simple scientific facts and had to be considered scientifically illiterate. There seemed to be a popular impression, for instance, that laser beams were composed of sound waves (rather than light waves) and that atoms are smaller than electrons (rather than the other way around).

This point might seem a little esoteric, but consider this: Twenty-one percent of those questioned were of the opinion that the Sun revolved about the Earth and an additional 7 percent didn't know which went around which.

Considering that it is now four centuries that science has been unanimous over the fact that the Earth goes about the Sun, how is it possible that a quarter of those asked didn't know about it? To my mind, there are three possibilities.

Those who didn't know either:

1. Had never gone to school and had never read any book that dealt with science in any significant way.

2. Had indeed gone to school and had read some books but had paid no attention whatever.

3. Had gone to school and had read books and had paid attention but hadn't been properly taught.

To me the first two possibilities are unthinkable, and I am forced to consider the third.

That Americans aren't properly taught is all too likely, considering the fact that a great many teachers must be as scientifically and mathematically illiterate as the general public. Yet how can any teacher, however poorly prepared, not teach the kids that the Earth goes around the Sun?

Well, there is a passage in the Bible that describes a fight between the Israelites under Joshua and the Gibeonites. The Israelites were winning, but it seemed the Gibeonites might escape under cover of darkness. To complete the victory, Joshua therefore commanded "Sun, stand thou still upon Gibeon. . . . And the sun stood still . . . and hasted not to go down about a whole day." (Joshua 10:12–13).

Now, how can Joshua have ordered the Sun to stand still and how could the sun have proceeded to stand still, if it weren't moving to begin with? These verses were used by people in the 1500s and 1600s to fight the notion that the Earth was moving around the sun. They kept quoting the passage in Joshua.

In actual fact, this story was told when everyone in the world thought the Sun did move. We now know better. And, even if the passage were divinely inspired, it may simply have been worded in a way that would make sense to the people of that time.

Nevertheless, there are millions of people in the United States who still firmly believe that every word of the Bible is inspired and absolutely, literally true; that the sun is moving and Joshua did command it to stand still, and it did stop moving temporarily.

Perhaps that means that in areas where such views are strong, teachers teach that the sun goes around the Earth, either out of stubborn belief or out of the fear that they will be fired if they don't. And perhaps that is why so many Americans are ignorant of so vital and elementary a point.

Imagine the harm things like this can do to our country!

This kind of backward thinking must not continue if America is to keep its role of the world's scientific leader.

KNOCK PLASTIC!

ONE OF MY FAVORITE STORIES (undoubtedly apocryphal, else why would I remember it?) concerns the horseshoe that hung on the wall over the desk of Professor Niels Bohr.

A visitor stared at it with astonishment and finally could not help exclaiming, "Professor Bohr, you are one of the world's great scientists. Surely you cannot believe that object will bring you good luck."

"Why, no," replied Bohr, smiling, "of course not. I wouldn't believe such nonsense for a moment. It's just that I've been informed it will bring me good luck whether I believe it will or not."

And I too have an amiable weakness—I am an indefatigable knocker of wood. If I make any statement which strikes me as too smug or self-satisfied, or in any way too boastful of good fortune, I look feverishly about for wood to knock.

Of course, I don't for one moment really believe that knocking wood will keep off the jealous demons who lie in wait for the unwary soul who boasts of his good luck without the proper propitiation of the spirits and demons on whom good and bad luck depend. Still—after all—you know—come to think of it—what can you lose?

I have been growing a little uneasy, in consequence, over the way in which natural wood is used less and less in ordinary construction, and is therefore harder and harder to find in an emergency. I might, in fact, have been heading for a severe nervous breakdown, had I not heard a casual remark made by a friend.

He said, some time ago, "Things are going very well for me lately." With that, he knocked on the tabletop and calmly said, "Knock plastic!"

Heavens! Talk about blinding flashes of illumination. Of course! In the modern world, the spirits will grow modern too. The old dryads, who inhabited trees and made sacred grooves sacred, giving rise to the modern notion of knocking wood,* must be largely unemployed now that more than half the world's forests have been ground up into toothpicks and newsprint. Undoubtedly they now make their homes in vats of polymerizing plastic and respond eagerly to the cry of "Knock plastic!" I recommend it to one and all.

But knocking wood is only one example of a class of notions, so comforting and so productive of feelings of security, that men will seize upon them on the slightest provocation or on none at all.

Any piece of evidence tending to support such a "Security Belief," however frail and nonsensical it might be, is grabbed and hugged close to the bosom. Every piece of evidence tending to break down a Security Belief, however strong and logical that evidence might be, is pushed away. (Indeed, if the evidence against a Security Belief is strong enough, those presenting the evidence might well be in danger of violence.)

It is very important, therefore, in weighing the merits of any widely held opinion, to consider whether it can be viewed as a Security Belief. If it is, then its popularity means nothing; it must be viewed with considerable suspicion.

Some people say that knocking wood is symbolic of touching the True Cross, but I don't believe that at all. I'm sure the habit must antedate Christianity.

It might, of course, be that the view is accurate. For instance, it is a comforting thought to Americans that the United States is the richest and most powerful nation in the world. But in all truth, it *is*, and this particular Security Belief (for Americans) is justified.

Nevertheless, the Universe is an insecure place, indeed, and on general principles Security Beliefs are much more likely to be false than true.

For instance, a poll of the heavy smokers of the world would probably show that almost all of them are firmly convinced that the arguments linking smoking with lung cancer are not conclusive. The same heavy majority would exist if members of the tobacco industry were polled. Why not? The opposite belief would leave them too medically insecure, or economically insecure, for comfort.

Then, too, when I was young, we kids had the firm belief that if one dropped a piece of candy into the incredible filth of the city streets, one need only touch the candy to the lips and then wave it up to the sky ("kissing it to God") to make it perfectly pure and sanitary. We believed this despite all strictures on germs, because if we didn't believe it, that piece of candy would go uneaten by ourselves, and someone else, who did believe it, would get to eat it.

Naturally, anyone can make up the necessary evidence in favor of a Security Belief. "My grandfather smoked a pack a day for seventy years and when he died his lungs were the last to go." Or "Jerry kissed candy to God yesterday and today he won the forty-yard dash."

If Grandfather had died of lung cancer at thirty-six, or if Jerry had come down with cholera—no problem, you cite other instances.

But let's not sink to special cases. I have come up with six very broad Security Beliefs that, I think, blanket the field—although the Gentle Reader is welcome to add a seventh, if he can think of one.

SECURITY BELIEF NO.1: *There exist supernatural forces that can be cajoled or forced into protecting mankind.*

Here is the essence of superstition.

When a primitive hunting society is faced with the fact that game is sometimes plentiful and sometimes not, and when a primitive agricultural society watches drought come one year and floods the next, it seems only natural to assume—in default of anything better—that some more-than-human force is arranging things in this way.

Since nature is capricious, it would seem that the various gods, spirits, demons (whatever you wish to call them) are themselves capricious. In one way or another they must be induced or made to subordinate their wild impulses to the needs of humanity.

Who says this is easy? Obviously, it calls for all the skill of the wisest and most experienced men of the society. So there develops a specialized class of spirit manipulators—a priesthood, to use that term in its broadest sense.

It is fair enough to call spirit manipulation "magic." The word comes from "magi," the name given to the priestly caste of Zoroastrian Persia.

The popularity of this Security Belief is almost total. A certain Influential Personage in science fiction, who is much given to adopting these Security Beliefs and then pretending he is a member of a persecuted minority, once wrote to me: "Every society but ours has believed in magic. Why should we be so arrogant as to think that everyone but ourselves is wrong?"

My answer at the time was: "Every society but ours has believed the Sun revolved about the Earth. Do you want to settle the matter by majority vote?"

Actually the situation is worse than even the Influential Personage maintains. Every society, *including our own,* believes in magic. Nor do I restrict the belief only to the naive and uneducated of our culture. The most rational elements of our society, the well educated, the scientist, retain scraps of belief in magic.

When a horseshoe hangs over Bohr's desk (assuming one really did), that is a magical warding-off of misfortune through the power of "cold iron" over a spirit world stuck in the Bronze Age. When I knock wood (or plastic) I too engage in spirit manipulation.

But can we argue, as the Influential Personage does, that there must be something to magic since so many people believe in it?

No, of course not. It is too tempting to believe. What can be easier than to believe that one can avoid misfortune by so simple a device as knocking on wood? If it's wrong, you lose nothing. If it's right, you gain so much. One would need to be woodenly austere indeed to refuse the odds.

Still, if magic doesn't work, won't people recognize that eventually and abandon it?

But who says magic doesn't work? Of course it works—in the estimation of those who believe.

Suppose you knock on wood and misfortune doesn't follow. See? Of course, you might go back in time and not knock on wood and find out that misfortune doesn't follow, anyway—but how can you arrange a control like that?

Or suppose you see a pin and pick it up on ten successive days, and on nine of those days nothing much happened one way or the other, but on the tenth you get good news in the mail. It is the work of a moment to remember that tenth day and forget the other nine— and what better proof do you want anyway?

Or what if you carefully light two on a match and three minutes later fall and break your leg. Surely you can argue that if you had lit that third cigarette, you would have broken your neck, not your leg.

You can't lose! If you want to believe, you can believe!

Indeed, magic can work in actual fact. A tightrope walker, having surreptitiously rubbed the rabbit's foot under his belt, can advance with such self-confidence as to perform perfectly. An actor, stepping out on stage just after someone has whistled in his dressing room, can be so nervous that he will muff his lines. In other works, even if magic doesn't work, belief in magic does.

But then, how do scientists go about disproving the usefulness of magic? They don't! It's an impossibility. Few, if any, believers would accept the disproof anyway.

What scientists do is to work on the *assumption* that Security Belief No. 1 is false. They take into account no capricious forces in their analysis of the Universe. They set up a minimum number of generalizations (miscalled "natural laws") and assume that nothing happens or can be made to happen that is outside those natural laws. Advancing knowledge may make it necessary to modify the generalizations now and then, but always they remain noncapricious.

Ironically enough, scientists themselves become a new priesthood. Some Security Believers see in the scientist the new magus. It is the scientist, now, who can manipulate the Universe, by mysterious rites understood by him only, so as to insure the safety of man under all circumstances. This belief, in my opinion, is as ill-founded as the earlier one.

Again, a Security Belief can be modified to give it a scientific tang. Thus, where once we had angels and spirits descending to Earth to interfere in our affairs and mete out justice, we now have advanced beings in flying saucers doing so (according to some). In fact, part of the popularity of the whole flying saucer mystique is, in my opinion, the ease with which the extraterrestrials can be looked upon as a new scientific version of angels.

SECURITY BELIEF NO. 9: *There is no such thing, really, as death.*

Man, as far as we know, is the only species capable of foreseeing the inevitability of death. An individual man or woman knows, for certain, as no other creature can, that someday he or she must die.

This is an absolutely shattering piece of knowledge and one can't help but wonder how much it, by itself, affects human behavior, making it fundamentally different from the behavior of other animals.

Or perhaps the effect is less than we might expect, since men so universally and so resolutely refuse to think of it. How many individuals live as though they expect to keep on going forever? Almost every one of us, I think.

A comparatively sensible way of denying death is to suppose that it is a family that is the real living entity and that the individual does not truly die while the family lives. This is one of the bases of ancestor worship, since the ancestor lives as long as he has a descendant to worship him.

Under these circumstances, naturally, the lack of children (especially sons, for in most tribal societies women didn't count) was a supreme disaster. It was so in early Israelite society, for instance, as the Bible tells us. Definite rules are given in the Bible that oblige men to take, as wives, the widows of their childless brothers, in order to give those wives sons who might be counted as descendants of the dead man.

The crime of Onan ("onanism") is not what you probably think it is, but was his refusal to perform this service for his dead brother (see Genesis 38:7–10).

A more literal denial of death is also very popular. Almost every society we know of has some notion of an "afterlife." There is someplace where an immortal residue of each human body can go. The shade can live a gray and dismal existence in a place like Hades or Sheol, but he lives.

Under more imaginative conditions, the afterlife, or a portion of it, can become an abode of bliss while another portion can become an abode of torment. Then, the notion of immortality can be linked with the notion of reward and punishment. There is a Security Belief angle to this too, since it increases one's security in the midst of poverty and misery to know you'll live like a god in Heaven, while that rich fellow over there is going straight to Hell, ha, ha, and good for him.

Failing an afterlife in some place beyond Earth, you can have one on Earth itself by arranging a belief in reincarnation or in transmigration of souls.

While reincarnation is no part of the dominant religious beliefs in the Western world, such are its Security Belief values that any evidence in its favor is delightedly accepted. When, in the 1950s, a rather silly book entitled *The Search for Bridey Murphy* appeared and seemed to indicate the actual existence of reincarnation, it became a best-seller at once. There was nothing to it, to be sure.

And, of course, the whole doctrine of spiritualism, the entire battery of mediums and table-rappings and ectoplasm and ghosts and poltergeists and a million other things are all based on the firm insistence of mankind that death does not take place; that something persists; that the conscious personality is somehow immortal.

Is there any use then in trying to debunk spiritualism? It can't be done. No matter how many mediums are shown to be fakes, the ardent believer will believe the next medium he encounters. He may do even better. He may denounce the proof of fakedom as itself a fraud and continue to have faith in the fake, however transparent.

Science proceeds on the assumption that Security Belief No. 2 is false also.

Yet scientists are human too, and individuals among them (as distinct from science in the abstract) long for security. Sir Oliver J. Lodge, a scientist of considerable reputation, depressed by the death of a son in World War I, tried to reach him through spiritualism and became a devotee of "psychic research."

My friend, the Influential Personage, has often cited Lodge and men like him as evidence of the value of psychic research. "If you believe Lodge's observations on the electron, why don't you believe his observations on spirits?"

The answer is, of course, that Lodge has no security to gain from an electron but does from spirits. —And scientists are human too.

SECURITY BELIEF NO. 3: *There is some purpose to the Universe.*

After all, if you're going to have a whole battery of spirits and demons running the Universe, you can't really have them doing it all for nothing.

The Zoroastrians of Persia worked out a delightfully complicated scheme of the Universe. They imagined the whole of existence to be engaged in a cosmic war. Ahura Mazda, leading countless spirits under the banner of Light and Good, encountered an equally powerful army under Ahriman fighting for Darkness and Evil. The forces were almost evenly matched and individual men could feel that with them lay the balance of power. If they strove to be good they were contributing to the "right side" in the most colossal conflict ever imagined.

Some of these notions crept into Judaism and Christianity, and we have the war of God versus the Devil. In the Judeo-Christian view, however, there is no question as to who will win. God must and will win. It makes things less exciting.

This Security Belief is also assumed to be false by science. Science does not merely ignore the possibility of a cosmic war, when it tries to work out the origins and ultimate fate of the Universe; it ignores the possibility of any deliberate purpose anywhere.

The most basic generalizations of science (the laws of thermodynamics, for instance, or quantum theory) assume random movement of particles, random collisions, random energy transfers, and so on. From considerations of probability one can assume that with many particles and over long periods of time, certain events are reasonably sure to take place, but concerning individual particles and over short periods of time, nothing can be predicted.

Possibly, no scientific view is so unpopular with nonscientists as this one. It seems to make everything so "meaningless."

But does it? Is it absolutely necessary to have the entire Universe or all of life meaningful. Can we not consider that what is meaningless in one context is meaningful in another; that a book in Chinese which is meaningless to me is meaningful to a Chinaman? And can we not consider that each of us can so arrange his own particular life so as to make it meaningful to himself and to those he influences? And in that case does not all of life and all the Universe come to have meaning *to him*?

Surely it is those who find their own lives essentially meaningless who most strive to impose meaning on the Universe as a way of making up for the personal lack.

SECURITY BELIEF NO. 4: *Individuals have special powers that will enable them to get something for nothing.*

"Wishing will make it so" is a line from a popular song and oh, how many people believe it. It is much easier to wish, hope, and pray, than to take the trouble to *do* something.

I once wrote a book in which a passage contained a description of the dangers of the population explosion and of the necessity for birth control. A reviewer who looked over that passage wrote in the margin, "I'd say this was God's problem, wouldn't you?"

It was like taking candy from a baby to write under that in clear print: "God helps those who help themselves."

But think of the popularity of stories in which characters get three wishes, or the power to turn everything they touch into gold, or are given a spear that will always find the mark, or a gem that will discolor in the presence of danger.

And just imagine if we had amazing powers all the time and didn't know it—telepathy, for instance. How eager we are to have it. (Who hasn't experienced a coincidence and at once cried out, "Telepathy!") How ready we are to believe in advanced cases elsewhere since that will improve the possibilities of ourselves possessing the power if we practiced hard enough.

Some wild powers represent the ability to foresee the future—clairvoyance. Or else one gains the knowledge to calculate the future by means of astrology, numerology, palmistry, tea leaves, or a thousand other hoary frauds.

Here we come close to Security Belief No. 1. If we foresee the future, we might change it by appropriate action and this is nearly the equivalent of spirit manipulation.

In a way, science has fulfilled the fairy tales. The jet plane goes far faster and farther than the flying horse and the seven-league boots of the fable writers of yore. We have rockets which seek out their targets, like Thor's hammer, and do far more damage. We have, not gems, but badges that discolor in the presence of too much accumulated radiation.

But these do not represent "something for nothing." They are not awarded through supernatural agency and don't act capriciously. They are the hard-earned products of the generalizations concerning the Universe built up by a science that denies most or all of the Security Beliefs.

SECURITY BELIEF NO. 5: *You are better than the next fellow.*

This is a very tempting belief, but it is often a dangerous one. You tell this to that big bruiser facing you and he's liable to break your neck. So you appoint a surrogate: Your father is better than his father; your college is better than his college; your accent is better than his accent; your cultural group is better than his cultural group.

Naturally this fades off into racism and it is not at all surprising that the more lowly the social, economic, or personal position of an individual, the more likely he is to fall prey to the racist temptation.

It is not surprising that even scientists as individuals have trouble with this one. They can rationalize and say that it must surely be possible to divide mankind into categories in such a way that some categories aresuperior to others in some ways. Some groups are taller than other groups, for instance, as a matter of genetic inheritance. Might it not be that some groups are, by birth and nature, more intelligent or more honest than others?

A certain Nobel Prize winner demanded, some time ago, that scientists stop ducking the issue; that they set about determining whether slumdwellers (English translation: Negroes) are not actually "inferior" to nonslumdwellers and whether attempts to help them were not therefore futile.

I was asked by a certain newspaper to write my views about this, but I said I had better tell them, in advance, what my views were going to be and save myself the trouble of writing an article they wouldn't print.

I said that, in the first place, it was very likely that those who were most enthusiastic for such an investigation were quite confident that they had set up measurement standards by which the slumdwellers would indeed prove to be "inferior." This would then relieve the superior nonslumdwellers of responsibility toward the slumdwellers and of any guilt feeling they might possess.

If I were wrong, I went on to say, then I felt the investigators should be as eager to find a superior minority as an inferior one. For instance, I strongly suspected that by the measurement standards prevailing in our society, it would turn out that Unitarians and Episcopalians would have a higher average IQ and a higher performance record than other religious groups.

If this proved to be so, I suggested, Unitarians and Episcopalians ought to wear some distinctive badge, be ushered to the front of the bus, be given the best seats at the theaters, be allowed to use the cleaner restrooms and so on.

So the newspaper said, "Forget it!" and it's just as well. No one wants to search out superiors to one's self—only inferiors.

SECURITY BELIEF NO. 6: *If anything goes wrong, it's not one's own fault.*

Virtually everyone has a slight touch of paranoia. With a little practice, this can easily lead one into accepting one of the conspiracy theories of history.

How comforting it is to know that if you're failing in business, it's the unfair crooked tactics of the Bulgarian who owns the store down the block; if you've got a pain, it's because of the conspiracy of Nigerian doctors all about you; if you tripped when you turned to look at a girl, it was one rotten Ceylonese who put that crack in the sidewalk there.

And it is here at last that scientists are touched most closely—for this Security Belief can turn directly against them for standing out against Security Beliefs in general.

When the Security Believers are stung by the explosion of the hoaxes and follies that deceive them, what is their last, best defense? Why, that there is a conspiracy of scientists against them.

I am myself constantly being accused of participating in such a conspiracy. In today's mail, for instance, I got a most violent and indignant letter, from which I will quote only a couple of mild sentences:

"Not only are we [the public] being played for fools by politicians . . . but now these tactics have spread to science as well. If your purpose is deceiving others for whatever intention, let this tell you that you are not one hundred percent successful."

I read the letter carefully through and it seemed that he had read some magazine article which had rebutted one of his pet beliefs. He was instantly sure, therefore, not that he himself might be wrong, but that scientists were in a conspiracy against him and were under orders from NASA to lie to him.

The trouble was that he was referring to some article which had been written by someone else, not me—and I didn't know what on earth he was talking about.

However, I am positive that the forces of Rationality will rise triumphant over the onslaughts of Security Believers despite everything. (Knock plastic!)

LOST
IN NON-
TRANSLATION

AT THE NOREASCON (the 29th World Science Fiction Convention), which was held in Boston on the Labor Day weekend of 1971, I sat on the dais, of course, since, as the Bob Hope of science fiction, it is my perennial duty to hand out the Hugos. On my left was my daughter, Robyn, sixteen, blond, blue-eyed, shapely, and beautiful. (No, that last adjective is not a father's proud partiality. Ask anyone.)

My old friend Clifford D. Simak was guest of honor, and he began his talk by introducing, with thoroughly justified pride, his two children, who were in the audience. A look of alarm instantly crossed Robyn's face.

"Daddy," she whispered urgently, knowing full well my capacity for inflicting embarrassment, "are you planning to introduce me?"

"Would that bother you, Robyn?" I asked.

"Yes, it would."

"Then I won't," I said, and patted her hand reassuringly.

She thought a while. Then she said, "Of course, Daddy, if you have the urge to refer, in a casual sort of way, to your beautiful daughter, that would be all right."

So you can bet I did just that, while she allowed her eyes to drop in a charmingly modest way.

But I couldn't help but think of the blond, blue-eyed stereotype of Nordic beauty that has filled Western literature ever since the blond, blue-eyed Germanic tribes took over the western portions of the Roman Empire, fifteen centuries ago, and set themselves up as an aristocracy.

. . . And the manner in which that has been used to subvert one of the clearest and most important lessons in the Bible—a subversion that contributes its little bit to the serious crisis that today faces the world, and the United States in particular.

In line with my penchant for beginning at the beginning, come back with me to the sixth century B.C. A party of Jews have returned from Babylonian Exile to rebuild the Temple at Jerusalem, which Nebuchadnezzar had destroyed seventy years before.

During the Exile, under the guidance of the prophet Ezekiel, the Jews had firmly held to their national identity by modifying, complicating, and idealizing their worship of Yahweh into a form that was directly ancestral to the Judaism of today. (In fact Ezekiel is sometimes called "the father of Judaism.")

This meant that when the exiles returned to Jerusalem, they faced a religious problem. There were people who, all through the period of the Exile, had been living in what had once been Judah, and who worshipped Yahweh in what they considered the correct, time-honored ritual. Because their chief city (with Jerusalem destroyed) was Samaria, the returning Jews called them Samaritans.

The Samaritans rejected the newfangled modifications of the returning Jews, and the Jews abhorred the old-fashioned beliefs of the Samaritans. Between them arose an undying hostility, the kind that is exacerbated because the differences in belief are comparatively small.

In addition, there were, of course, also living in the land, those who worshipped other gods altogether—Ammonites, Edomites, Philistines, and so on.

The pressures on the returning band of Jews were not primarily military, for the entire area was under the more or less beneficent rule of the Persian Empire, but it was social, and perhaps even stronger for that. To maintain a strict ritual in the face of overwhelming numbers of nonbelievers is difficult, and the tendency to relax that ritual was almost irresistible. Then, too, young male returnees were attracted to the women at hand and there were intermarriages. Naturally, to humor the wife, ritual was further relaxed.

But then, possibly as late as about 400 B.C., a full century after the Second Temple had been built, Ezra arrived in Jerusalem. He was a scholar of the Mosaic law, which had been edited and put into final form in the course of the Exile. He was horrified at the backsliding put through a tub-thumping revival. He called the people together, led them in chanting the law and expounding upon it, raised their religious fervor, and called for confession of sins and renewal of faith.

One thing he demanded most rigorously was the abandonment of all non-Jewish wives and their children. Only so could the holiness of strict Judaism be maintained, in his view. To quote the Bible (and I will use the recent New English Bible for the purpose):

"Ezra the priest stood up and said, 'You have committed an offense in marrying foreign wives and have added to Israel's guilt. Make your confession now to the Lord the God of your fathers and do his will, and separate yourselves from the foreign population and from your foreign wives.' Then all the assembled people shouted in reply, 'Yes; we must do what you say. . . .'" (Ezra 10:10–12)

From that time on, the Jews as a whole began to practice an exclusivism, a voluntary separation from others, a multiplication of peculiar customs that further emphasized their separateness; and all of this helped them maintain their identity through all the miseries and catastrophes that were to come, through all the crises, and through exiles and persecutions that fragmented them over the face of the Earth.

The exclusivism, to be sure, also served to make them socially indigestible and imparted to them a high social visibility that helped give rise to conditions that made exiles and persecutions more likely.

Not everyone among the Jews adhered to this policy of exclusivism. There were some who believed that all men were equal in the sight of God and that no one should be excluded from the community on the basis of group identity alone.

And one who believed this (but who is forever nameless) attempted to present this case in the form of a short piece of historical fiction. In this fourth-century-B.C. tale the heroine was Ruth, a

Moabite woman. (The tale was presented as having taken place in the time of the judges, so the traditional view was that it was written by the prophet Samuel in the eleventh century B.C. No modern student of the Bible believes this.)

Why a Moabite woman, by the way?

It seems that the Jews, returning from Exile, had traditions concerning their initial arrival at the borders of Canaan under first Moses, then Joshua, nearly a thousand years before. At that time, the small nation of Moab, which lay east of the lower course of the Jordan and of the Dead Sea, understandably alarmed at the incursion of tough desert raiders, took steps to oppose them. Not only did they prevent the Israelites from passing through their territory, but, tradition had it, they called in a seer, Balaam, and asked him to use his magical abilities to bring misfortune and destruction upon the invaders.

That failed, and Balaam, on departing, was supposed to have advised the king of Moab to let the Moabite girls lure the desert raiders into liaisons, which might subvert their stern dedication to their task. The Bible records the following:

"When the Israelites were in Shittim, the people began to have intercourse with Moabite women, who invited them to the sacrifices offered to their gods; and they ate the sacrificial food and prostrated themselves before the gods of Moab. The Israelites joined in the worship of the Baal of Peor, and the Lord was angry with them." (Numbers 25:1–3)

As a result of this, "Moabite women" became the quintessence of the type of outside influence that by sexual attraction tried to subvert pious Jews. Indeed Moab and the neighboring kingdom to the north, Ammon, were singled out in the Mosaic code:

"No Ammonite or Moabite, even down to the tenth generation, shall become a member of the assembly of the Lord . . . because they did not meet you with food and water on your way out of Egypt, and because they hired Balaam . . . to revile you. . . .You shall never seek their welfare or their good all your life long." (Deuteronomy 23:3–4, 6)

And yet there were times in later history when there was friendship between Moab and at least some men of Israel, possibly because they were brought together by some common enemy.

For instance, shortly before 1000 B.C. Israel was ruled by Saul. He had held off the Philistines, conquered the Amalekites, and brought Israel to its greatest pitch of power to that point. Moab naturally feared his expansionist policies and so befriended anyone rebelling against Saul. Such a rebel was the Judean warrior David of Bethlehem. When David was pressed hard by Saul and had retired to a fortified stronghold, he used Moab as a refuge for his family.

"David . . . said to the king of Moab, 'Let my father and mother come and take shelter with you until I know what God will do for me.' So he left them at the court of the king of Moab, and they stayed there as long as David was in his stronghold." (1 Samuel 22:3–4)

As it happened, David eventually won out, became king first of Judah, then of all Israel, and established an empire that took in the entire east coast of the Mediterranean, from Egypt to the Euphrates, with the Phoenician cities independent but in alliance with him. Later, Jews always looked back to the time of David and of his son Solomon as a golden age, and David's position in Jewish legend and thought was unassailable. David founded a dynasty that ruled over Judah for four centuries, and the Jews never stopped believing that some descendant of David would yet return to rule over them again in some idealized future time.

Yet, on the basis of the verses describing David's use of Moab as a refuge for his family, there may have arisen a tale to the effect that there was a Moabite strain in David's ancestry. Apparently, the author of the Book of Ruth determined to make use of this tale to point up the doctrine of nonexclusivism by using the supremely hated Moabite woman as his heroine.

The Book of Ruth tells of a Judean family of Bethlehem—a man, his wife, and two sons—who are driven by famine to Moab. There the two sons marry Moabite girls, but after a space of time all three men die, leaving the three women—Naomi, the mother-in-law, and Ruth and Orpah, the two daughters-in-law—as survivors.

Those were times when women were chattels and when unmarried women, without a man to own them and care for them, could subsist only on charity. (Hence the frequent biblical injunction to care for widows and orphans.)

Naomi determined to return to Bethlehem, where kinsmen might possibly care for her, but urged Ruth and Orpah to remain in Moab. She does not say, but we might plausibly suppose she is thinking, that Moabite girls would have a rough time of it in Moab-hating Judah.

Orpah remains in Moab, but Ruth refuses to leave Naomi, saying, "Do not urge me to go back and desert you. . . . Where you go, I will go, and where you stay, I will stay. Your people shall be my people, and your God my God. Where you die I will did, and there I will be buried. I swear a solemn oath before the Lord your God: nothing but death shall divide us." (Ruth 1:16–17)

Once in Bethlehem, the two were faced with the direst poverty and Ruth volunteered to support herself and her mother-in-law by gleaning in the fields. It was harvesttime and it was customary to allow any stalks of grain that fell to the ground in the process of gathering to remain there to be collected by the poor. This gleaning was a kind of welfare program for those in need. It was, however, backbreaking work, and any young woman, particularly a Moabite, who engaged in it, underwent certain obvious risks at the hands of the lusty young reapers. Ruth's offer was simply heroic.

As it happened, Ruth gleaned in the lands of a rich Judean farmer named Boaz, who coming to oversee the work, noticed her working tirelessly. He asked after her, and his reapers answered, "She is a Moabite girl . . . who has just come back with Naomi from the Moabite country." (Ruth 2:6)

Boaz speaks kindly to her and Ruth says, "Why are you so kind as to take notice of me when I am only a foreigner?" (Ruth 2:10) Boaz explains that he has heard how she has forsaken her own land for love of Naomi and how hard she must work to take care of her.

As it turned out, Boaz was a relative of Naomi's dead husband, which must be one reason why he was touched by Ruth's love and fidelity. Naomi, on hearing the story, had an idea. In those days, if a widow was left childless, she had the right to expect her dead husband's brother to marry her and offer her his protection. If the dead husband had no brother, some other relative would fulfill the task.

Naomi was past the age of childbearing, so she could not qualify for marriage, which in those days centered about children; but what about Ruth? To be sure, Ruth was a Moabite woman and it might well be that no Judean would marry her, but Boaz had proven kind. Naomi therefore instructed Ruth how to approach Boaz at night and, without crudely seductive intent, appeal for his protection.

Boaz, touched by Ruth's modesty and helplessness, promised to do his duty, but pointed out that there was a kinsman closer than he and that, by right, this other kinsman had to have his chance first.

The very next day, Boaz approached the other kinsman and suggested that he buy some property in Naomi's charge and, along with it, take over another responsibility. Boaz said, "On the day when you acquire the field from Naomi, you also acquire Ruth the Moabitess, the dead man's wife. . . . " (Ruth 4:5)

Perhaps Boaz carefully stressed the adjectival phrase "the Moabitess," for the other kinsman drew back at once. Boaz therefore married Ruth, who in time bore him a son. The proud and happy Naomi held the child in her bosom and her women friends said to her, "The child will give you new life and cherish you in your old age; for your daughter-in-law who loves you, who has proved better to you than seven sons, has borne him." (Ruth 4:15)

This verdict of Judean women on Ruth, a woman of the hated land of Moab, in a society that valued sons infinitely more than daughters, a verdict that she "has proved better to you than seven sons" is the author's moral—that there is nobility and virtue in all groups and that none must be excluded from consideration in advance simply because of their group identification.

And then, to clinch the argument for any Judean so nationalistic as to be impervious to mere idealism, the story concludes: "Her neighbors gave him a name: 'Naomi has a son,' they said; 'we will call him Obed.' He was the father of Jesse, the father of David." (Ruth 4:17)

Where would Israel have been, then, if there had been an Ezra present then to forbid the marriage of Boaz with a "foreign wife"?

Where does that leave us? That the Book of Ruth is a pleasant story, no one will deny. It is almost always referred to as a "delightful idyl" or words to that effect. That Ruth is a most successful characterizations of a sweet and virtuous woman is beyond dispute.

In fact, everyone is so in love with the story and with Ruth that the whole point is lost. It is, by right, a tale of tolerance for the despised, of love for the hated, of the reward that comes of brotherhood. By mixing the genes of mankind, by forming the hybrid, great men will come.

The Jews included the Book of Ruth in the canon partly because it is so wonderfully told a tale but mostly (I suspect) because it gives the lineage of the great David, a lineage that is *not* given beyond David's father, Jesse, in the soberly historic books of the Bible that anteceded Ruth. But the Jews remained, by and large, exclusivistic and did not learn the lesson of universalism preached by the Book of Ruth.

Nor have people taken its lesson to heart since. Why should they, since every effort is made to wipe out that lesson? The story of Ruth has been retold any number of times, from children's tales to serious novels. Even movies have been made of it. Ruth herself must have been pictured in hundreds of illustrations. And in every illustration I have ever seen, she is presented as blond, blue-eyed, shapely, and beautiful—the perfect Nordic stereotype I referred to at the beginning of the article.

For goodness sake, why shouldn't Boaz have fallen in love with her? What great credit was there in marrying her? If a girl like that had fallen at your feet and asked you humbly to do your duty by her and kindly marry her, you would probably have done it like a shot.

Of course she was a Moabite woman, but so what? What does the word "Moabite" mean to you? Does it arouse any violent reaction? Are there many Moabites among your acquaintances? Have your children been chased by a bunch of lousy Moabites lately? Have they been reducing property values in your neighborhood? When was the last time you heard someone say, "Got to get those rotten Moabites out of here. They just fill up the welfare rolls."

In fact, judging by the way Ruth is drawn, Moabites are English aristocrats and their presence would raise property values.

The trouble is that the one word that is *not translated* in the Book of Ruth is the key word "Moabite," and as long as it is not translated, the point is lost; it is lost in non-translation.

The word Moabite really means "someone of a group that receives from us and deserves from us nothing but hatred and contempt." How should this word be translated into a single word that means the same thing to, say, many modern Greeks? . . . Why, "Turk." And to many modern Turks? . . . Why, "Greek." And to many modern White Americans? . . . Why, "Black."

To get the proper flavor of the Book of Ruth, suppose we think of Ruth not as a Moabite woman but as a Black woman.

Reread the story of Ruth and translate Moabite to Black every time you see it. Naomi (imagine) is coming back to the United States with her two black daughters-in-law. No wonder she urges them not to come with her. It is a marvel that Ruth so loved her mother-in-law that she was willing to face a society that hated her unreasonably and to take the risk of gleaning in the face of leering reapers who could not possibly suppose they need treat her with any consideration whatever.

And when Boaz asked who she was, don't read the answer as "She is a Moabite girl," but as "She is a black girl." More likely, in fact, the reapers might have said to Boaz something that was the equivalent of (if you'll excuse the language), "She is a nigger girl."

Think of it that way and you find the whole point is found in translation and only in translation. Boaz's action in being willing to marry Ruth because she was virtuous (and not because she was a Nordic beauty) takes on a kind of nobility. The neighbors' decision that she was better to Naomi than seven sons becomes something that could have been forced out of them only by overwhelming evidence to that effect. And the final stroke that out of this miscegenation was born none other than the great David is rather breathtaking.

We get something similar in the New Testament. On one occasion a student of the law asks Jesus what must be done to gain eternal life, and answers his own question by saying, "Love the Lord your God with all your heart, with all your soul, with all your strength, and with all your mind; and your neighbor as yourself." (Luke 10:27)

These admonitions are taken from the Old Testament, of course. That last bit about your neighbor comes from a verse that says, "You shall not seek revenge, or cherish anger towards your kinsfolk; you shall love your neighbor as a man like yourself." (Leviticus 19:18)

(The New English Bible translations sound better to me here than the King James's: "Thou shalt love thy neighbor as thyself." Where is the saint who can truly feel another's pain or ecstasy precisely as he feels his own? We must not ask too much. But if we simply grant that someone else is "a man like yourself," then he can be treated with decency at least. It is when we refuse to grant even this and talk of another as our inferior that contempt and cruelty come to seem natural, and even laudable.)

Jesus approves the lawyer's saying, and the lawyer promptly asks, "And who is my neighbor?" (Luke 10:29) After all, the verse in Leviticus first speaks of refraining from revenge and anger toward *kinsfolk*; might not, then, the concept of "neighbor" be restricted to kinsfolk, to one's own kind, only?

In response, Jesus replies with perhaps the greatest of the parables—of a traveler who fell in with robbers, who was mugged and robbed and left half dead by the road. Jesus goes on, "It so happened that a priest was going down by the same road; but when he saw him, he went past on the other side. So too a Levite came to the place, and when he saw him went past on the other side. But a Samaritan who was making the journey came upon him, and when he saw him was moved to pity. He went up and bandaged his wounds, bathing them with oil and wine. Then he lifted him on to his own beast, brought him to an inn, and looked after him there." (Luke 10:31–34)

Then Jesus asks who the traveler's neighbor was, and the lawyer is forced to say, "The one who showed him kindness." (Luke 10:37)

This is known as the Parable of the Good Samaritan, even though nowhere in the parable is the rescuer called a *good* Samaritan, merely a Samaritan.

The force of the parable is entirely vitiated by the common phrase "good" Samaritan, for that has cast a false light on who the Samaritans were. In a free-association test, say "Samaritan" and probably every person being tested will answer, "Good." It has become so imprinted in all our brains that Samaritans are good that we take it for granted that a Samaritan would act like that and wonder why Jesus is making a point of it.

We forget who the Samaritans were, in the time of Jesus!

To the Jews, they were *not* good. They were hated, despised, contemptible heretics with whom no good Jew would have anything to do. Again, the whole point is lost through non-translation.

Suppose, instead, that it is a White traveler in Mississippi who has been mugged and left half dead. And suppose it was a minister and a deacon who passed by and refused to "become involved." And suppose it was a Black sharecropper who stopped and took care of the man.

Now ask yourself: Who was the neighbor whom you must love as though he were a man like yourself if you are to be saved?

The Parable of the Good Samaritan clearly teaches that there is nothing parochial in the concept "neighbor," that you cannot confine your decency to your own group and your own kind. All mankind, right down to those you most despise, are your neighbors.

Well, then, we have in the Bible two examples—in the Book of Ruth and in the Parable of the Good Samaritan—of teachings that are lost in non-translation, yet are terribly applicable to us today.

The whole world over, there are confrontations between sections of mankind defined by race, nationality, economic philosophy, religion, or language as belonging to different groups, so that one is not "neighbor" to the other.

These more or less arbitrary differences among peoples who are members of a single biological species are terribly dangerous and nowhere more so than here in the United States where the most perilous confrontation (I need not tell you) is between white and black.

Next to the population problem generally, mankind faces no danger greater than this confrontation, particularly in the United States.

It seems to me that more and more, each year, both whites and blacks are turning, in anger and hatred, to violence. I see no reasonable end to the steady escalation but an actual civil war.

In such a civil war, the whites, with a preponderance of numbers and an even greater preponderance of organized power would, in all likelihood, "win." They would do so, however, at an enormous material cost and, I suspect, at a fatal spiritual one.

And why? Is it so hard to recognize that we are all neighbors, after all? Can we, on both sides—on *both* sides—find no way of accepting the biblical lesson?

Or if quoting the Bible sounds too mealymouthed and if repeating the words of Jesus seems too pietistic, let's put it another way, a practical way:

Is the privilege of feeling hatred so luxurious a sensation that it is worth the material and spiritual hell of a white-black civil war?

If the answer is really "yes," then one can only despair.

LOOK LONG UPON A MONKEY

CONSIDERING THAT I WORK SO HARD at establishing my chosen persona as a man who is cheerfully self-appreciative, I am sometimes absurdly sensitive to the fact that every once in a while people who don't know me take the persona for myself.

I was interviewed recently by a newspaper reporter who was an exceedingly pleasant fellow but who clearly knew very little about me. I was curious enough, therefore, to ask why he had decided to interview me.

He explained without hesitation. "My boss asked me to interview you," he said. Then he smiled a little and added, "He had strong, ambivalent feelings about you."

I said, "You mean he likes my writing but thinks I am arrogant and conceited."

"Yes," he said, clearly surprised. "How did you know?"

"Lucky guess," I said, with a sigh.

You see, it's *not* arrogance and conceit; it's cheerful self-appreciation, and anyone who knows me has no trouble seeing the difference.

Of course, I could save myself this trouble by choosing a different persona, by practicing aw-shucks modesty and learning how to dig my toe into the ground and bring the pretty pink to my cheeks at the slightest word of praise.

But no, thanks. I write on just about every subject and for every age level, and once I begin to practice a charming diffidence, I will make myself doubt my own ability to do so, and that would be ruinous.

So I'll go right along the path I have chosen and endure the ambivalent feelings that come my way, for the sake of having the self-assurance to write my wide-ranging essays—like this one on evolution.

I suspect that if man* could only have been left out of it, there would never have been any trouble about accepting biological evolution.

Anyone can see, for instance, that some animals resemble each other closely. Who can deny that a dog and a wolf resemble each other in important ways? Or a tiger and a leopard? Or a lobster and a crab? Twenty-three centuries ago, the Greek philosopher Aristotle lumped different types of species together and prepared a "ladder of life," by arranging those types from the simplest plants upward to the most complex animals, with (inevitably) man at the top.

Once this was done, we moderns could say, with the clear vision of hindsight, that it was inevitable that people should come to see that one type of species had changed into another; that the more complex had developed from the less complex; that, in short, there was not only a ladder of life but a system whereby life forms climbed that ladder.

Not so! Neither Aristotle nor those who came after him for more than two thousand years moved from the ladder of life as a static concept to one that was a dynamic and evolutionary one.

The various species, it was considered, were *permanent*. There might be families and hierarchies of species, but that was the way in which life was created from the beginning. Resemblances has existed from the beginning, it was maintained, and no species grew to resemble another more—or less—with the passage of time.

Anyone who reads these essays knows that I am a women's-libber, but I also have a love for the English language. I try to circumlocute "man" when I mean "human being" but the flow of sound suffers sometimes when I do. Please accept, in this article, "man" in the general, embracing "woman." (Yes, I know what I said.)

My feeling is that the insistence on this constancy of species arose, at least in part, out of the uncomfortable feeling that once change was allowed, man would lose his uniqueness and become "just another animal."

Once Christianity grew dominant in the Western world, views on the constancy of species became even more rigid. No only did Genesis 1 clearly describe the creation of the various species of life as already differentiated and in their present form, but man was created differently from all the rest. "And God said, Let us make man in our image, after our likeness . . ." (Genesis 1:26)

No other living thing was made in God's image and that placed an insuperable barrier between man and all other living things. Any view that led to the belief that the barriers between species generally were not leakproof tended to weaken that all-important barrier protecting man.

It would have been nice, of course, if all the other life forms on Earth were enormously different from man so that the insuperable barrier would be clearly reflected physically. Unfortunately, the Mediterranean world was acquainted, even in early times, with certain animals we now call "monkeys."

The various monkeys with which the ancients came in contact had faces that, in some cases, looked like those of shriveled little men. They had hands that clearly resembled human hands and they fingered things as human beings did and with a clearly lively curiosity. However, they had tails and that rather saved the day. The human being is so pronouncedly tailless and most of the animals we know are so pronouncedly tailed that that, in itself, would seem to be a symbol of that insuperable barrier between man and monkey.

There are, indeed, some animals without tails or with very short tails, such as frogs, guinea pigs, and bears, but these, even without tails, do not threaten man's status. And yet—

There is a reference to a monkey in the Bible, one for which the translators used a special word. In discussing King Solomon's trading ventures, the Bible says (1 Kings 10:22), ". . . once in three years came the navy of Tharshish, bringing gold, and silver, ivory, and apes, and peacocks."

Tharshish is often identified as Tartessus, a city on the Spanish coast just west of the Strait of Gibraltar, a flourishing trading center in Solomon's time that was destroyed by the Carthaginians in 480 B.C. In northwestern Africa across from Tartessus, there existed then (and now) a type of monkey of the macaque group. It was this macaque that was called an "ape," and in later years, when northwestern Africa became part of "Barbary" to Europeans, it came to be called "Barbary ape."

The Barbary ape is tailless and therefore more resembles man than other monkeys do. Aristotle, in his ladder of life, placed the Barbary ape at the top of the monkey group, just under man. Galen, the Greek physician of about A.D. 200, dissected apes and showed the resemblance to man to be internal as well as external.

It was the resemblance to man that made the Barbary ape amusing to the ancients, and yet annoying as well. The Roman poet Ennius is quoted as saying, "The ape, vilest of beasts, how like to us!" Was the ape really the "vilest of beasts"? Objectively, of course not. It was its resemblance to man and its threat, therefore, to man's cherished uniqueness that made it vile.

In medieval times, when the uniqueness and supremacy of man had become a cherished dogma, the existence of the ape was even more annoying. They were equated with the Devil. The Devil, after all, was a fallen and distorted angel, and as man had been created in God's image, so the ape was created in the Devil's.

Yet no amount of explanation removed the unease. The English dramatist William Congreve wrote in 1695: "I could never look long upon a monkey, without very mortifying reflections." It is not so hard to guess that those "mortifying reflections" must have been to the effect that man might be described as a large and somewhat more intelligent ape.

Modern times had made matters worse by introducing the proud image-of-God European to animals, hitherto unknown, which resembled him even more closely than the Barbary ape did.

In 1641 a description was published of an animal brought from Africa and kept in the Netherlands in a menagerie belonging to the Prince of Orange. From the description it seems to have been a chimpanzee. There were also reports of a large manlike animal in Borneo, one we now call the orangutan.

The chimpanzee and the orangutan were called "apes" because, like the Barbary ape, they lacked tails. In later years, when it was recognized that the chimpanzee and orangutan resembled monkeys less and men more, they came to be known as "anthropoid" (manlike) apes.

In 1758 the Swedish naturalist Carolus Linnaeus made the first thoroughly systematic attempt to classify all species. He was a firm believer in the permanence of species and it did not concern him that some animal species closely resembled man—that was just the way they were created.

He therefore did not hesitate to lump the various species of apes and monkey together, *with man included as well,* and call that group "Primates," from a Latin word for "first," since it included man. We still use the term.

The monkeys and apes, generally, Linnaeus put into one subgroup of Primates and called that subgroup "Simia," from the Latin word for "ape." For human being, Linnaeus invented the subgroup "Homo," which is the Latin word for "man." Linnaeus used a double name for each species (called "binomial nomenclature," with the family name first, like Smith, John, and Smith, William), so human beings rejoiced in the name *"Homo sapiens"* (Man, wise). But Linnaeus placed another member in that group. Having read the description of the Bornean orangutan, he named it "Homo troglodytes" (Man, cave-dwelling).

"Orangutan" is from a Malay word meaning "man of the forest." The Malays, who were there on the spot, were more accurate in their description, for the orangutan is a forest dweller and not a cave dweller, but either way it cannot be considered near enough to man to warrant the Homo designation.

The French naturalist Georges de Buffon was the first, in the middle 1700s, to describe the gibbons, which represent a third kind of anthropoid ape. The various gibbons are the smallest of the anthropoids and the least like man.

They are sometimes put to one side for that reason, the remaining anthropoids being called the "great apes."

As the classification of species grew more detailed, naturalists were more and more tempted to break down the barriers between them. Some species were so similar to other species that it was uncertain whether any boundary at all could be drawn between them. Besides, more and more animals showed signs of being caught in the middle of change, so to speak.

The horse, Buffon noted, had two "splints" on either side of its leg bones, which seemed to indicate that once there had been three lines of bones there and three hoofs to each leg.

Buffon argued that if hoofs and bones could degenerate, so

might entire species. Perhaps God had created only certain species and that each of these had, to some extent, degenerated and formed additional species. If horses could lose some of their hoofs, why might not some of them have degenerated all the way to donkeys?

Since Buffon wished to speculate on what was, after all, the big news in man-centered natural history, he suggested that apes were degenerated men.

Buffon was the first to talk of the mutability of species. Here, however, he avoided the worst danger—that of suggesting that man-the-image-of-God had once been something else—but he did say that man could *become* something else. Even that was too much, for once the boundaries were made to leak in one direction, it would be hard to make it leakproof in the other. The pressure was placed on Buffon to recant, and recant he did.

The notion of the mutability of species did not die, however. A British physician, Erasmus Darwin, had the habit of writing long poems of indifferent quality in which he presented his ofttimes interesting scientific theories. In his last book, *Zoonomia,* published in 1796, he amplified Buffon's ideas and suggested that species underwent changes as a result of the direct influence upon them of the environment.

This notion was carried still further by the French naturalist Jean Baptiste de Lamarck, who, in 1809, published *Zoological Philosophy* and was the first scientist of note to advance a theory of evolution, a thoroughgoing description of the mechanisms by which an antelope, for instance, could conceivably change, little by little over the generations, into a giraffe. (Both Darwin and Lamarck were virtually ostracized for their views by the Establishments, both scientific and nonscientific, of those days.)

Lamarck was wrong in his notion of the evolutionary mechanism, but his book made the concept of evolution well known in the scientific world and it inspired others to find a perhaps more workable mechanism.**

The man who turned the trick was the English naturalist

**Antievolutionists usually denounce evolution as "merely a theory" and cite various uncertainties in the details, uncertainties that are admitted by biologists. In this, the antievolutionists are being fuzzy-minded. That evolution has taken place is as nearly a fact as anything nontrivial can be. The exact details of the mechanism by*

Charles Robert Darwin (grandson of Erasmus Darwin), who spent nearly twenty years gathering data and polishing his argument. This he did, first, because he was a naturally meticulous man. Secondly, he knew the fate that awaited anyone who advanced an evolutionary theory, and he wanted to disarm the enemy by making his arguments cast-iron.

When he published his book *On the Origin of Species by Means of Natural Selection* in 1859, he carefully refrained from discussing man in it. That didn't help, of course. He was a gentle and virtuous person, as nearly a saint as any cleric in the kingdom, but if he had bitten his mother to death, he couldn't have been denounced more viciously.

Yet the evidence in favor of evolution had kept piling up. In 1847 the largest of the anthropoid apes, the gorilla, was finally brought into the light of European day, and it was the most dramatic ape of all. In size, at least, it seemed most nearly human, or even superhuman.

Then, too, in 1856 the very first fossil remnants of an organism that was clearly more advanced than any of the living anthropoids and as clearly more primitive than any living man was discovered in the Neander valley in Germany. This was "Neanderthal man." Not only was the evidence in favor of evolution steadily rising, but so was the evidence in favor of *human* evolution.

In 1863 the Scottish geologist Charles Lyell published *The Antiquity of Man*, which used the evidence of ancient stone tools to argue that mankind was much older than the six thousand years allotted him (and the Universe) in the Bible. He also came out strongly in favor of the Darwinian view of evolution.

And in 1871 Darwin finally carried the argument to man with his book *The Descent of Man.*

The antievolutionists remain with us, of course, to this day, ardent and firm in their cause. I get more than my share of letters from them, so that I know what their arguments are like.

which evolution proceeds, however, remain theoretical in many respects. The mechanism, however, is not the thing.

Thus, very few people really understand the mechanism by which an automobile runs, but those who are uncertain of the mechanism do not argue from that that the automobile itself does not exist.

They concentrate on one point, and on one point only—the descent of man. I have never once received any letter arguing emotionally that the beaver is *not* related to the rat or that the whale is *not* descended from a land mammal. I sometimes think they don't even realize that evolution applies to all species. Their only insistence is that man is not, *not*, NOT descended from or related to apes or monkeys.

Some evolutionists try to counter this by saying that Darwin never said that man is descended from monkeys; that no living primate is an ancestor of man. This, however, is a quibble. The evolutionary view is that man and the apes had some common ancestor that is not alive today but that looked like a primitive ape when it was alive. Going farther back, man's various ancestors had a distinct monkeyish appearance—to the nonzoologist at least.

As an evolutionist, I prefer to face that fact without flinching. I am perfectly prepared to maintain that man *did* descend from monkeys, as the simplest way of stating what I believe to be the fact.

And we've got to stick to monkeys in another way, too. Evolutionists may talk about the "early hominids," about "Homo erectus," the "Australopithecines," and so on. We may use that as evidence of the evolution of man and of the type of organism from which he descended.

This, I suspect, doesn't carry conviction to the antievolutionists or even bother them much. Their view seems to be that when a bunch of infidels who call themselves scientists find a tooth here, a thigh bone there, and a piece of skull yonder and jigsaw them all together into a kind of ape man, that doesn't mean a thing.

From the mail I get and from the literature I've seen, it seems to me that the emotionalism of the anitevolutionist boils itself down to man and monkey, and nothing more.

There are two ways in which an antievolutionist, it seems to me, can handle the man-and-monkey issue. He can stand pat on the Bible, declare that is divinely inspired and that it says man was created out of the dust of the Earth by God, in the image of God, six thousand years ago, and that's it. If that is his position, his views are clearly nonnegotiable, and there is no point in trying to negotiate. I will discuss the weather with such a person, but not evolution.

A second way is for the antievolutionist to attempt some rational justification for his stand; a justification that is, that does not rest on authority, but can be tested by observation or experiment and argued logically. For instance, one might argue that the differences between man and all other animals are so fundamental that it is unthinkable that they be bridged and that no animal can conceivably develop into a man by the operation of nothing more than the laws of nature—that supernatural intervention is required.

An example of such an unbridgeable difference is a claim, for instance, that man has a soul and that no animal has one, and that a soul cannot be developed by an evolutionary procedure. —Unfortunately, there is no way of measuring or detecting a soul by those methods known to science. In fact, one cannot even define a soul except by referring to some sort to mystical authority. This falls outside observation or experiment, then.

On a less exalted plane, an antievolutionist might argue that man has a sense of right and wrong; that he has an appreciation of justice; that he is, in short, a moral organism while animals are not and cannot be.

That, I think, leaves room for argument. There are animals that act as though they love their young and that sometimes give their lives for them. There are animals that cooperate and protect each other in danger. Such behavior has survival value and it is exactly the sort of thing that evolutionists would expect to see developed bit by bit, until it reaches the level found in man.

If you were to argue that such apparently "human" behavior in animals is purely mechanical and is done without understanding, then once again we are back to argument by mere assertion. We don't know what goes on inside an animal's mind and, for that matter, it is by no means certain that our own behavior isn't as mechanical as that of animals—only a degree more complicated and versatile.

There was a time when things were easier than they are now, when comparative anatomy was in its beginnings, and when it was possible to suppose that there was some gross physiological difference that set off man from all other animals. In the seventeenth century, the French philosopher René Descartes thought the pineal gland was the seat of the soul, for he accepted the then-current notion that this gland was found only in the human being and in no other organism whatever.

Alas, not so. The pineal gland is found in all vertebrates and is most highly developed in a certain primitive reptile called the tuatara. As a matter of fact, there is no portion of the physical body which the human being owns to the exclusion of all other species.

Suppose we get more subtle and consider the biochemistry of organisms. Here the differences are much less marked than in the physical shape of the body and its parts. Indeed, there is so much similarity in the biochemical workings of *all* organisms, not only if we compare men and monkeys, but if we compare men and bacteria, that if it weren't for preconceived notions and species-centered conceit, the fact of evolution would be considered self-evident.

We must get very subtle indeed and begin to study the very fine chemical structure of the all but infinitely versatile protein molecule in order to find something distinctive for each species. Then, by the tiny differences in that chemical structure, one can get a rough measure of how long ago in time two organisms may behave branched away from a common ancestor.

By studying protein structure, we find no large gaps; no differences between one species and all others that is so huge as to indicate a common ancestor so long ago that in all the history of Earth there was no time for such divergence to have taken place. If such a large gap existed between one species and all the rest, then that one species would have arisen from a different globule of primordial life than that which gave birth to all the rest. It would still have evolved, still have descended from more primitive species, but it would not be related to any other earthly life form. I repeat, however, that no such gap has been found and none is expected. *All* earthly life is interrelated.

Certainly man is not separated from other forms of life by some large biochemical gap. Biochemically, he falls within the Primates group and is not particularly more separate than the others are. In fact, he seems quite closely related to the chimpanzee. The chimpanzee, by the protein structure test, is closer to man than to the gorilla or orangutan.

So it is from the chimpanzee, specifically, that the antievolutionist must protect us. Surely, if, in Congreve's words, we "look long upon the monkey," meaning the chimpanzee in this case, we must admit it differs from us in nothing vital but the brain. The human brain is four times the size of the chimpanzee brain!

It might seem that even this large difference in size is but a difference in degree, and one that can be easily explained by evolutionary development—especially since fossil hominids had brains intermediate in size between the chimpanzee and modern man.

The antievolutionist, however, might dismiss fossil hominids as unworthy of discussion and go on to maintain that it is not the physical size of the brain that counts, but the quality of the intelligence it mediates. It can be argued that human intelligence so far surpasses chimpanzee intelligence that any thought of a relationship between the two species is out of the question.

For instance, a chimpanzee cannot talk. Efforts to teach young chimpanzees to talk, however patient, skillful, and prolonged, have always failed. And without speech, the chimpanzee remains nothing but an animal: intelligent for an animal, but just an animal. With speech, man climbs to the heights of Plato, Shakespeare, and Einstein.

But might it be that we are confusing communication with speech? Speech is, admittedly, the most effective and delicate form of communication ever conceived. (Our modern devices from books to television sets transmit speech in other forms, but speech still.) —But is speech all?

Human speech depends upon human ability to control rapid and delicate movements of throat, mouth, tongue, and lips and all this, seems to be under the control of a portion of the brain called "Broca's convolution." If Broca's convolution is damaged by a tumor or by a blow, a human being suffers from aphasia and can neither speak nor understand speech. —Yet such a human being retains intelligence and is able to make himself understood by gesture, for instance.

The section of the chimpanzee brain equivalent to Broca's convolution is not large enough or complex enough to make speech in the human sense possible. But what about gesture? Chimpanzees use gestures to communicate in the wild—

Back in June 1966, then, Beatrice and Allen Gardner at the University of Nevada chose a one-and-a-half-year-old female chimpanzee they named Washoe and decided to try to teach her a deaf-and-dumb language. The results amazed them and the world.

Washoe readily learned dozens of signs, using them appropriately to communicate desires and abstractions. She invented new modifications which she also used appropriately. She tried to teach the language to other chimpanzees, and she clearly enjoyed communicating.

Other chimpanzees have been similarly trained. Some have been taught to arrange and rearrange magnetized counters on a wall. In so doing, they showed themselves capable of taking grammar into account and were not fooled when their teachers deliberately created nonsense sentences.

Nor is it a matter of conditioned reflexes. Every line of evidence shows that chimpanzees know what they are doing, in the same sense that human beings know what they are doing when they talk.

To be sure, the chimpanzee language is very simple compared to man's. Man is still enormously the more intelligent. However, Washoe's feat makes even our ability to speak differ from the chimpanzee's in degree only, not in kind.

"Look long upon a monkey." There are no valid arguments, save those resting on mystical authority, that serve to deny the cousinship of the chimpanzee to man or the evolutionary development of *Homo sapiens* from non-Homo non-sapiens.

THINKING
ABOUT
THINKING

I HAVE JUST RETURNED FROM A VISIT to Great Britain. In view of my antipathy to traveling (which has not changed), I never thought I would walk the streets of London or stand under the stones of Stonehenge, but I did. Of course, I went by ocean liner both ways, since I don't fly.

The trip was an unqualified success. The weather during the ocean crossing was calm; the ships fed me (alas) all I could eat; the British were impeccably kind to me, even though they did stare a bit at my varicolored clothes, and frequently asked me what my bolo ties were.

Particularly pleasant to me was Steve Odell, who was publicity director of Mensa, the organization of high-IQ people which more or less sponsored my visit. Steve squired me about, showed me the sights, kept me from falling into ditches and under cars, and throughout maintained what he called his "traditional British reserve."

For the most part, I managed to grasp what was said to me despite the funny way the British have of talking. One girl was occasionally incomprehensible, however, and I had to ask her to speak more slowly. She seemed amused by my failure to understand her, although I , of course, attributed it to her imperfect command of the language. "You," I pointed out, "understand *me.*"

"Of course I understand you, " she said. "You speak slowly in a Yankee drool."

I had surreptitiously wiped my chin before I realized that the poor thing was trying to say "drawl."

But I suppose the most unusual part of the trip (which included three speeches, three receptions, innumerable interviews by the various media, and five hours of book signing at five bookstores in London and Birmingham) was being made a vice-president of International Mensa.

I took it for granted that the honor was bestowed upon me for the sake of my well-known intelligence, but I thought of it during my five-day return on the *Queen Elizabeth 2* and it dawned on me that I didn't really know much about intelligence. I *assume* I am intelligent, but how can I *know?*

So I think I had better think about it—and where better than here among all my Gentle Friends and Readers?

One common belief connects intelligence with (1) the ready accumulation of items of knowledge; (2) the retention of such items, and (3) the quick recall, on demand, of such items.

The average person, faced with someone like myself (for instance) who displays all these characteristics in abundant degree is quite ready to place the label of "intelligent" upon the displayer and to do so in greater degree the more dramatic the display.

Yet surely this is wrong. One may possess all three characteristics and yet give evidence of being quite stupid; and, on the other hand, one may be quite unremarkable in these respects and yet show unmistakable signs of what would surely be considered intelligence.

During the 1950s, the nation was infested with television programs in which large sums were paid out to those who could come up with obscure items of information on demand (and under pressure). It turned out that some of the shows weren't entirely honest, but that is irrelevant.

Millions of people who watched thought that the mental calisthenics indicated intelligence.* The most remarkable contestant was a postal employee from St. Louis who, instead of applying his expertise to one category as did others, took the whole world of factual items for his province. He amply displayed his prowess and struck the nation with awe. Indeed, just before the quiz program fad collapsed, there were plans to pit this man against all comers in a program to be entitled "Beat the Genius."

Genius? Poor man! He had barely competence enough to make a poor living and his knack of total recall was of less use to him than the ability to walk a tightrope would have been.

But not everyone equates the accumulation and ready regurgitation of names, dates, and events with intelligence. Very often, in fact, it is the lack of this very quality that is associated with intelligence. Have you never heard of the absent-minded professor?

According to one kind of popular stereotype, all professors, and all intelligent people generally, are absent-minded and couldn't remember their own names without a supreme effort. But then what makes them intelligent?

I suppose the explanation would be that a very knowledgeable person bends so much of his intellect to his own sector of knowledge that he has little brain to spare for anything else. The absent-minded professor is therefore forgiven all his failings for the sake of his prowess in his chosen field.

Yet that cannot be the whole story either, for we divide categories of knowledge into a hierarchy and reserve our admiration for some only, labeling successful jugglery in those and those only as "intelligent."

We might imagine a young man, for instance, who has an encyclopedic knowledge of the rules of baseball, its procedures, its records, its players, and its current events. He may concentrate so thoroughly on such matters that he is extremely absent-minded with respect to mathematics, English grammar, geography, and history. He is not then forgiven his failure in some respects for the sake of his success in others; he is *stupid!* On the other hand, the

---

I was asked to be on one of these shows and refused, feeling that I would gain nothing by a successful display of trivial mental pyrotechnics and would suffer needless humiliation if I were human enough to muff a question.

mathematical wizard who cannot, even after explanation, tell a bat boy from a home run is; nonetheless, *intelligent*.

Mathematics is somehow associated with intelligence in our judgments and baseball is not, and even moderate success in grasping the former is enough for the label of intelligent, while supreme knowledge of the latter gains you nothing in that direction (though much, perhaps, in others).

So the absent-minded professor, as long as it is only his name he doesn't remember, or what day it is, or whether he has eaten lunch or has an appointment to keep (and you should hear the stories about Norbert Wiener), is still intelligent as long as he learns, remembers, and recalls a great deal about some category *associated* with intelligence.

And what categories are these?

We can eliminate every category in which excellence involves merely muscular effort or coordination. However admirable a great baseball player or a great swimmer, painter, sculptor, flutist, or cellist may be, however successful, famous, and beloved, excellence in these fields is, in itself, no indication of intelligence.

Rather it is in the category of theory that we find an association with intelligence. To study the technique of carpentry and write a book on the various fashions of carpentry through the ages is a sure way of demonstrating intelligence even though one could not, on any single occasion, drive a nail into a beam without smashing one's thumb.

And if we confine ourselves to the realm of thought, it is clear that we are readier to associate intelligence with some fields than with others. We are almost sure to show more respect for a historian than for a sports writer, for a philosopher than for a cartoonist, and so on.

It seems an unavoidable conclusion to me that our notions of intelligence are a direct inheritance from the days of ancient Greece, when the mechanical arts were despised as fit only for artisans and slaves, while only the "liberal" arts (from the Latin world for "free men") were respectable, because they had no practical use and were therefore fit for free men.

So nonobjective is our judgment of intelligence, that we can see its measure change before our eyes. Until fairly recently, the proper education for young gentlemen consisted very largely in the brute inculcation (through beatings, if necessary) of the great Latin writers. To know no Latin seriously disqualified anyone for enlistment in the ranks of the intelligent.

We might, of course, point out that there is a difference between "educated" and "intelligent" and that the foolish spouting of Latin marked only a fool after all—but that's just theory. In actual fact, the uneducated intelligent man is invariably downgraded and underestimated and, at best, is given credit for "native wit" or "shrewd common sense." And women, who were not educated, were shown to be unintelligent by their lack of Latin and that was the excuse for not educating them. (Of course that's circular reasoning, but circular reasoning has been used to support all the great injustices of history.)

Yet see how things change. It used to be Latin that was the mark of intelligence and now it is science, and I am the beneficiary; I know no Latin except for what my flypaper mind has managed to pick up accidentally, but I know a great deal of science—so without changing a single brain cell, I would be dumb in 1775 and terribly smart in 1975.

You might say that it isn't knowledge itself, not even the properly fashionable category of knowledge, that counts, but the *use* that is made of it. It is, you might argue, the manner in which the knowledge is displayed and handled, the wit, originality, and creativity with which it is put to use, that counts. Surely, *there* is the measure of intelligence.

And to be sure, though teaching, writing, scientific research are examples of professions often associated with intelligence, we all know there can be pretty dumb teachers, writers, and researchers. The creativity or, if you like, the intelligence can be missing and still leave behind a kind of mechanical competence.

But if creativity is what counts, that, too, only counts in approved and fashionable areas. A musician, unlearned, uneducated, unable to read music perhaps, may be able to put together notes and tempos in such a way as to create, brilliantly, a whole new school of music. Yet that in itself will not earn him the accolade of "intelligent." He is merely one of those unaccountable "creative geniuses" with a "gift from God." Since he doesn't know how he does it, and cannot explain it after he's done it,** how can he be considered intelligent?

**The great trumpeter Louis Armstrong, on being asked to explain something about jazz, is reported to have said (translated into conventional English), "If you've got to ask, you aren't ever going to know."—These are words fit to be inscribed on jade in letters of gold.

The critic who, after the fact, studies the music, and finally, with an effort, decides it is not merely an unpleasant noise by the old rules, but is a great accomplishment by certain new rules—why *he* is intelligent. (But how may critics would you exchange for one Louis Armstrong?)

But in that case, why is the brilliant scientific genius considered intelligent? Do you suppose he knows how his theories come to him or can explain to you how it all happened? Can the great writer explain how he writes so that you can do as he does?

I am not, myself, a great writer by any standard I respect, but I have my points and I have this value for the present occasion—that I am one person, generally accepted as intelligent, whom I can view from within.

Well, my clearest and most visible claim to intelligence is the nature of my writing—the fact that I write a great many books in a great many fields in complex yet clear prose, displaying great mastery of much knowledge in doing so.

So what?

No one ever taught me to write. I had worked out the basic art of writing when I was eleven. And I can certainly never explain what that basic art is to anyone else.

I dare say that some critic, who knows far more of literary theory than I do (or than I would ever care to), might, if he chose, analyze my work and explain what I do and why, far better than I ever could. Would that make him more intelligent than I am? I suspect it might, to many people.

In short, I don't know of any way of defining intelligence that does not depend on the subjective and the fashionable.

Now, then, we come to the matter of intelligence testing, the determination of the "intelligence quotient" or "IQ."

If, as I maintain and firmly believe, there is no objective definition of intelligence, and what we call intelligence is only a creation of cultural fashion and subjective prejudice, what the devil is it we test when we make use of an intelligence test?

I hate to knock the intelligence test, because I am a beneficiary of it. I routinely end up on the far side of 160 when I am tested and even then I am invariably underestimated because it almost always takes me less time to do a test than the time allotted.

In fact, out of curiosity, I got a paperback book containing a sizable number of different tests designed to measure one's IQ. Each test had a half-hour time limit. I worked on each one as honestly as I could, answering some questions instantly, some after a bit of thought, some by guesswork, and some not at all. —And naturally, I got some answers wrong.

When I was done, I worked out the results according to directions and it turned out I had an IQ of 135. —But wait! I had not accepted the half-hour limit offered me, but broke off each section of the test at the fifteen-minute mark and went on to the rest. I therefore doubled the score and decided I have an IQ of 270. (I'm sure that the doubling is unjustified, but the figure of 270 pleases my sense of cheerful self-appreciation, so I intend to insist on it.)

But however much all this soothes my vanity, and however much I appreciate being vice-president of Mensa, an organization which bases admission to its membership on IQ. I must, in all honesty, maintain that it means nothing.

What, after all, does such an intelligence test measure but those skills that are associated with intelligence by the individuals designing the test? And those individuals are subject to the cultural pressures and prejudices that force a subjective definition of intelligence.

Thus, important parts of any intelligence test measure the size of one's vocabulary, but the words one must define are just those words one is apt to find in reading approved works of literature. No one asks for the definition of "two-bagger" or "snake eyes" or "riff," for the simple reason that those who design the tests don't know these terms or are rather ashamed of themselves if they do.

This is similarly true of tests of mathematical knowledge, of logic, of shape visualization, and of all the rest. You are tested in what is culturally fashionable—in what educated men consider to be the criteria of intelligence—i.e., of minds like their own.

The whole thing is a self-perpetuating device. Men in intellectual control of a dominating section of society define themselves as intelligent, then design tests that are a series of clever little doors that can let through only minds like their own, thus giving them more evidence of "intelligence" and more examples of "intelligent people" and therefore more reason to devise additional tests of the same kind. More circular reasoning!

And once someone is stamped with the label "Intelligent" on the basis of such tests and such criteria, any demonstration of stupidity no longer counts. It is the label that matters, not the fact, I don't like to libel others, so I will merely give you two examples of clear stupidity which I myself perpetrated (though I can give you two hundred, if you like):

1. On a certain Sunday, something went wrong with my car and I was helpless. Fortunately, my younger brother, Stan, lived nearby and since he is notoriously goodhearted, I called him. He came out at once, absorbed the situation, and began to use the Yellow Pages and the telephone to try to reach a service station, while I stood by with my lower jaw hanging loose. Finally, after a period of strenuous futility, Stan said to me with just a touch of annoyance, "With all your intelligence, Isaac, how is it you lack the brains to join the AAA?" Whereupon, I said, "Oh, I belong to the AAA," and produced the card. He gave me a long, strange look and called the AAA. I was on my wheels in half an hour.

2. Sitting in Ben Bova's room at a recent science fiction convention, I was waiting, rather impatiently, for my wife to join us. Finally, there was a ring at the door. I sprang to my feet with an excited "Here's Janet!", flung open a door, and dashed into the closet—when Ben opened the room door and let her in.

Stan and Ben love to tell these stories about me and they're harmless. Because I have the label "intelligent," what would surely be evidence of stupidity is converted into lovable eccentricity.

This brings us to a serious point. There has been talk in recent years of racial differences in IQ. Men like William B. Shockley, who has a Nobel Prize (in physics), point out that measurements show the average IQ of blacks to be substantially lower than that of whites, and this created quite a stir.

Many people who, for one reason or another, have already concluded that blacks are "inferior" are delighted to have "scientific" reason to suppose that the undesirable position in which blacks find themselves is their own fault after all.

Shockley, of course, denies racial prejudice (sincerely, I'm sure) and points out that we can't deal intelligently with racial problems if, out of political motives, we ignore an undoubted scientific finding; that we ought to investigate the matter carefully and study the intellectual inequality of man. Nor is it just a matter of blacks versus whites; apparently some groups of whites score less well than do other groups of whites, and so on.

Yet to my mind the whole hip-hurrah is a colossal fraud. Since intelligence is (as I believe) a matter of subjective definition and since the dominant intellectuals of the dominant sector of society have naturally defined it in a self-serving manner, what is it we say when we say that blacks have a lower average IQ than whites have? What we are saying is that the black subculture is substantially different from the dominant White subculture and that the Black values are sufficiently different from dominant white values to make blacks do less well on the carefully designed intelligence tests produced by the whites.

In order for blacks, on the whole, to do as well as whites, they must abandon their own subculture for the white and produce a closer fit to the IQ-testing situation. This they may not want to do; and even if they want to, conditions are such that it is not made easy for them to fulfill that desire.

To put it as succinctly as possible: blacks in America have had a subculture created for them, chiefly by white action, and have been kept in it chiefly by white action. The values of that subculture are defined as inferior to those of the dominant culture, so that the black IQ is arranged to be lower; and the lower IQ is then used as an excuse for the continuation of the very conditions that produced it. Circular reasoning? Of course.

But then, I don't want to be an intellectual tyrant and insist that what I speak must be the truth.

Let us say that I am wrong; that there *is* an objective definition of intelligence, that it *can* be measured accurately, and that blacks *do* have lower IQ ratings than whites do, on the average, not because of any cultural differences but because of some innate, biologically based intellectual inferiority. Now what? How should whites treat blacks?

That's a hard question to answer, but perhaps we can get some good out of supposing the reverse. What if we test blacks and find out, more or less to our astonishment, that they end up showing a *higher* IQ than do whites, on the average?

How should we *then* treat them? Should we give them a double vote? Give them preferential treatment in jobs, particularly in the government? Let them have the best seats in the bus and theater? Give them cleaner restrooms than whites have, and a higher average pay scale?

I am *quite* certain that the answer would be a decided, forceful, and profane negative for each of these propositions and any like them. I suspect that if it were reported that blacks had higher IQ ratings than Whites do, most whites would at once maintain, with considerable heat, that IQ could not be measured accurately and that it was of no significance if it could be, that a person was a person regardless of book learning, fancy education, big words, and fol-de-rol, that plain ordinary horsesense was all anyone needed, that *all* men were equal in the good old United States, and those damned pinko professors and their IQ tests could just shove it—

Well, if we're going to ignore IQ when *we* are on the low end of the scale, why should we pay such pious attention to it when *they* are?

But hold on. I may be wrong again. How do I know how the dominants would react to a high-IQ minority? After all, we *do* respect intellectuals and professors to a certain extent, don't we? Then, too, we're talking about oppressed minorities, and a high-IQ minority wouldn't be oppressed in the first place, so the artificial situation I set up by pretending the blacks scored high is just a straw man, and knocking it down has no value.

Really? Let's consider the Jews, who, for some two millennia, have been kicked around whenever Gentiles found life growing dull. Is this because Jews, as a group, are low-IQ? —You know, I *never* heard that maintained by anyone, however anti-Semitic.

I do not, myself, consider Jews, as a group, to be markedly high-IQ. The number of stupid Jews I have met in the course of a lifetime is enormous. That, however, is not the opinion of the anti-Semite, whose stereotype of the Jews involves their possession of a gigantic and dangerous intelligence. Although they may make up less than half a percent of a nation's population, they are forever on the point of "taking over."

But then, shouldn't they, if they are high-IQ? Oh, no, for that intelligence is merely "shrewdness," or "low cunning," or "devious slyness," and what really counts is that they lack the Christian, or the Nordic, or the Teutonic, or the what-have-you virtues of other sorts.

In short, if you are on then receiving end of the game-of-power, any excuse will do to keep you there. If you are seen as low-IQ you are despised and kept there because of that. If you are seen as high-IQ you are feared and kept there because of that.

Whatever significance IQ may have, then, it is, at present, being made a game for bigots.

Let me end, then, by giving you my own view. Each of us is part of any number of groups corresponding to any number of ways of subdividing mankind. In each of these ways, a given individual may be superior to others in the group, or inferior, or either, or both, depending on definition and on circumstance.

Because of this, "superior" and "inferior" have no useful meaning. What *does* exist, objectively, is "different." Each of us is different. I am different, and you are different, and you, and you, and you—

It is this difference that is the gory of *Homo sapiens* and the best possible salvation, because what some cannot do, others can, and where some cannot flourish, others can, through a wide range of conditions. I think we should value these differences as mankind's chief asset, as a species, and try never to use them to make our lives miserable, as individuals.

COPYRIGHT NOTICES